HIGH STAKES

BO BLACKMAN
BOOK THREE

HELEN HARPER

✽ Created with Vellum

For Adrianna, Kimchi, Molly, Tux and Mumpkin

CHAPTER 1
CLIENTS

Dr Love knits his hands together and gazes at me with a fatherly smile. I've elected to come to his office rather than continue to run the gauntlet of the Montserrat mansion. Even though I left the Family with the secret encouragement of Michael, Lord Montserrat, the vast majority of my 'siblings' regard me as a traitor.

The small room is sparsely decorated and possesses a remarkable lack of personality. I suppose Love's clients make up for it. There's a wall calendar and an impressive array of scholarly medical tomes on a heavy bookshelf, but the walls themselves are an unobtrusive beige and there's no artwork. There's not even a family photo on his tidy desk. The smell of bleach mingles with some potent kind of herbal tea. I can see several soggy, discarded teabags lying in the bottom of his wastepaper basket. Unless he has a team of extremely lazy cleaners, I can only surmise that he's already on his seventh cup. But then again, it is 7pm in the evening.

As a newly-fledged vampire, I'm not strong enough yet to withstand the sun's rays. Consequently I have to wait until dusk before I can venture outside. To say living nocturnally makes my life complicated would be the understatement of the year. At least with winter approaching, the days are shortening. I've never looked forward to November before: in England, even here in the warmer south, it's typically a grey affair, with depressing skies, endless rain and little prospect of sunshine. I can't wait.

'So, Bo, how have you been?' Dr Love asks the question with absolute sincerity, as if the weight of the world lies on my answer.

'Fine.' I rearrange my limbs. Every part of me wants to hunch over, cross my legs and fold my arms to create as much of a barrier as possible between myself and the psychiatrist. I need him to think that I trust him, however, so I force myself to relax and look open and receptive.

He raises his eyebrows. 'Have there been any more hallucinations?'

I shake my head. 'No. In fact, I feel remarkably chipper.' I beam at him to add credibility to my answer.

'You can tell me the truth,' he says.

No, I really can't. If I told him that a Kakos daemon with the catchy nomenclature of 'X' had touched my temples and sucked out whatever darkness was rattling around in there, he'd probably throw me in the nearest loony bin. And then X would eat Dr Love's heart. I am under strict instructions from the daemon not to tell a living soul. There are only three people who genuinely terrify me: X, my grandfather and Michael Montserrat. And as far as the latter is concerned it might be my own feelings and desires that are scary rather than the vampire himself. I haven't quite made up my mind yet.

'Honestly, I feel great. I mean, I'm worried about how things are going with the humans and their growing hatred towards bloodguzzlers. And goodness only knows when Medici is going to make a move. But, yeah,' I shrug, 'other than that, I feel fantastic.'

Dr Love rests his chin on his hands. 'It's interesting that you use the term bloodguzzler.'

I stiffen. 'Is it? I think you'll find it's the word most of the world uses to describe vampires. And it's what we do. We guzzle blood. We suck it from the tender jugulars of fresh, innocent people. We thrive on its iron-rich goodness.' My voice is bitter.

'You continue to feel an aversion towards drinking blood then?'

I start to cross my legs then stop, planting both feet firmly back on the floor. 'I wouldn't call it an aversion, exactly.'

'Really? What would you call it then?'

Disgust. Hatred. 'A mild dislike of the process,' I say.

'Do you drink every day?'

'I have to. I can't function unless I do.'

Dr Love rubs his chin thoughtfully. 'And you still use Connor? The ginger man who works with you at New Order?'

'Yes. He says he enjoys it.' My lip curls.

'You don't believe him?'

'I have no reason to think he's lying.'

'Tell me, Bo. Are you still seeking a cure?'

I don't have to. It's hiding behind a slab of chocolate in my fridge. 'No,' I answer truthfully. I choose my words with care. 'I'm told a cure doesn't exist.'

Unfortunately for me, the good doctor deals in half-truths all day long so he's not about to ignore mine. 'You're told? You mean you think it might still be out there?'

'Some people tell me there's a God. Some people tell me we're descended from aliens. Some people say that Jack the Ripper was a human.' I shrug. 'I like to keep an open mind.'

I receive a faintly disapproving look in return. 'I'm going to set you a little challenge,' he says. 'Once a week, you need to step out of your comfort zone and drink from someone else.'

'Why?'

'Well, for one thing it can't be good for Connor to lose so much blood so regularly.'

'I don't take a lot.'

'You're not the only vampire working in the office though.'

'Matt doesn't use Connor. He goes back to the Montserrat mansion during the day to sleep and drink from the vampettes who line up there.'

'It's unusual for two fledglings to be given such freedom.'

It's more than unusual, it's unique. 'I suppose we're special cases.' I look the doctor directly in the eye, challenging him to question this further. Instead, he glances at his watch.

'Time is almost up. What are you planning on doing with the rest of your night?'

'Work.'

'New Order has been open for almost a fortnight?' I nod. 'Have you had much interest?'

'Nothing so far that's going to help us change any attitudes.' I try to remain ambivalent. 'It's early days yet though.'

NEW ORDER IS the brainchild of Michael Montserrat. Ignorant of the fact that the majority of the Families are made up of reformed criminals, the media used to glamorise vampires while the general populace admired their longevity and increased physical prowess. All that changed when a recent recruit called Nicky subverted a daemon's virility enhancement spell to bend male vampires to her will. There were a lot of deaths, and the fallout from her actions was considerable. There's a growing antipathy towards our kind that shows no sign of abating. We may have succeeded in bringing Nicky down but I often wonder whether it was her who had the real success.

New Order is acting as a conduit between the vampires and humans. It is a sort of investigative agency, tasked with dealing with complaints, queries and delicate incidents. There are six of us in the agency: two humans, two Sanguines and two vampires. We all have some sort of tie with the Montserrat Family but, if things work well, the other Families will join the organisation. Except for the Medici Family. Their Lord is determined to maintain the status quo; he thinks that giving any ground to the humans will ultimately weaken every vampire in the country and he's prepared to go to almost any lengths to stop our little agency from prospering. Not that there've been many signs of prosperity recently. The constant picketing outside the office puts most humans off. The dentist using the ground floor space has already complained to the council twice. I can't blame him really; his business must be suffering too.

It's fairly early when I get back to Covent Garden so the group of humans chanting and holding placards above their heads is still quite large. Not big enough to make headline news but enough to create a headache. When they see me coming, their shouts get louder.

'Murderer!'

'Baby-killer!'

'Fuck off back to where you came from, bitch!'

I'm from London, so that's a non-starter.

As if they'd pre-planned it, the group forms a barrier between me and the office entrance. I do my best to ignore their yells and search for a route inside. We're going to have to use the back windows as our exit and entrance point if this keeps up. That's easy enough for me and Matt, and Peter would probably manage it too. But Arzo is still in a wheelchair and I'm doubtful that there are the necessary muscles within Connor's skinny freckled body. Besides, even if my grandfather was spry enough to manage it, there's no way he'd demean himself in such a fashion.

I'm tempted to push through the protesters. The danger is that if I so much as touch any of them, they'll call foul and claim I assaulted them. And there's no point in attempting to reason with them. There may only be thirty or so of them but they have a crowd mentality and are goading each other on. I bite my lip then shrug. I'll just have to show off.

I loosen my knees slightly, trying not to tense my muscles too much and inadvertently make myself fall. It certainly wouldn't do to screw this up and have them witness my embarrassment. I've already clocked the German tourists who have their smartphones out so they can record the action; I don't need to end up on the wrong side of a viral video. Taking a deep breath, I launch upwards, springing from my toes until I'm several feet in the air and high above the protestors' heads. Several of them reach up to try and hit me with their placards but I'm too fast; I'm already somersaulting then landing on the opposite side of the crowd. I curse inwardly as I have to step backwards to maintain my balance; it's a move I'll have to practise if I want to get it perfect. Still, despite the jeers, I've made it to the door. Without a backward glance, I slip inside and run up the stairs.

When I enter the office, Connor is perched on Peter's desk, chatting amiably. Peter's not paying any attention to him. He catches my eye and looks relieved.

'Bo! Great!' Leaving Connor in mid-sentence, Peter scoops up his jacket and almost runs out of the door. I open my mouth to warn him about the protestors but he's already vanished. A beat later there's a roar of delighted disapproval from outside as he exits the building. I listen carefully in case he needs help but, when the crowd subsides after a few seconds, I realise he must have made his escape on his own.

'Mr Blackman said you were to go and see him as soon as you got in,' Connor says brightly.

I raise my eyebrows. 'Mr Blackman?' I suppose we should at least be thankful he declined that bloody knighthood when he retired from MI7 a few years ago.

Connor's eyes dart from side to side and he lowers his voice. 'I called him Arbuthnot yesterday. He wasn't very pleased. In fact, he made me feed the cat as a punishment.'

I would laugh if I didn't possess similar feelings of antipathy towards my grandfather's fat ginger moggy. For some reason he insists on bringing the sodding thing with him to the office every day where it gets in everyone's way. Even Arzo, who reeks of power, is afraid of it. Last week, he spent a full hour rearranging the filing cabinet rather than use his computer because the cat was asleep on the keyboard. In fact, the only person other than my grandfather who doesn't seem to tiptoe round the damn thing is Peter. Peter only seems wary of humans or tribers who try to pass the time of day with him .

Leaving Connor to dwell over the horror of his punishment, I knock on my grandfather's door. It swings open to admit me, the result of a simple spell to reward lazy people. My grandfather doesn't usually hold with such 'white-magic-fangled rubbish' as he puts it, but after three days he was so fed up of us walking in whenever we felt like it that he engaged the services of a local witch to set it up.

When I stroll in, he's sitting behind his desk with the ramrod-straight posture of an army drill sergeant. I'd thought – or perhaps hoped – that he'd only work a few hours every day as a result of his advanced age. Unfortunately for me, he doesn't do things by half-measures; he completes full shifts, crossing over from day to night to accommodate the needs of both Matt and I, as well as Peter and Arzo. He arrives at 3pm on the dot and departs at 11pm, immediately after winding his fob watch and ensuring it's set to match the distant – and from here inaudible – chimes of Big Ben. I'm a stickler for punctuality, and there are no prizes for guessing where I get that from, but one can be too officious.

My grandfather looks up at me and frowns. 'Bo. It's about time you got here. We've had a busy day and I need to run through the adapted client list with you.'

I raise my eyebrows. 'Busy day?'

'Two phone queries and one walk-in.'

I don't say anything. I don't need to.

He tuts. 'I told you when you when we started this venture that business would take time to pick up. People need to learn to trust us first.'

I snort. 'People need to come and talk to us if that's ever going to happen.'

'Three is a good number.'

'What did these three clients want?'

'The first phone call was a search request. Peter dealt with most of it. A woman named Melanie Jones is looking for her husband and thought he might have been recruited. He was found with the Stuart Family.'

I wonder whether knowing that he's still live and kicking, rather than a corpse floating in the Thames, made the woman happy or sad.

'She wants to know whether she can sue him for desertion,' he continued.

Ah. I guess she's not happy then. 'And the second phone call?'

'Someone wanting a pizza delivery.' I bite my tongue very, very hard. 'I have no idea why people insist on eating such a poor excuse for food.'

'Have you ever tried pizza?'

He gazes at me blankly. 'Why on earth would I do that?'

Life is too short. I change the subject. 'The walk-in?'

'Now this is more intriguing. A young man with a most peculiar name is convinced that his dog has been bitten and is now a vampire.'

'A vampire dog? That's impossible. The only animals that have ever been bloodguzzlers are bats.'

'All the same, he wants someone to go round to his house and investigate so I've pencilled you in. You can take Matthew with you if you promise to look after him.' For some reason my grandfather has taken a shine to Matt. It's probably because Matt's compelled to do whatever he's told by anyone who speaks to him.

I sigh. 'It's a complete waste of time. It's probably some attack dog that the owner can't control properly and it's going around biting people as a result. He's looking for an excuse to blame us for him being a shitty pet owner.'

'Language, Bo, please.'

'Sorry,' I mutter. Arbuthnot Blackman is the only person in the world who can make me feel like I'm five years old again.

'Of course it's a ridiculous theory. But,' he continues, 'we can do with the story being contained. Having the populace believe that their beloved pets are about turn vampire is not going aid your cause.'

The cat uses that moment to leap into my grandfather's lap. It flicks its yellow eyes at me with the sort of disdain that only cats can achieve. I can't help thinking that it would probably be improved if it actually were a vampire cat. It certainly couldn't be any worse.

'You're the head of this agency. Surely, it should be "our" cause?' I say it mildly but the challenge is there.

'I'm not going to deign to answer that,' he sniffs. 'Call in when you get to the house. It's in Richmond.'

I snap out a salute. 'Yessir.'

'Bo, that kind of flippant attitude is not helpful.'

I start to leave before I say anything I might regret. The last thing I want is to end up on cat-feeding duty.

'Oh, and Bo?' Grandfather calls out after me. 'Lord Montserrat requested that you telephone him at your earliest convenience. You may do that when you return from the,' the corners of his mouth turn down, 'vampire dog.'

'Great,' I mumble. The only reason I'm not taking umbrage at the implicit order in my grandfather's words is because I'm really not sure I want to talk to Michael Montserrat at all.

CHAPTER 2
KIMCHI

Matt and I take the motorbike. It was an expensive gift that I should have returned but I couldn't help myself. It fits too well with the badass persona I like to think I've created for myself and is such a sleek joy to ride that I can't imagine giving it up. I even have an over-sized leather jacket to match the look, although it's currently being repaired after receiving a large scorching hole as a result of a hybrid black-and-white witch's attentions. It's probably just as well. My lack of height allows me to get away with a lot but, as my grandfather keeps reminding me, I'm supposed to do what I can to appear approachable and non-threatening. Personally I don't think leather makes people throw up their hands and run away shrieking, but he's determined to keep me looking 'lady-like'. Apparently a man's leather jacket doesn't achieve that effect. Still, image aside, having the bike makes it far easier to zip through the city traffic and we arrive at the dog-owner's address in a satisfyingly short space of time.

There's a small patch of garden in front with a neatly trimmed lawn and one of those whirly contraptions for drying clothes. A single abandoned sock hangs from it. I'm tempted to rescue it but I damp down the urge. Matt looks at me question-ingly and I nod, so he steps up and rings the doorbell. For a second there's silence, then loud, excited barking erupts from somewhere inside. So far so normal. There's a shout and the dog subsides but I can hear it whining.

'I had a pet goldfish when I was little,' Matt informs me as the door finally opens. 'It died when I tried to take it out of the tank to play with.'

'You tried to play with a goldfish?'

'I was six! It looked lonely!'

I look up at the man standing in the doorway. He's staring at Matt as if he's crazy. I don't blame him.

'Mr Brinkish?' I ask, directing his attention back to me. 'My name is Bo Blackman. I'm from New Order. You called us about your dog?'

He blinks rapidly. He's not much taller than I am, which makes a change, but he's remarkably broad. His head is shaven and his shiny forehead seems massive as a result. 'Good,' he mutters. 'Come in.'

I must have looked surprised at his willingness to invite two vampires into his home because he produces a wooden crucifix from behind his back and holds it up. 'I'm not afraid of blood-guzzlers but you should be afraid of me.'

Matt snickers and I jab him sharply in the ribs. 'Sir, I should inform you that crosses don't actually harm vampires in any way.'

He frowns then, as if testing my words, thrusts it towards my face. When I don't flinch, he reaches out and presses it against my skin. Nothing happens. He pulls the cross back and shakes it as if he's hoping there's a wire loose inside. 'I paid good money for this,' he says. He tosses it aside. 'It doesn't matter. I've got plenty of garlic.'

'Garlic doesn't affect us either,' Matt interjects cheerfully.

'Oh yeah?' Brinkish says. 'Well, my dog hates it.'

'Is that why you think he's a vampire?'

The man bares his teeth. Distractingly, one of his molars is gold-plated; if he had an eye-patch and a parrot, he'd make a perfect pirate. 'I don't think he's a vampire,' he says. 'I know.'

He steps back so we can come inside. I'm about to move past him into the small hallway when he clicks his tongue. I glance at him askance and realise he's pointing at my feet. 'Shoes,' he grunts.

I see several low-lying shelves brimming with all kinds of footwear. I look at Brinkish's feet. He's wearing a pair of fluffy slippers that don't quite fit with his tough-guy attitude. 'Wife doesn't like dirt tracked in from outside,' he says by way of explanation.

I nod dutifully and bend down to pull off my boots. Embarrassingly, there's a hole in one of my socks that my big toe gapes through. Brinkish doesn't seem to notice.

Matt clears his throat. 'Uh, Bo? Is it okay if I stay outside?' He drops his voice to a loud stage whisper. 'My feet are really smelly.'

I pat his shoulder reassuringly. 'No problem.'

Brinkish's lip curls. 'Just don't mess up my lawn,' he says, slamming the door shut in poor Matt's face. He turns back to me. 'The mutt is this way.'

I follow him through to a small living room. To say it's over decorated would be an understatement: the sofa is covered in chintz, the wallpaper is a bright, repetitive floral design and everywhere I look there are china ornaments. I'd think it was all his wife's doing but Brinkish absently places a hand on a large porcelain ballerina in mid-pirouette and strokes its head.

In the middle of the room, almost camouflaged by the contrasting patterns and clutter, is a dog. As soon as it sees me, it charges over, tongue lolling. It leaps up, placing its front paws on my legs, and yelps.

'He's, uh, very friendly,' I comment, patting its head and doing what I can to avoid its doggy-breath licks.

Brinkish watches the pair of us with narrowed eyes. 'Like seeks like,' he says.

I extricate myself and sit on the edge of the sofa. The dog returns to its former spot in the middle of a garish rug and drools. 'What's he called?' I ask.

'Kimchi.'

'Isn't that a Korean food?'

'Yeah.'

'Don't Koreans eat dogs?'

His bottom lip juts out. 'A few. It's hardly a staple part of their diet.'

I get the impression this is a conversation he has had many times. 'Kimchi,' I call softly to see what the dog will do. His ears perk up and he bounds over to me, then jumps up and plonks himself onto my lap so my vision is almost obscured. Kimchi certainly verges on the more rotund side of canine.

'So,' I say, peering round first one floppy ear, then the other. 'What makes you think he's a vampire?' I feel ridiculous even saying the words.

'Check his teeth,' Brinkish tells me.

Somewhat warily, I place my hands on Kimchi's hindquarters and gently encourage him to look at me. My face is immediately slathered in several wet licks.

'Dogs should be afraid of vampires. Instinct should tell them to attack or run. He thinks you're his new best friend,' Brinkish continues, as I try to peer into Kimchi's mouth while avoiding any further collisions with his tongue. The reek of digested Pedigree Chum is off-putting. I can't see anything out of the ordinary about his teeth, however. Not that I'd try and pass myself off as any kind of animal expert.

'Um...' I begin. 'What exactly am I looking for?'

'His fangs!' Brinkish says, exasperated.

I look again. They seem perfectly normal to me. I glance at Brinkish, letting my guard down as I do. Kimchi swoops in for another lick. 'It's normal for a dog's canine teeth to be long,' I say, giving myself the air of a knowledgeable professional, while twisting away from the dog.

'Yeah?' he challenges. 'Then explain why he won't go outside during the day. He refuses point blank to be taken for a walk unless it's dark.'

Kimchi whines as if sensing he's the focus of our discussion. I stroke his ears and he subsides but I can feel his eyes on me. 'Perhaps if you take him to a vet...'

'I cut myself a few days ago,' Brinkish interrupts, his voice rising. 'Some blood dropped on the floor. Before I could get a cloth, he was licking it up.'

Tired of dodging Kimchi's slobber, I scoot him off my lap. He pants, tail wagging, then disappears out of the room. I sigh. 'Look, Mr Brinkish, can you see my eyes? The red in the centre of my pupil indicates I'm a vampire. Kimchi doesn't have that.'

'Oh yeah? Kimchi, come here,' he calls.

The dog returns, my right boot in his mouth. I gape. In the space of a few seconds he's managed to rip off a chunk of the expensive leather. Brilliant.

Brinkman grabs a small torch from a side table. He's obviously prepared for this. He passes it over to me. 'Shine it in his eyes.'

I'm doubtful; I don't want to damage the dog's vision by shoving a bright light into them. Brinkish, however, seems insistent so I do as he asks. As soon as the torch is turned on, I can see it: there's definitely some kind of red pigmentation there. It's in Kimchi's iris though, not his pupil.

I put the torch down and stand up. 'He's just a dog. The vampire mutation only occurs in humans and bats. It's widely accepted that other animals are immune.'

'It was widely accepted once that you could either be a black witch or a white witch,' Brinkish sneers. 'Look where we are now.'

I rub my forehead. The hybrid witches created as a result of O'Connell's desire to make the world a better place went public not long after he was charged with murder. Most people seem to think they're a good thing. Having met a few of them, I would beg to differ.

'I really do think you should just take him to a vet.'

'No. There must be a test you can do. Something to prove it.'

I grit my teeth. 'I suppose I could take a sample of blood...'

'Take the dog.'

I stare at him. 'Take it where?'

'You vampires have got state-of-the-art laboratories. Don't think I don't know that! Get him properly tested by bloodguzzlers who know what they're doing.'

'And then what? When I prove to you that your dog is just a dog?'

His eyes shift. 'Bring him back, of course.'

'He's your pet, Mr Brinkish. Your responsibility.'

'Responsibility is not letting a potentially lethal animal out on the streets. There are children living round here!'

I close my eyes briefly. I need to humour him; New Order is supposed to take all complaints and concerns about vampires seriously. As my grandfather suggested, it wouldn't take much to create a panic about people's pets turning guzzler overnight. A few well-placed internet articles and ... poof! We become even more hated than ever. I'm not stupid; I know that the British are more inclined to feel sympathy for a dog than they are for a human. In fact, it's not just Brits. There's a reason why the dog always survives in disaster movies: people just don't enjoy seeing animals suffer. I chew my lip.

'I came here on a motorbike,' I say finally. 'I can't take Kimchi now. I'll have to send someone round later.'

He shakes his head. 'You've come round to solve my vampire problem.' His eyes harden. 'Solve it.'

I look at Kimchi. His tail thumps on the rug as he registers my attention. Red irises aside, his large eyes are soulful and expressive. I can't stop myself from smiling at him. I guess I can put his owner's mind at rest. 'Fine,' I sigh, unable quite to believe I'm doing this. 'But if there's an accident...'

'He's a vampire dog. If there's an accident, he'll heal.'

Kimchi drops my poor boot. I can see the saliva on the ripped lining. The sooner I can get an official piece of paper to appease Mr Brinkish, the better.

Our return journey is frankly ridiculous. Kimchi is entirely unafraid of the motorbike but Matt and I are forced to wedge him between us to keep him stable. That means that I have to endure repeated wet slobbers on the back of my neck. I've always scorned side-cars in the past but I'm starting to see their appeal. When we pull up at a set of traffic lights, the family in the car opposite us are horrified. The only good thing is that – with our helmets on – they can't tell that we're vampires. I dread to think what the animal rights' lobbyists would say. In truth, they'd be right.

It takes every ounce of concentration I have to avoid the dips and minor potholes in the road to make Kimchi's journey as unstressful as possible. When we pull up outside the New

Order offices, he jumps off and barks once. I swear he's grinning in delight. He gives the motorbike one long sniff, then sits back as if giving it the doggy stamp of approval.

It's later now so the majority of the protestors have vanished, off to the safety of their own homes. There are still a few stragglers, however. When one spots us, he moves in our direction, pockmarked face twisting. I hear a low rumble and realise that it's Kimchi growling. I lunge for his collar, just managing to grab it before he leaps towards the protestor and into what would be disastrous action.

'Night beast!' the protestor yells.

'No, it's just a dog.'

Kimchi's growl intensifies.

'Since when do vampires have familiars?'

'It's not a familiar.' I speak evenly but I'm starting to get pissed off. 'It's a dog.'

'Bo,' Matt says nervously, 'maybe we should just go inside.'

I'm tempted to loosen my hold on Kimchi's collar just to see what happens. It's a pointless desire, though. The protestors hold all the cards: we can't intimidate them or threaten them or even politely ask them to leave. Our remit is to encourage free speech and open dialogue, even if that means letting these idiots make our lives as difficult as possible. I take Matt's advice and gently pull Kimchi round. Then we go through the main door.

There's still a light on in Pearls of Wisdom on the ground floor. I ignore it and start climbing the stairs but, before I get too far, the door opens and Dr Drechlin's voice rings out behind me. 'No animals allowed.'

'Matt, take Kimchi upstairs.' He nods his head vigorously and does as he's told. I turn round and face the good dentist. 'It's only temporary,' I tell him. Thank goodness he's not spotted the cat yet.

'First a cat, now a dog.' Damn. 'It's against the lease regulations.'

I move down so I'm level with him. Well, I say level: my feet are next to his but I'm a good foot shorter. I admit it's a ploy I've used before. Men – especially human men – are comforted when they feel physically superior, even if it is all an illusion.

'They won't get in your way,' I soothe.

'All you bloodguzzlers have done since you moved in is get in my fucking way.'

I open my mouth to placate him when there's the sudden sound of a scuffle from upstairs and an agonised yell from Matt, followed by a thunderous roar of paws rushing back down the stairs. Kimchi appears, ignoring me in favour of flinging himself at Drechlin. The dentist is knocked backwards against the wall. The dog bounces up, his paws scrabbling at Drechlin's shirt.

Drechlin is flustered. He pats Kimchi's head but glares at me. 'You shouldn't keep dogs if you can't train them properly.'

'He's not my dog,' I begin, before faltering. Somehow I don't think explaining that I'm investigating the possibility that the animal slobbering over him might be vampiric would endear either of us to the dentist.

There's a faint whine. Drechlin glowers and reaches inside the pocket of his white coat. To my surprise he pulls out a biscuit and gives it to Kimchi, who delicately snaps it from his fingers. Then the dentist whirls round and re-enters his office, slamming the door.

I raise my eyebrows at Kimchi, who is licking off the last few remaining crumbs. 'You're smarter than you look.' He wags his tail.

Matt's pale face peers round from the top of the stairs. 'Sorry, Bo.'

'Don't worry,' I call up. 'I think Kimchi might get on better with our neighbours than we do.'

'That's good,' Matt responds, 'because I don't think your grandfather's cat is very impressed.'

I roll my eyes. Of course not.

WHEN I finally drag Kimchi back upstairs, he eyes my grandfather's closed door with trepidation then shuffles over to the furthest corner away from it and curls up. My grandfather, unfortunately, is on the wrong side of the door.

'You were supposed to reassure the client that his canine was not a vampire, not bring it home with you. What kind of dog is that anyway?'

I eye Kimchi. 'Pure mutt, I think.'

'It's obese.'

I feel insulted on the dog's behalf. Goodness knows why. 'It's big boned.' My grandfather raises his eyebrows. 'I need to get a blood test done so Mr Brinkman has an official document to prove his dog is vampire-free. He isn't going to accept anything else.'

'Bo, you shouldn't let people walk all over you. It's demeaning and quite unbecoming for a Blackman.'

I put my hands on my hips. 'You mean walking all over me like you're trying to do right now?'

'I am your employer.'

I bite back my reply. It wouldn't do any good, even if calling himself my 'employer' is taking it a bit too far. Connor and Matt's heads are both down, as if they don't know where to look. Even Kimchi is avoiding eye contact. The last thing any of us need at this juncture is to have everyone in the office tiptoe around because of a frosty atmosphere caused by poor family relations. I like to think my silence makes me the better person; it's got nothing to do with the fact that any argument with my grandfather always finishes with him running circles around me. Fortunately, the phone rings so it looks less like I'm capitulating and more like I'm merely busy.

'New Order, Bo Blackman speaking. How may I help you?'

'Hello.' Michael's voice is soft. In my imagination, however, it's still laced with danger.

I start. Damn it. I wanted to be more prepared before I spoke to him. 'Uh, hi.'

'You were supposed to call me.'

'I only just got back,' I say, wishing I didn't have a sudden flurry of butterflies squirming around my stomach.

My grandfather checks his fob watch. It's almost 11pm and time for him to leave. Thank goodness. He throws Kimchi a dirty look then carefully opens the office door. There's a single plaintive meow before he closes it behind him.

'Back from where?' Michael asks, oblivious to the tension on this side of the line. 'It wasn't anything dangerous, was it?'

I ignore the flip-flop in my heart at his apparent concern. To stay grounded, I remind myself of all my unanswered questions about his murky past. 'No. I was just seeing a man about a dog.'

'Anything I can help with?'

I frown. It would be easiest to follow Brinkish's suggestion and use the Montserrat labs to test Kimchi's blood but an outside agency would remove any taint of bias. I'll get Connor to take him to a vet tomorrow before his shift starts. 'No,' I answer finally, 'everything's good.'

'Excellent,' he purrs. 'In that case, would you like to meet me for breakfast once you're done for the night?'

I hesitate. The last time we met for a meal it didn't go very well. 'Uh...'

'It doesn't have to be a vampette establishment, Bo. Not if you've already drunk today.'

Thankfully Connor provided that service before I left for

therapy. 'I have. How about a drink? Alcoholic, I mean,' I quickly add, 'not blood.' Facing him with some Dutch courage to help me along seems like a good idea.

He's silent for a moment before answering. 'Okay.'

'Have you heard anything from Medici?'

'No,' he says grimly. 'Have you?'

'Nada. He's going to bring Dahlia out of the woodwork sooner or later,' I say, referring to Arzo's ex-fiancée, whom Lord Medici illegally turned.

'I'm tempted to force the issue.'

'I don't think...' I trail off as I register Connor's face paling dramatically as he stares at his computer screen. Matt leans over, his eyes widening in dismay.

'What is it?'

'Hold on,' I mutter, going over to see what the problem is.

My grandfather's door opens and he strides out as if he's sensed that there is a problem. He joins our little cluster. A reporter's mouth moves silently from a live news feed. The scrolling words on the bottom of the screen read: 'Unprovoked vampire attack.'

'Turn up the sound.'

Connor does as he's told. The office fills with the reporter's flat, received pronunciation. '...The woman in question called an ambulance early this evening. Police are already on the scene and making a formal request for witnesses. The victim's name is currently being withheld but we understand she has been viciously beaten as well as raped. Sources say that she has identified her attacker as a vampire.'

I close my eyes. Bugger it all to hell. That's the last thing we need.

'Bo?' Michael's voice floats in from the receiver.

I hold it back up to my ear. 'We've got a serious problem.'

CHAPTER 3

EVIDENCE

I hover around the London General Hospital entrance, keeping far enough away to ensure the gaggle of journalists at the front don't spot me. It's imperative that I talk to the woman but I can't risk being identified. All it will take is one blurry photo and the tabloids will scream intimidation.

I chew my lip. There has to be a way to manage this. I could skirt round the back and look for a side entrance – or even clamber up to the roof to see whether I can gain access that way – but it doesn't take a genius to realise that the entire building will be on high alert for bloodguzzlers. The chance of me slipping in unnoticed is miniscule. And much as I need to talk to the victim, if I barge into her room and demand answers while she lies prone and hurting in a hospital bed, it *is* intimidation regardless of how pure my motives are.

I wonder how many Family members were rapists before they were recruited. Michael told me that new vampire recruits have their slates wiped clean; the few who don't take to the rehabilitation becoming a bloodguzzler affords are executed immediately if they step out of line. He views recruiting criminals as giving them a second chance; it's a way to make society better for everyone. I can't help thinking that once a rapist, always a rapist.

I check my watch. It's already well after midnight so, tempting as it is to contact Rogu3 and see whether he can infiltrate each Family's network and pull the files on any supposed ex-shitheads who would try this sort of thing, it wouldn't be fair. He's just a kid, after all. Besides, Medici aside, the Families pledged to cooperate with any investigations we started. Now is as good a time as any to test that promise.

I pull out my phone and dial. As I expect, Matt answers. I tell him what I need, adding that he's not to take no for an answer. He'll doggedly do everything necessary to get the information I need. I'm just hanging up when I spot a familiar figure striding out of the hospital's main entrance to address the press. My eyes narrow while the journalists rush forward. Perhaps they're not just called 'the press' because of their old printing equipment.

'At nine twenty-five this evening, police were called to a location on the South Bank. They were responding to an alleged sexual attack. On arrival, they discovered a woman aged thirty-five who had been badly beaten. There were also visible signs of sexual assault. To date, no suspects have been identified but door-to-door enquiries are taking place.'

'Was it a bloodguzzler?'

'No suspects have yet been identified,' Inspector Foxworthy repeats.

'The vampires are above human law. If her attacker turns out to be one, what action will the police take?'

Even from this distance, I see the inspector's eyes harden. 'This was a brutal and sustained attack. The victim is lucky to have escaped with her life. Regardless of who the perpetrator is, when they are caught justice will be served.'

Several cameras flash, illuminating his grim face. I mull over his choice of words. Justice can mean many things to many people. For humans, it only involves life imprisonment. For a fleeting moment, I hope it *is* a bloodguzzler who's done this. I quash down the thought as quickly as it arrives. Prior to my own turning, I'd believed that capital punishment was both futile and wrong. It's more than just my lifespan that's altered in recent months. I shiver and tell myself my opinions haven't changed, and that I'm just reacting to the brutality of the crime.

'He drove a stake through her palms to pin her to the ground,' a soft voice says behind me.

I jump half a foot in the air. So much for enhanced senses. I twist round, recognising Foxworthy's sidekick. Oh joy. She moves a step closer.

'Her mouth was stuffed full of dirt so she couldn't scream but she still bit off part of her tongue. Both her legs are broken.' Sergeant Nicholls raises her eyebrows. 'Have you ever seen someone who's been beaten so badly that their body is not only purple with bruises but swollen to almost twice its normal size?'

I stare at her.

'He was going to kill her,' she continues. 'It's only because she ripped free from the stakes that she managed to get away. You should see her hands, Ms Blackman. I wonder whether even a bloodguzzler like you would have the strength to tear your own flesh like that.'

I find my voice. 'Is she going to make it?'

Nicholls shrugs. 'Probably. But even if her wounds heal, she'll have nightmares for the rest of her life.'

'Was it a vampire?'

She meets my eyes. 'You tell me.'

'What's her name?'

'We're not releasing any details. Victims have rights too.'

'I can help!' I burst out. 'If a vampire did this...'

Her lip curls. 'Then she'll never get peace. Your kind don't like sharing. Even if the prick who did this is slaughtered, you won't tell us. We'll chase our tails for months while you sit back and laugh.'

'No,' I shake my head. 'It's not like that any more. We're changing. We're going to be more open and share what goes on. It's not going to be like it used to be.'

She leans in until her face is barely an inch from mine. 'I'll believe it when I see it.' Then she turns on her heel and stalks off.

Bile rises in my throat. I squeeze my eyes shut. It's going to take more than my words to prove that the Families are finally adapting to the modern world. The only thing that'll do it is action. I think of the broken woman lying less than a hundred feet away and make her a silent promise. No matter what, I'll find out the truth for her so she knows. I can't heal her bones or ease the pain in her mind but I can get her the justice she deserves, whatever form it takes. This isn't just about improving the Families' battered reputations.

Foxworthy let slip that the woman was found at the South Bank. Deciding that trying to breach hospital security is pointless, I head straight there instead, hoping there are still enough crime scene investigators around so I can find the exact location. I park the bike directly across the river from the Houses of Parliament and take a brief moment to stare up at Big Ben's illuminated clock face as painful memories flash through my mind. Then I shake myself and get to work.

I walk briskly along the waterfront, passing large, glittering buildings. The London Eye stares down at me, illuminated in blue. It's not the wheel itself that catches my attention, however – it's the other blue lights that are flashing nearby at the edge of Jubilee Park.

I frown. It's a well travelled and public place for such a prolonged attack; it's a wonder that the bastard who did this wasn't interrupted by someone wandering past. It must have been barely dark when the victim was attacked; either the rapist didn't care about getting caught or he had a point to prove. I think about her being held in place by stakes and shudder. It can't be a coincidence that the traditional weapon used for killing bloodguzzlers was used to pin down a human woman. It's not looking good for the Families. For us.

There's a small crowd of gawkers behind the police cordon. Distastefully, more than one is using a smartphone to record the apparently titillating action. White-suited investigators pick over the ground and there's a makeshift tent near a large oak tree: it's the sort that's normally used to conceal dead bodies from prying eyes. My stomach lurches at the thought of just how horrific the scene is that it needs to be hidden.

I ignore the onlookers and try to find the best vantage point. I can't just stroll nonchalantly onto the scene, I'm going to have to surreptitiously piggyback onto the police investigation and use what they discover to my own advantage. Right now, however, my chances of either seeing or hearing anything appear slim.

The principle behind any crime scene is that every contact made by both victim and perpetrator can be counted as a silent witness. Disruptive as it is to people who are live or work close to such scenes, every trace of evidence needs to be examined, from flecks of blood to smudged footprints to displaced blades of grass. It's a painstaking process. Most investigators try to preserve evidence by creating two cordons: an inner one where the main crime took place, and an outer one to keep away anyone who shouldn't be there. That includes me.

The only thing I have on my side is that the outer cordon here at Jubilee Park is fairly small; that means I'll have a better chance of learning something useful because I can get closer to the action. Most of the other onlookers are on the north side because that's where the tent is. I head towards the start of the approach path, where small metal footpads have been placed to give the investigators access to the site without disturbing the scene too much.

A uniformed officer stands to the side so, careful to avoid being identified as a bloodguzzler, I stay away from him. People trail past me and I strain to listen to what they say about the scene. Unfortunately they're all too sodding tight-lipped and engaged in their own sombre business to let anything slip. I'm going to have to be more canny.

I back away carefully. Because of the large temporary lamps set up to light the crime scene and the flashing police vehicles, the area is so bright that it could be midday rather than the middle of the night. I keep my head down whenever someone passes near me so they don't look in my eyes and spot my vampiric ethnicity. Then I step right until I'm next to the closest car.

The window is down and a tinny voice echoes out from the radio. 'Foxtrot Delta. The vic's flat is clear. Do we have the go-ahead to begin sweeps?'

There's a crackle of reply from somewhere across the city. Too many people monitor the radios; the police are not daft enough to give out hard information over such an unsecure line.

I glance around the car's interior but it's completely empty. Not that I am expecting to see a file marked 'Secret Evidence Regarding Jubilee Park Rape', but it is still frustrating.

I move to the next vehicle. There's a crumpled chocolate

wrapper, some empty evidence bags and very little else. I wrinkle my nose. This isn't going well.

I hear a rustle of movement further away and twist my head round to track it. One of the investigators pads over in his blue bootees to a nearby van and gives several clear evidence bags to someone inside. I scan the contents as quickly as I can before they're swallowed up. This time the lights are working in my favour and I spot a few cigarette butts, some dead leaves – which I suppose include traces of blood – and a scrap of ripped material. Nothing that will aid my cause right now but they do give me an idea.

Double-checking that no one is looking in my direction, I reach behind me and test the car door. The driver clearly thought it was safe to leave the car unlocked given the police presence surrounding us. I open the door slightly and squeeze my hand inside until I can grab the corner of one of the empty evidence bags. I pull it out and walk away, using a tree to block myself from everyone else's view. I scuff up some dirt from the tree roots, scoop it into the bag and seal it. I shake it a few times then I muss up my fringe until it covers half my eyes.

Striding over to the van, I hold out the bag. Naturally, I'm not wearing the necessary protective clothing so it's touch and go whether I'll get away with this. Fortunately, the technician inside is obviously exhausted and concerned more with getting back to his bed than who is handing him another scrap of prob-ably useless evidence.

'Here,' I say gruffly.

'From which sector?' he asks in a bored voice.

Shit. 'Uh, three.'

He rolls his eyes. 'Three what?'

I blink.

'A, B or C?'

'3A,' I squeak, hoping this isn't going to cause problems

with the investigation. It's only dirt, so I very much doubt it but I can't help feeling guilty.

He takes the bag and scribbles something on a clipboard. I crane my neck over his shoulder. Evidence bags are neatly stacked on shelves behind him, one of which contains an ID card. I shift my weight to my left foot and move so I can see it more clearly. There's a photo of an unsmiling woman and a name: Corinne something. Damn it, her surname is completely obscured. I grit my teeth.

'Sign here,' the tech grunts, holding out his clipboard and a pen.

I scribble something illegible and return it, although I keep hold of the pen. He gestures. 'I need the pen too.'

I pretend to look startled and glance down. 'Oh, yes, silly me!' I start to pass it over but fumble and trip so it falls to the ground. He curses as I kick it underneath the exhaust. 'Shit, sorry,' I apologise, getting down to look for it. After a moment or two, I stand up. 'I can't see it. Do you have a torch?'

He sighs and goes into the back of the van. I quickly go inside after him.

'You can't come in here!' he shouts.

I take another step and look down at the evidence bag. Corinne Matheson. Then I hold up my palms as he faces me. 'Sorry.' I say as I back away.

'Don't you know anything about chain of evidence?' he snaps. 'Who are you anyway?'

I give up on the pretence and sprint out of the van. The tech yells after me and several heads turn in my direction. A few people give chase but I'm a vampire. Even on my worst day and even as a fledgling, I could outrun any human. I speed out of the park, down the street and away.

～

I DON'T SLOW to a walk until I'm a good distance away. I curse my lack of foresight in parking the bike so near to the crime scene. I'll have to retrieve it later. Still, I now have something to go on, even if it's only a name. I dig out my phone, connect to the internet and search for Corinne.

It's such an unusual name that there are only three Corinne Mathesons using social media in London. I hope that the one I want is among them. Given that the first Corinne appears to be in school uniform – and remembering that Foxworthy's statement mentioned the victim was thirty-five – I narrow the names down to two. Both have high privacy settings and I can only see their profile pictures. The second one, who has bouncy blonde curls and a friendly lipsticked smile, is standing next to a small coffee shop called Huggamug. It takes less than a minute to discover it's located out towards the East End.

I flag down a taxi. The one good thing about only being able to venture outside when the sun is down is that the traffic is minimal. It won't take long to get there.

The driver is chatty and I have to respond, even though I'd prefer to be left to my own thoughts. Every vampire in the city has been ordered to be as friendly and amenable as possible; the more people we can prove our lack of evil leanings to, the better. Technically I can escape that rule as I'm the only known bloodguzzler without a Family and am therefore free from such strictures, but promoting good relations is the sensible thing to do.

'So,' the cabbie says in a strong London drawl, 'I'm betting you're trying track down a certain nonce.' He turns his head back in the direction of the park. 'The coppers are really going all out on this one.'

By now the news is probably all over the city, less because of the rape than because the main suspect is vamp. I rub my forehead. 'It's not surprising. If it turns out that the prick who did this is a vampire…'

He glances in the rear view mirror and nods. 'Yeah. You lot are up shit creek. You need to find him before they do.'

I stare at the back of his head. 'Does that bother you?'

'I've got no truck with bloodguzzlers. No offence,' he adds hastily, 'it's just the blood thing. Gives me the heebie-jeebies.' Him and me both. 'But at least if you get to him first, he'll get what he deserves. We should take a leaf out of your book – it's better than our taxes paying for him to live in a comfy cell for the rest of his days. Satellite TV and three meals a day,' he scoffs. 'It's not right.'

I think there's probably more to being in prison than that, but I stay quiet on the matter. Instead, I ask, 'Do you think a bloodguzzler could have done it?'

He speaks quietly as if he's afraid of being overheard. 'I've got a mate works at London General. Not a doctor or anything, he's just a porter. But he sees things. He called me earlier. Said she's got bite wounds on her neck. Not just one.' He shudders. 'There are lots.'

I feel sick. The only thing worse than Corinne's attacker being a vampire would be Corinne's attacker being *several* vampires. If it were true, it could be the nail in the Families' coffin. The human government is adept at knee-jerk reactions. First, they'll introduce legislation forcing the vampires to become subject to human law, then they'll prevent recruitments from taking place. The five Families keep their numbers steady at about five hundred apiece but, contrary to myth, bloodguzzlers aren't immortal. We enjoy extended life spans but within a few generations we could be all but wiped out of existence. Maybe that would be a good thing but, on the whole, the Families are better at keeping triber peace than the witches or the daemons. Unbalance the triber population and goodness knows what might happen.

The driver drops me off outside the darkened windows of Huggamug. I pass over several crumpled notes and a hefty tip. I wait until he drives off before I turn to the shop. If I need to break in, I'm going to have to make damned sure there aren't any witnesses.

There are a couple of posters in the window. One refers to a petition to stop a large coffee chain from settling in down the street while the other is for an amateur historical society. There's a photo on the front of a group of smiling people next to the Tower of London. The one in the centre is Corinne Matheson.

I press my face against the glass and peer inside the café. It's a small place with only eight little tables inside. Each one has a white vase filled with dried flowers. There's a strip of counter along the left-hand side and a large industrial-sized coffee maker. It looks completely deserted, although that's hardly surprising at this time of night. I test the door and the lock rattles. Short of breaking the glass, I'm not going to get in from here. In the interior gloom, however, I spot a door at the back. Maybe I'll find another way in if I skirt round the building.

Corinne Matheson is my only lead right now. Perhaps if I find out more about her, I'll find out more about her attacker. Surprisingly few rapes are committed by strangers. Odds are the vampire – or vampires – who did this already knew her.

I glance down the street. This is a terrace of buildings so I'll have to walk to the end of the road and double back to find a rear entrance. I only walk a few paces before I stop. Next to the coffee shop, there's a door leading to three flats. There are three buzzers with names inscribed behind plastic panels – and the bottom one is Matheson. She's probably the owner of Huggamug; living next to her business makes sense. And it makes my life considerably easier.

It's very late. If Corinne is not lying in London General, then she's fast asleep in her bed. The fact that there are no police anywhere near here suggests I've got the wrong woman but I have to be sure. If the worst I do is wake her up, then she's lucky. I take a deep breath and press the buzzer with my thumb. I hold it there, feeling the tension in my shoulders, and start to count silently in my head. One. Two. Three. Four. Five. Six. Seven. Eight. Ni—

The door bursts open.

A furious man glares at me. He seems remarkably clear eyed so, although he's wearing striped pyjamas, I don't think I actually woke him up. 'What?'

I stay calm. 'I need to speak to Corinne.'

His expression darkens. 'You've got the wrong fucking one! Don't you people ever quit? She's not a goddamn whore!'

Interesting. 'Is she here?'

'Where else would she be? It's not enough that we've changed our phone number, is it? Does she need to change her name too?'

A sleepy voice calls down. 'James? Who is it?'

'Go back to bed, Corinne. I'll deal with this.'

'I'm sorry, James,' I say softly. His eyes turn to me. 'But there's been a vicious attack on a woman called Corinne Matheson and I need to make sure it's not related to your girlfriend.'

'Wife,' he snarls.

I bow my head. 'My apologies. Your wife. I take it that she's frequently mistaken for someone else?'

'Ever since she changed her name and we got married. Dirty old men calling us up at all hours of the night. Bloodguzzlers like you,' he sneers.

'Do you happen to know where the other Corinne Matheson lives?'

'No, I fucking don't.' He slams the door shut so hard that the frame shakes. I hear one final muffled, 'Piss off!' before he stomps upstairs to his flat.

I stay where I am. James Matheson has a lot of pent-up anger to deal with. Still, he's given me some useful information. The Corinne Matheson who's fighting for her life in hospital is a prostitute; that explains why she has the vampire bite marks of on her neck. As I discovered not too long ago, offering herself up for feeding can be an easy and lucrative sideline for women like her. Maybe she was the victim of a client who took things too far. Then I remember what Nicholls told me about the stakes. It's unlikely. I've made some progress though.

CHAPTER 4
DATE NIGHT

By the time I finally get back to New Order, dawn is less than a couple of hours away. Other than the occasional distant siren, the streets are silent. Indoors, however, is an entirely different matter. Two vampires I've never seen before are sitting uncomfortably on the sofa in the waiting room. Kimchi is directly in front of them, a pool of slobber on the floor beside his paws. Both of them are remonstrating loudly with Matt.

'You can't keep us here!'

'At the very least, you can provide us with some O neg while we wait!'

'I can offer you Connor,' Matt begins.

'No way,' the ginger-headed human complains. 'I'm reserved for Bo.'

I wince. It makes him sound like he's my own personal drinking bottle. 'Fellows,' I say, holding up my palms and doing my best to look benign. 'I'm sure your Family Heads made it clear how important it is we talk to you.'

I receive curled lips in response. A matching pair, how

sweet. 'They told us to cooperate, not sit here cooling our heels for three hours,' the one on the left snaps.

Matt looks at me helplessly. 'Don't worry,' I reassure him. 'You did exactly what I asked you to do.' I look over the pair. The chattier one is wearing white, signifying his allegiance to the Bancroft Family, while his companion is dressed in silver, making him a Gully bloodguzzler. I wonder briefly how they manage to keep their clothes so clean. The colours aren't exactly inconspicuous either.

'Only two of you?' I ask.

'I spoke to all the Heads themselves.' Matt swallows. 'But Lord Medici, um, refused to cooperate. Mr Blackman told me to leave him alone.'

Unsurprising. At least Medici didn't try to recruit Matt again.

'So out of four Families, there are only two rapists?'

'Hey!' the Bancroft vampire protests, 'ex-rapist.'

Acid curdles my stomach. I point to him and nod towards our tiny conference room. It's really more like a cupboard but grandfather insists we give it a proper name. 'You first.'

The vampire grumbles but gets stiffly to his feet. As he walks inside, I pull Matt over so the other bloodguzzler can't hear me. 'Do you think they were telling the truth? The Heads?' Despite being forced to obey orders unquestioningly, Matt is often surprisingly sensitive to what's going on around him.

'As far as I can tell,' he whispers.

I chew my bottom lip. Two out of two thousand: I'm not sure those statistics are credible. But then again, rape is one of the most under-reported crimes. Who knows how many other undeclared shitheads like these two lurk in the Family closets? Right now, I can only work with what I've got.

'Bo?' Connor asks quietly. 'Would you like some company in there?'

I note the worried furrow across his brow and feel an odd rush of tenderness. 'I'm a vampire too, Connor,' I remind him gently.

'Yes, but...'

'It's okay,' I tell him. The Gully bloodguzzler eyes the pair of us. I narrow my gaze in his direction, daring him to say something. Fortunately for him, he keeps his mouth firmly buttoned. 'This won't take long,' I say grimly, then march into the conference room and close the door behind me.

The Bancroft bloodguzzler has made himself comfortable, leaning back in his chair with his legs propped up on the table and his hands knotted casually behind his head. I don't bother to hide my dislike of him. 'What's your name?'

He blinks at me lazily. 'Show me yours, darling, and I'll show you mine.'

I'm not in the mood for this. I kick upwards, connecting with his legs and forcing them down to the floor. Then I stand over him, hands planted on my hips.

'I like a woman with attitude,' he grunts.

'Your name,' I repeat.

He sighs dramatically. 'Nick. And I've got a great big...'

I smack him hard across his face with the back of my hand. He rocks backwards. 'That was unnecessary.'

'What did you do, Nick? When you were human?'

'You're frightened of me.'

I ignore him. 'How many did you rape?'

He glares at me. 'It wasn't technically rape. They didn't say no. And besides, I'm reformed now. This is all a waste of time.'

'If it wasn't rape then why did Lord Bancroft send you here?'

He lifts his eyes to the ceiling. 'I may have had sexual relations with some women who were drunk. Six or seven.'

I force my emotions down. It's not easy. 'When you say drunk...'

'Unconscious. They were unconscious, alright? It's not like I forced them to drink or anything. They shouldn't have gotten themselves in that state in the first place.'

I step towards him. 'So you're saying that it was all their fault?'

He starts to nod then registers my expression. 'No. It was my doing. I shouldn't have done it and I regret my actions. I have learnt the error of my ways.'

He sounds like he's repeating someone else's words verbatim. Without realising it, I've balled my fists tightly. I slowly release my fingers. 'When was the last one?'

'Eight months before I turned.' He forestalls my next question by adding, 'And I was turned nine years ago.'

That makes him very young by vampire standards. Young enough to not be fully assimilated into the Family – and willing to break rank by raping again?

'Look, lady,' he sneers. 'I know what you're thinking.'

I'm thinking you're a disgusting, perverted excuse for a vampire. 'What?' I ask him, playing along.

'You're thinking I might have had something to do with that woman who was attacked. It wasn't me.'

'Really.' My tone is dry. 'Do you have an alibi?'

The corners of his mouth lift and he bares his teeth. 'I don't need one.' He stands up suddenly, kicking the chair backwards. I tense, ready for a fight. Nine years isn't so much, I can take a bloodguzzler of that age. He starts undoing his belt buckle. No sodding way. For a moment I feel sheer, unadulterated terror. Except I'm learning to be a fight-rather-than-flight kind of girl. I pick up the chair behind me to smash over his head while he drops his trousers.

'Look,' he says.

'I know what a tiny penis looks like.' I prepare to swing.

'Not like this you don't.'

My eyes move downwards of their own accord. Then I gape. Nick has no penis and no testicles; his groin looks more like that of a woman than a man. There's not even any pubic hair. I blink several times then look up at his face.

'Happy now?' he asks me.

'What...?'

'Castration and total penectomy. It was a condition of my recruitment. Lady Bancroft demanded it.' A muscle twitches in his cheek. There's a challenge in his eyes but also a lot of shame.

I draw in a deep breath. 'You may get dressed. You're free to go.'

'What? You don't want a piece of this? You don't think I'm sexy?'

I walk out. I shouldn't be surprised. After all, Lady Bancroft executed one of her own bloodguzzlers in front of me simply because I took him unawares. She wasn't someone who's afraid of stamping her authority.

I try to compose myself then look at the Gully suspect. In my absence, Kimchi has drifted closer towards him. From the expression on the man's face, he's not much of a dog lover.

'Have you been...?' I pause and attempt to rephrase. 'Does everything still work?'

He looks confused but, when Nick comes out of the conference room, still tucking in his shirt and winking at me as if he'd just got his leg over, his face clears. 'Yes.' He scratches his neck and looks away. 'Yes, it does.'

'Come on then.' I turn on my heel, forcing him to follow. Sensing less aggression from him than Nick, I sit down this time. He picks up the fallen chair and places it carefully upright before doing the same.

'You were getting quite lippy in there,' I comment.

He shifts uncomfortably. 'Sorry. I'm hungry.'

I take a softer approach. 'Do you know why you're here?'

'You think I'm the sort of guy who goes around raping women.'

I raise my eyebrows. 'You're not?'

'I wouldn't be, er, intact if I was.'

'So why did Lord Gully send you here then?'

He looks away. 'It's on my record. Rape, I mean. But it's not what you think.'

'Apparently it never is. Why don't you enlighten me?'

He twitches. He's baby faced: I reckon he must have been very young when he was turned. His cheeks are round and slightly chubby but there are high points of colour on his cheekbones. 'I had sex with my girlfriend,' he mutters. 'I was seventeen and she was fifteen.'

I manage to avoid cursing aloud. Statutory rape. 'Did she agree? Was it consensual?'

'Of course! We'd been going out for two years. We were in love.' He drops his head. 'Then her father found out and...'

'Where is she now?'

'Married to an investment banker. Twin girls. Big house in the country.'

'Love's young dream turned sour, then?' He nods. 'Where were you yesterday between eight and nine pm?'

'Work. I'm responsible for the upkeep and maintenance of the Gully properties.'

'Can anyone verify you were there?'

'Lord Gully can. He was checking I'd done a good enough job repairing the perimeter wall. It was damaged recently when some humans drove a car into it. We think they were trying to, you know, get inside and do some mischief.'

I grit my teeth. If Lord sodding Gully knew all along that this vampire was innocent, why the hell did he send him here? I could say the same about the new Lord Bancroft. The pair of them were simply wasting my time.

'Fine,' I snap. 'Do you have a phone number where I can reach you if I need to ask more questions?'

He reels off a number. I make a note of it and stand up.

'That's it?'

'Well, you did say you were hungry.'

He stumbles over his own feet in his haste to get to the door. I watch him leave and drop my head into my hands. I'd wanted cooperation, not mindless suspicion.

Connor appears in the doorway. 'Bo?'

'Mm.'

'You're meeting Lord Montserrat in twenty minutes.'

I roll my eyes up to the heavens. Just brilliant. A shitty end to a shitty night.

THE BAR IS ALMOST DESERTED. I can't understand how twenty-four hour establishments like this justify staying open all night. There are only five other people in the place, lined up on bar stools and staring at themselves in the fingerprint-smudged mirror opposite. Or perhaps they're not gazing at their own reflections but the long line of multi-coloured bottles. Either way, it's a miracle the place stays afloat.

I order a martini while Kimchi settles at my feet. Michael Montserrat had better bloody well be on time. I don't fancy spending the whole day here because I strayed past sunrise.

The television on the far wall is on mute. For some unfathomable reason, it's broadcasting aerobics. For an equally unfathomable reason I watch it, my eyes tracking the lycra-clad gym bunnies as they glow their way through the routine. The brunette in front needs to invest in a better sports bra.

The door opens but I avoid looking towards it. I don't want to see the sexy five o'clock shadow tracing Michael's jawline or the way his perfectly tailored suit fits his well-toned body. Instead, I keep my gaze fixed on the brilliant white smiles of the aerobics extras.

'You made it,' he says, settling onto the stool nearest to me.

I sip my drink. I can do casual. 'Why wouldn't I?'

'You've been known to avoid such meetings in the past.'

I wrinkle my nose. 'Every time I've failed to show, I've had a very good reason.' It's true. And it's only happened twice. It's not as if I make a habit of it; I like being punctual.

'Well, it's good to see you anyway.'

I'm in the middle of another sip which goes down the wrong way so I end up coughing and spluttering. Really slick. 'Is it?' I choke as the brunette tosses back her hair and performs a complicated step routine that is impossible to follow.

'Bo. Look at me.'

Unwillingly, I turn my head. Kimchi mistakes my movement for something exciting and immediately bounces up, tail wagging.

Michael blinks. 'That's not yours, is it?'

I sigh. 'No. His owner thinks he might be a vampire.'

'A vampire dog?'

'He's a bloodhound.'

My joke falls flat and Michael seems puzzled. 'He looks like a mutt.'

Kimchi starts gnawing Michael's shoelace. 'He likes you. He only eats the shoes of people he likes.'

'Is that so?'

I shrug. 'It's what I've decided anyway.'

He orders a beer then eyes me carefully. 'You seem ... pissed off.'

'It's been a long night.'

'I mean pissed off with me.'

I bite my lip. It's not his fault that being near him makes me feel as skittish as newborn kitten. 'I just feel a bit awkward, that's all,' I admit.

'I realised that when you said you wanted to meet in a bar.' He sighs. 'Bo, is this about what happened in the vampette restaurant?'

That and the fact I've got a photo underneath my mattress that suggests you're a cold-blooded killer who enjoys chopping people's heads off. 'Sort of,' I say. 'You tell me you like me but you don't want to be with me.' I scrunch up my face. 'And there's the whole "you must do what I say because I'm Lord Montserrat" gig you've got going on.'

He takes my hands and heat surges through my veins. 'What I said was that you're under my skin. That I dream about you. But you need to come to terms with being a vampire first. I'm not going to be your recruit-rebound guy.'

'My what?'

'It happens a lot. Newbie vampire gets all flushed with their new power and lease of life. Shags the first available guy – or girl – then moves on. And as for the "you must do what I say" part, I've not really done that with you.'

I meet his eyes. It's not fair that he can be so laid back while my stomach is in knots. 'You wouldn't tell me what you did with the Medici bloodguzzler you knocked unconscious in the middle of the street.'

'I seem to recall that you did most of the damage, Bo,' he says mildly.

'You know exactly what I mean.'

He runs a hand through his hair. 'Does it make a difference?'

'I don't know,' I say quietly. 'Besides, what if the only reason we're attracted to each other is because you're the one who turned me?'

'Who cares what the reason is?'

'I care.'

'You're over-thinking things.'

I take another drink. 'I can't help it.'

He stares at me, his dark eyes hooded. 'Why don't we simply start over then?' he says finally. 'My name's Michael.'

I swallow. 'Bo.'

The corner of his mouth quirks up and I have to resist the urge to reach out and touch it. 'Nice to meet you.'

I give him a small smile and fiddle with my glass. 'So is this good morning for you or good night?'

He grimaces. 'At bit of both. I was up most of the night trying to find out what happened to the woman in Jubilee Park. The police were not cooperative.'

'Neither were the Families.' I tell him about the Gully and Bancroft 'suspects'.

'I forget sometimes how new you are to all this. It's pretty standard.'

'Castrating rapists?'

He shrugs. 'It's what we do. Don't tell me you disagree?'

'Well, yes. Not that I don't think they're absolute bastards but I don't see how it solves any problems. Rape is about power, not sex. Castration's just so ... extreme.' I shake my head.

'It's a choice, Bo. We don't go to them and ask if they want to be recruited. They come to us. Those are our terms.'

'So you lot were telling Matt the truth? That in four Families there are only two rapists? One of whom isn't really a rapist anyway?' I twist my fingers together. 'Although I admit that now I'm no longer surprised.'

He frowns. 'Four Families?'

'Medici wouldn't play ball.'

He snarls quietly. 'We need to do something about him.'

'I know. Grandfather seems to think we're better off waiting for Medici to make a move first.' I look at him pointedly. 'I don't agree but you're the one who thought the old man would be good for New Order.'

'So did Arzo.' Michael punches me lightly on the arm. 'And so did you, even if you won't admit it.'

I glance up at him through my eyelashes. 'Yeah, yeah.'

He smiles. 'So that was your night? Rounding up dogs and interviewing dodgy vampires?'

'I found out who the victim was too.'

He starts. 'The police told you?'

'No, I did a little digging.' I know I sound smug; I can't seem to help it. 'Her name is Corinne Matheson. I'm pretty certain she's a prostitute.'

'Really?' He looks thoughtful. 'That puts a different spin on things.'

I nod. 'Her attacker could have been a client. From what little the police did tell me, whoever it was tortured her.' I look away. 'There were stakes, Michael. They impaled her hands with wooden stakes.'

He blanches. 'Sweet Jesus.'

Kimchi whines and licks my hand. As he does, I feel the odd prickle across the back of my neck alerting me to the sun's impending approach.

'I have to go.' I hop off the stool.

'I can walk you back if you wish.'

'It's okay. I have Kimchi to protect me.'

He gives me a funny look. 'The dog's name is Kimchi? Isn't that...'

I bob my head. 'Believe me, I've already gone through this.' I twist my hands nervously. 'Well, see you.'

'Bo,' he calls softly, when I'm already halfway out the door. 'Let's do this again. It wasn't so bad, was it?'

'I guess not.' I smile at him while my stomach somersaults. Maybe next time I'll ask him about the photo.

CHAPTER 5

PUPPY LOVE

When I open my eyes eight hours later, my small flat is a scene of utter devastation. I spring to my feet, eyes wide as I take in clouds of white stuffing, some unidentifiable beige material, and my clothes strewn about. I'd been tired, sure, but the thought that someone could wander while I was fast asleep and trash the place sends my heart racing. I don't own anything of value so a thief would get little joy from rifling through my belongings. Then it occurs to me what the intruder may have been after. I sprint to the tiny kitchen and fling open the fridge door, scrabbling towards the back. Relief floods through me: X's little vial of dark red blood – and the theoretical cure for vampirism – is still there. I close my eyes and rock back on my heels until something cold nudges my back.

Twisting round, I'm greeted by Kimchi. He thumps his tail on the floor. I frown at him. 'Did you do this?' I scoop up the nearest ball of fluff and hold it out while he looks away, suddenly unable to meet my eyes. 'You're in the doghouse, buster,' I tell him sternly.

There's a scrawled note on the kitchen table from Connor,

informing me that he took the dog to the vet but it would be a day or two before we received the blood tests back. I wonder what the vet's face was like when Connor told him he wanted the mutt checked for vampirism. I'm also tempted to ask him to return my key. Dropping in unannounced is one thing; dropping in and leaving the Drool Master is something entirely different.

Sighing, I fill a bowl with water and place it on the floor, before opening various cupboards to find something doggy friendly for Kimchi to eat. Given how many of my belongings he's managed to chew through, he'll probably eat just about anything. I find a tin of tuna hiding behind some teabags and gaze at it. I must have bought it during one of my 'I'm going to eat normal food like a human' shopping expeditions. I don't have to eat anything – vampires can survive on blood alone, but most still enjoy eating real food sometimes. Ria, in one of her more benevolent moods, gave me a specially created vampire cookbook not long after I moved in here. Most of the recipes seem to incorporate blood and, quite frankly, turn my stomach. It was a nice thought though.

I open the tin and tip out the tuna onto a plate. Kimchi scarfs it down in five seconds flat and doesn't seem to suffer from any immediate ill effects. I'll have to buy some real dog food pronto, though. He licks the plate shiny clean then sneaks a look up at me. There's a faint whine.

'Are you saying that because you want more to eat?' I ask. 'Or is that an apology for destroying my soft furnishings?'

He barks once and leaps up, placing his paws on my legs. His saliva-dripping tongue veers perilously close to my bare skin so I extricate myself carefully.

'Sit,' I tell him in as commanding a tone as I can manage.

He looks delighted and jumps again. I'm about to try again when his ears prick up. He bounds to the front door, tail wagging so fervently I'm amazed it's still attached to his body. Three seconds later, the doorbell rings and, on cue, Kimchi starts barking.

Unable to reach the door handle thanks to Kimchi's ecstatically vibrating body, I grab his collar and try to pull him away. 'No!' I say firmly.

He ignores me and continues yelping. Idiot dog. Or, to be more accurate, idiot me. Even Brinkish had managed to control him; I'm clearly not cut out to be a dog handler. For expediency's sake, I scoop him up into my arms. Kimchi seems to think this is some kind of new game and wriggles around in delight. I get him into the bedroom and shut the door – then it occurs to me that now he can gnaw on my bedsheets as well as my clothes and cushions. As he's fallen suspiciously quiet, no doubt that's what he's immediately set about doing.

Giving up on the dog, I open the door and peer out. When I see who it is, I fall back in surprise. It's been a while since I saw Rogu3 face to face and he's grown about a foot and a half in the intervening months. Gallingly, he's now taller than I am. He still has the gangliness of a teenager, however, and grins at me awkwardly.

'Hi, Bo.' He glances at my clothes. 'Oh, did I wake you?'

I realise I'm still wearing my rather threadbare pyjamas, dotted all over with teddy bears. Hardly a kickass vampire PI, then.

'I keep different hours these days,' I mutter, feeling somewhat embarrassed. I beckon him inside. 'What are you doing here, Rogu3?'

He scratches his neck. 'Do you want me to go?'

Realising how easily my question could have been misconstrued, I backtrack. 'No, of course not! It's great to see you.' To emphasise my words, I lean over and give him a hug. 'It's just that you normally prefer the whole incognito thing.'

'I thought you'd want this.' He gives me a slim file.

I flip it open. The first sheet is a mugshot of woman in her twenties. Typed next to the photo are the words 'Matheson, Corinne'. I raise my eyebrows. 'Is telepathy a new trick of yours?'

Rogu3 shrugs. 'It was all over the news. I figured it was the kind of thing you'd be after.'

'It is.' My suspicions, however, are on full alert. I can't believe he stayed up half the night to pull all the information he could extricate from the virtual world merely on the off-chance that I'd want it. He's a great kid but he's smart enough to charge market value for his services. Given that I still owe him money, something else is going on. 'What do you really want?'

'Um,' he flushes. 'Nothing, just...'

I suddenly realise something is different. I grin at him. 'Your voice! It's broken!'

'Yeah,' he admits, smiling. 'I was pretty much the last one in my class, which was kind of embarrassing, especially when it kept cracking at the wrong moments. But last week's word of the week was "stentorian". Mainly because when I'm not concentrating, I sound like my old primary school teacher who enjoyed bellowing loudly about decimal points.'

I'm glad he's not grown up so much that he's putting aside his more endearing personality quirks. 'Try me,' I say.

Rogu3 clears his throat. 'No, you foolish child,' he booms, 'calculators are reserved for the arithmetically challenged!'

I clap my hands. 'Impressive. And definitely stentorian. Now tell me why you're here.'

There's a snuffling sound at my bedroom door. He throws me a look. 'Either you've really changed since you've become a bloodguzzler, Bo, or you've got a new friend.'

'It's a case I'm working on. Answer the question.'

He swallows. 'You can say no...'

'Granted. Go on.'

He stands back up, thrusting his hands into his pockets. 'This is stupid,' he mumbles. 'Forget I was ever here.'

'Rogu3, sit down. You can ask me anything. I won't bite.' His eyes fly to mine and I smile softly. 'I promise.'

'Okay, yes,' he nods. 'I can trust you. I've known you for like forever.'

Forever clearly means something different to a teenager than it does to me. 'Sure.' I wait for him to speak but he just shuffles his feet. For some reason, neither of his shoelaces are tied. 'Rogu3, are you in trouble? Is it the hacking?'

His head swings dejectedly in dissent.

'Your exams? You were taking your GCSEs early, weren't you?'

'Only Maths. It went fine.'

'Your parents?'

'No. It's not them.'

'Rogu3,' I say gently, 'you're going to have to give me something here.'

His bottom lip juts out and for one horrifying moment I think he's about to cry. He draws in a deep breath and manages to keep hold of himself. 'Her name is Natasha,' he says.

It's just as well he's staring down at his trainers rather than looking at me because my mouth drops open. I shut it quickly. I should probably have guessed what the problem is, but he's always struck me as particularly confident and together. I suppose it doesn't matter who you are – when you fall in love, you get the same tinge of madness along with it.

'She's your girlfriend?'

He kicks at the chair leg. 'I wish.' He sighs. 'I'm a geek. A nerd who hides in his parents' garage and messes around on computers all day long.'

'Who's probably more successful now than any of your

peers will ever be,' I point out. Then I add hastily, 'Not that I condone illegal activity.'

'If you don't want those files, I can take them back.' He gestures to Corinne Matheson's folder in my hands.

'You know I'm going to keep them.' I put the folder down. 'Let's focus on Natasha, shall we?'

'She's a goddess. She's smart and pretty and cool.' Rogu3 sniffs. 'And popular.'

'Have you asked her out?'

'She's not going to look twice at me.'

'You don't know until you...'

'Try? Yeah, yeah, yeah. Except I do know, Bo. Believe me, I know. Why do you think I'm here?'

'For advice,' I say.

'Um, yeah. Advice. Sure.'

His expression makes me think that I'm the last person he'd come to for that. Given the state of my own love life, that's hardly surprising. It still doesn't explain why he's here.

'Spit it out. What can I help you with?'

'No, you're right. Advice is good. That's what I came here for.'

'Rogu3, you're not going to hurt my feelings if you don't want to listen to any of my wisdom.'

His relief is palpable. 'Oh, okay. Good.' He nods. Then everything comes out in a rushed babble. 'You're a vampire now, so you're cool and glamorous and if you showed up at my school with that leather jacket and that pout you always have and you come to talk to me, then maybe...'

'You'll be cool by association?' I ask drily. It's not a word I've ever related to myself but I could go with it. Then I frown. 'Hold on, what pout?'

He ignores my question. 'I know you can't come during the day but there's a band playing on Friday night in the gym.

There'll even be a bar. It's for under-eighteens,' he adds, when he spots my doubtful look. 'It is at school, remember? Everyone will be there. We could have a code and then, when she's nearby, you could come in and, you know, pretend to recognise me.'

'Except it wouldn't be pretending because I would recognise you.'

His face clears. 'Right! That makes it even better!'

He looks so hopeful and earnest, I'm reminded of Kimchi.

'Considering the way vampires are viewed right now, I don't think being mates with one is going to improve your street cred.'

A calculating expression appears on his face. 'Well, instead of being my friend, you could, you know, be mean and evil. You could show your fangs and threaten everyone and then I could,' he shifts his feet, 'knock you out or something.'

'Rogu3,' I sigh. 'You're one of the most intelligent people I know. You don't need to put on a show or be something you're not. Just be yourself. You're eloquent and articulate. You don't need to do this.'

'You don't get it.' He clenches his jaw in frustration. 'I'm a freak. I've got spots and I'm skinny and my friends are more interested in binary code than normal teenage things.'

I raise my eyebrows. 'Normal? You're kidding me, right? There's no such thing as normal.'

'I'm fourteen years old, Bo. It's all about being normal. Surely you're not so old that you can't remember what it's like?'

I choose not to answer that one. 'Rogu3, I can't go and threaten someone. Especially not kids! The vampires are trying to improve their reputations, not make them worse.'

'You talk about the bloodguzzlers as if you're not one of them.'

I run a hand through my hair. 'I've had some, um, acceptance issues. But I *am* one of them and I can't do what you're asking. Look, why don't I...'

'Forget about it,' he interrupts. 'I should have known you wouldn't help.' He turns and walks out.

'Rogu3!' I call out, inwardly cursing. I run after him. 'Wait!' I'm just in time to see him push past a figure on the stairs. 'Come back!'

'Ms Blackman, I sincerely hope you are not drinking blood from a minor. That would not go down well at all. Particularly considering you are no longer under the protection of a Family.'

It's sodding Inspector Foxworthy. I glare at him. 'Get out of my way.'

'I need to talk to you first.' The outside door slams shut as Rogu3 makes his escape into the night air. Bloody hell.

'Can't it wait?' I ask through gritted teeth.

The smile I receive reminds me of a clown with a painted grin on his mouth but with flinty eyes of stone behind the make-up. 'No,' he says, 'it can't.' He looks me up and down. 'Cute pyjamas though.'

Letting Kimchi out of the bedroom and sternly telling him to guard the room, I leave Foxworthy to cool his heels while I pull on something more appropriate. When I emerge, the dog is curled up on Foxworthy's lap.

I give the policeman an amused look. 'You realise he's here because his owner thinks he might be a vampire.' I shouldn't have said it but I couldn't resist.

He leaps up, knocking Kimchi to the floor where the dog immediately starts gnawing on a leg of the coffee table. 'A bloodguzzling dog? I didn't think that was possible.'

I'm tempted to prolong his concern but I yield to my better nature. 'It's not.'

Foxworthy doesn't relax, edging as far away from the dog as possible. I'm surprised; I hadn't thought the bullish inspector would be scared of much, let alone a daft mutt with more saliva than fight. I eye Foxworthy with as much suspicion as he's eyeing the dog. Last time we met, he locked me up in a cell with a black witch. It didn't go well.

'You said I'm no longer under Family protection. I think Lord Montserrat might beg to differ on that one.'

The inspector perches on the arm of the sofa and folds his arms. 'So the jury's still out. We've never had a loose vampire to contend with. What happens if you go all psycho like that other one?'

'The other one was an anomaly.'

'So are you. If other bloodguzzlers follow your lead and go solo, well,' he shrugs, 'let's just say I think the legislation might change. And for the better.'

I don't actually disagree with him. I set a dangerous precedent when I walked out on the Montserrat Family, even if it was with Michael's tacit blessing. I don't want Foxworthy to know I'm on his side with this, however, so I mirror his body language by folding my own arms. 'What do you want?'

'I want you to know this isn't my idea.'

'But?' I prompt.

'But it would be appreciated if you would come to London General and talk to the victim.'

'Corinne Matheson?' I ask, taken aback.

If he's surprised that I know her name, he doesn't show it. 'Indeed.' The disapproving arch to his spine makes it clear what he thinks of the plan. 'You might provide some insight into her story.'

'Story' is an interesting choice of words. 'You think she's lying,' I say softly.

'Oh, she was definitely attacked. And with a viciousness I've not seen in years.'

'Except you don't think it was a vampire who did it.' He doesn't answer, which is answer enough. 'It's nice that you're coming to me for help,' I comment. 'Last night, your buddy Nicholls was not exactly forthcoming.'

He stands up and steps towards me. Kimchi starts to growl from behind my legs, and Foxworthy hastily sits back down again. 'Yeah, except it didn't stop you from interfering. You really screwed us over with that. Your antics compromised every piece of evidence we collected from the scene. It's going to cause us problems if we ever nail the prick that did this and drag him to court.' He smirks at me. 'We've impounded your bike, by the way.'

I curse inwardly. 'Do I get it back?'

'I'll consider releasing it if you cooperate.' He reaches into his coat pocket and pulls out a set of handcuffs. I don't need to see the Magix logo to know that they've been bespelled to be particularly effective against vampires. He dangles them at me. 'For our own protection.'

'I'm not putting those on.'

He lifts an eyebrow. I sense he's pleased. 'Then I will waste no more of your precious time.'

Shit. He called my bluff and won. 'Fine,' I snap. 'Give them to me.'

Foxworthy doesn't speak as I hold out my bare wrists. Avoiding touching my skin, he puts them on me. The effect is instantaneous; they sap all my energy so any movement I make is slow and sluggish, like I'm wading through jelly. For the first time he smiles genuinely.

The protestors, who have regrouped outside, let out a

raucous cheer when Foxworthy leads me out. One lets fly hawks a ball of phlegm that lands in a glistening green mass on my shoulder.

'Aren't you going to do anything about that?' I say to the inspector, as he puts me into a waiting car.

'We live in a free country, Ms Blackman. People are allowed to protest.'

'Doesn't spitting count as assault?'

His eyes drift down to the phlegm dripping down my front then up to my face. 'I didn't see anything,' he says, slamming the car door shut behind me.

CHAPTER 6
FLASH OF GOLD

Foxworthy drags me through a series of labyrinthine, antiseptic-smelling corridors. He seems irritated that I'm struggling to keep up but, when I tell him that he'll have to remove the vampire inhibitor handcuffs if he wants us to move faster, he merely grunts. Everyone gives us a wide berth, even when there's little room for them to do so. One nurse lets out a small shriek and darts away as fast as her comfortable shoes can carry her. This fear of bloodguzzlers may be a recent development and a result of over-hyped media spin and one solitary psychopath, but every reaction serves to remind me that I really hate being a vampire.

Eventually we arrive at a small, private room. A uniformed copper stands outside. His gaze is friendly and I flash him a big smile, relieved that not everyone thinks I'm a monster. Then Foxworthy nudges me inside.

I'd been prepared to see someone battered and bruised but the state of Corinne Matheson takes my breath away. Her head has been shaved and there's a line of stitches across her skull that are reminiscent of those on Frankenstein's monster. Her right eye is massively swollen and her skin is mottled with angry-looking bruises. I glance down at her hands, which are wrapped in huge swathes of white bandages. Her one good eye blinks at me and a single bloodstained tear falls from it. I swallow hard.

'Pretty, ain't I?' she croaks.

'I need to know whether the blood is a problem for you,' Foxworthy says to me.

I don't answer immediately; I'm still too horrified by the nightmare vision of what used to be an attractive young woman.

'Blackman!' he snaps.

My head jerks. 'Sorry,' I mumble. 'It's fine.'

'Good.' He moves to the far wall, leaning his large body against it, his brows shoved together in a frown as he tracks my every move.

I do what I can to ignore him and sit down on the white plastic chair next to Corinne's bed. 'I'm Bo,' I say gently. 'I'm a vampire.'

I'm sure she'd scowl if her face were still capable of expression. 'I've not been fucking brain-damaged, you know.'

'I'm sorry. It's just I'd like to talk to you about what happened and I'll understand if you're not comfortable discussing it with a vampire.'

Her eye slides away. 'Got a dick?'

'No.'

'Then I ain't got a problem.'

I nod. 'I might ask you questions you've already answered, but it'd really help if you could repeat what you said before.'

Her head turns towards Foxworthy. 'How many times am I going to have to do this?'

I touch her hand lightly. She flinches but doesn't pull away. 'As often as it takes to make sure the bastard who did this doesn't ever do it again.'

She sniffs disgustedly but I sense her acquiescence.

'Where were you when he attacked?'

'On my way to meet a friend. I was waiting for a bus and he came out of nowhere. Had some kind of sedan car. He asked me if I wanted a lift and, when I declined, he grabbed me, punched me in the face and threw me into the back seat.'

'Do you know what time it was?'

'Around seven.'

It's late enough in the year that seven o'clock is already dark. That doesn't make a difference as far as most vampires are concerned – other than Matt and myself, bloodguzzlers aren't allowed on the streets until they're strong enough to cope with the sun – but the darkness would make it easier to abduct someone.

I glance at Foxworthy. 'Were there any witnesses?' He shakes his head, his eyes dark and brooding. 'CCTV?'

'No.'

'What happened then, Corinne?'

'I tried to get out but he locked the doors. He hit me again and I passed out. When I woke up I was in the park.'

'Jubilee?' She nods. 'It's a busy place,' I comment. 'He must have done something to avoid being noticed.'

She closes her eye. 'He waited until I came to. He wanted me awake to see what he was doing. To make sure I wouldn't miss a second.' Her voice is cold and bitter. 'When he started with the stakes, hammering them into my hands, I was screaming like a banshee. Someone should have heard.'

'We're looking into spell traces,' Foxworthy interrupts.

There are privacy spells all over the place. They're usually used in residential areas, and I've heard they're a godsend these days for adult children who are unable to afford to fly the family nest. No matter how good the spell was though, the perp was taking a hell of a risk by choosing such a public area.

'What did he look like?'

'When I came round, he was wearing a balaclava and I couldn't see a damn thing,' Corinne says. 'After I fainted a second time, he took it off. I guess he thought I was going to die so it didn't matter what I saw. Six foot, brown hair, nose, eyes, mouth.' She is obviously tiring of the questions.

'Here.' Foxworthy waves a piece of paper. When it becomes clear he's not going to bring it to me, I struggle to my feet and shuffle forward. The longer these bloody handcuffs are on for, the more debilitating they become.

It's a photofit. The man is good-looking, even with the harsh angles provided by the computer programme. I know it makes no sense but it seems unfair that he's not as ugly on the outside as he is on the inside. He has a square jaw, short, wavy chocolate-brown hair and a brilliant white smile. His eyes are hazel and include the little red dot that signifies vampire. It's a detailed photofit. It wouldn't take long to compare him against the databases of the Families' vampires. That's if Medici finally cooperates, of course.

I scrub the base of my thumb over the photo, smoothing it across his mouth to wipe away a smudge. Then I frown as I realise the mark is part of the picture itself.

'What's this?'

'Gold tooth.'

Ah. I look at Corinne, who's staring at the bedsheet. 'Are you sure about this?'

Her eyes fly to mine. 'The gold tooth? It's not a detail I'm likely to forget.'

I think of Brinkish and his gleaming molar. There can't be many dentists these days who provide that kind of service. It's not the link between Kimchi's owner and the perverted perp that makes me pause, however. 'Gold's a fairly soft metal,' I say.

'Compared to most others it's malleable and allows for a lot of give.'

Corinne's brow creases until she winces when the action tugs on the edges of a deep wound higher up on her forehead. 'So?' she asks. Her tone is steely but I reckon I detect nervousness lurking there too.

Foxworthy straightens. He nods with dawning comprehension.

'It's still a solid,' I continue. 'So it's basic chemistry, really.' Corinne doesn't understand what I'm getting at. Despite her allegations, my heart goes out to her. 'Vampires don't have teeth like humans. Sometimes we have fangs,' I open my mouth and allow my own ones to lengthen, 'and sometimes we don't.' I retract them again. 'Our tooth enamel is constantly shifting. I can't explain the biology behind it, but I do know that it would be impossible for a bloodguzzler to have a gold tooth. Even if it was a back tooth, it wouldn't last more than a week or two before the repeated loosening and tightening of the gums made it fall out. Which means either your attacker was faking his vampirism, Corinne, or you're lying.'

She presses her lips together. The silence grows, becoming more and more uncomfortable with each passing second. Foxworthy steps forward but I give him a warning glare. He's annoyed but he blinks in agreement, thrusting his hands in his suit pockets to wait Corinne out. Voices at the far end of the corridor drift down and I'm painfully aware of the loud ticking of the clock in the corner of the room.

Eventually, she takes a deep breath. 'I didn't do this to myself.'

'We know that.'

She points at the photofit in my hands. 'And he did look like that.' She stares glassily upwards. 'He just wasn't a vampire.'

'Was he human, Corinne?'

'Yes,' she whispers.

'Why did you lie? You must know we'd have found out sooner or later. There aren't enough bloodguzzlers in the country for a rapist to hide. The police can't catch this prick if they're looking in the wrong places.'

'I'm a whore.'

I'm taken aback by her vehemence. 'Corinne, I don't think...'

'I sell myself for sex and the occasional hungry guzzler. Women like me get raped all the time.' She looks at Foxworthy. 'You know that.'

He doesn't respond. But, then again, he doesn't need to.

'The only way I'd be taken seriously,' she says bitterly, 'is if you thought a bloodguzzler did this. Otherwise I'm just another tramp who got what she deserved. I know the way the world works. There wouldn't be reporters outside here screaming for justice if they knew the truth.' Her bandaged hands paw uselessly at the white sheet that covers her frail body. 'It was going to come out sooner or later. I ain't a fucking dimwit. I just thought...'

'...that if they started to care, they wouldn't suddenly stop.'

She nods. I regard her with empathy. Her lies are causing the vampires a lot of problems at a time when we can least afford them but I understand why she chose this path.

'He was going to kill me,' Corinne says. 'His eyes were so cold. He's evil.' She shakes her head. 'I ain't lying about that. That man is pure evil.'

FOXWORTHY ESCORTS ME BACK OUTSIDE. Despite his hardened exterior, I think he's as shaken by what happened to Corinne as I am.

'How did you know?' I ask him, when he finally releases me from the cuffs. 'How did you know she was lying?'

'I didn't,' he answers, 'not for sure. But actually there was a witness when she got into his car. It's an old lady with bottle tops for glasses and she was on the other side of the street. She swore that Corinne got into the car voluntarily.'

'That's why he thought he could get away with picking her up so easily,' I muse, 'and why she spoke to him. She thought he was a john.'

'It was a small detail,' he agrees. 'And it didn't mean I thought he wasn't a bloodguzzler. But...' his voice trails off. He's a better copper than I gave him credit for. And a better human being. 'If your records were open to us, we'd have discounted vampires much more quickly.'

'We're working on that. And I can still get access to most of the Families if you want to double-check what I've told you.'

Foxworthy runs a hand through his hair. 'If it's not from *every* Family, then there's no point, is there?' He pockets the handcuffs. 'Time was, we'd never have got to the truth. She could have said "vampire" from every rooftop in town and you lot wouldn't have bothered to comment.'

'Many things are different these days,' I say.

He grunts. 'It would be a good idea if you kept this to yourself for the time being.'

I stiffen. 'We're in a bad spot right now, Inspector. If people continue to think a vampire was responsible for this, then the antagonism will escalate.'

'You misunderstand me. I know how dangerous it could be if things get even more stirred up with the Families.' He looks at me darkly. 'I'm fully aware of how much strength bloodguzzlers have at their disposal. No, we'll release the information that the perp is a human as soon as I've cleared it with those higher up. It'll be out by morning at the latest. I just mean that it'll go better for Corinne if you keep quiet about her day job.'

I'm filled with distaste. 'You really believe I'd run to the tabloids to tell them she's a prostitute?'

'Quite frankly, Ms Blackman, these days I'm prepared to believe almost anything.'

ALTHOUGH I FEEL like the good inspector and I had a moment together, he is still lukewarm towards me. He leaves me in the hospital car park with some vague remark about me being able to collect my impounded bike within the next few days. I suppose it's better than his previous hostility but I could really have done with a lift back to Covent Garden.

I decide to stretch my legs and test my burgeoning vampiric skills so I stride over the road and use a nearby fire escape to pull myself up to the roof. Once there, I crick my neck from side to side and make a few unnecessary stretches, as if to warm up. It makes me feel more human. Then I brace my right leg backwards and focus on a tall, illuminated building in the distance. I glance down at my watch, making a careful note of the time. If I were human, it'd take me at least fifteen minutes to reach the building via the pavements below, even if I ran at full pelt. I reckon I can halve that time.

I suck air deep into my lungs then I'm off. My toes pivot off the edge of the first building and I sail over the gap. I pick up speed as soon as I land, scaring off a nesting pigeon. The next leap is harder because I have to spring upwards as well as over. I grab the edge of the rooftop with my fingers and pull myself up. This building has a sloping roof so I have to balance along the top. My foot slips on a patch of slimy moss and I start to slide down towards the gutter. I jump up in the air, twisting my body sideways so that when I land I can use the edge of my boot to dig in and halt my momentum. Then I force myself back up to the top of the slope.

The crescent moon, obscured until now by a bank of clouds, appears momentarily, although it seems dim against the twinkling lights of the city. I remind myself to breathe then sprint forward, trying out some new moves to avoid any more mossy obstacles. I use an old chimney top from which to perform a handstand flip, and the vertical wall of a rooftop emergency exit to run along and push myself even faster. I even execute a perfect somersault landing. Better late than never.

When I finally reach my self-imposed destination, I stop and check my time. I raise my eyebrows and give myself a mental pat on the back. Just over five minutes; I'm improving. Much as I loathe being a vampire, the exhilaration provided by the changes to my strength and speed delight me.

As I force my heart rate to slow, I spot a shadow of movement far below. I tiptoe to the building's edge and peer down. It's a fox. It pauses for a moment, nose quivering as it catches my scent. Then the wind changes and it relaxes, nosing towards a collection of rubbish bins. Unfortunately, a group of late-night partygoers lurch past, causing the animal to run for cover. It's quickly swallowed up by the darkness. I feel an odd, painful kinship with the fox; we're both scavengers – though it is seeking food and I'm looking for information.

I jar my knees slightly as I drop back down to street level. I pad over to a parked car and use its wing mirror to check my appearance. I do my best to smooth down my unruly curls and wipe away a smudge of dirt from my cheek before straightening up and heading to a door nearby that is marked in the corner with a red design. I'm taking a risk coming here but this will be my fourth visit and, so far, nothing untoward – or even remotely exciting – has happened. After the trouble it took me to find this place, I'm not about to act like a frightened rabbit and simply hang back to observe.

I make a series of elaborate knocks and wait patiently until the small shutter set in the centre slides back and a fanged face appears. There's a smear of blood at the corner of his lips which is frankly repellent, but I keep my expression blank.

'Let me in.'

The vampire blinks at me. 'We told Lord Medici you'd been hanging around here.'

I shrug. I'd expected as much. 'So?'

He doesn't respond, merely moves back and opens the door. I duck inside, allowing my fangs to grow as I pass the bouncer. It might be a dick move to make but I want him to know that I'm not intimidated by him or his boss. For his part, he's totally disinterested.

I walk into the darkened, smoky room. There aren't many places in London now where you can have a cigarette. Getting cancer is not a problem for vampires and after the smoking ban some of them flaunted that fact across the city. I think the smokers finally realised that such actions were petty and point-less, so now any bloodguzzlers who do suck on nicotine tend to stick to the human laws and avoid public places. This joint, however, doesn't count. I had heard a rumour that applications to join the Families and turn vampire increased considerably in recent years as there were a lot of smokers unwilling to give up the habit. It strikes me as one of the more stupid reasons to want to be a bloodguzzler; however, I realised on my last visit here that I could use the smokers' addiction to my advantage. It worked when I was human, anyway. So far, I've avoided approaching any of the patrons here as the only way this will work is if they come to me first.

I walk up to the bar and perch on a stool. As unpleasant as this place is, at least it's not providing television aerobics as entertainment. The bartender, with a flicker of recognition in her eyes, wanders over.

'Bloody Mary?' she asks.

I nod my head.

'Sure I can't tempt you with the real thing?' She points to a comfortable looking cubicle that houses several bored looking humans. I wonder which one is Mary.

'No, thanks.'

She shrugs, busying herself with creating my cocktail. It's nothing more than vodka, blood, Worcestershire sauce and a celery stalk. Although the blood is fresh – rarely more than a day or two old – to really satisfy a vampire's hunger it should be drunk directly from the vein. Despite Dr Love's instructions to me to venture out and make myself drink from humans other than Connor, while I'm here I'm going to stick to my principles. Even decanted blood can provide enough nourishment to see me through until I catch up with Connor again.

I stare into space, trying to appear as if I'm ignoring the other customers. I've already clocked the trio by the door, none of whom I recognise. They're rather loud and raucous but I've received several covert looks from them; they're not as drunk as they're pretending to be. There's a solitary drinker in the far corner who's been here every time I have come in and who seems to have a penchant for rum. A couple are playing footsie in a nearby booth – although the girl was here last time with a different guy. A tall thin is man playing on the bandit machine next to the toilets. I purse my lips. Slim pickings tonight, then. It might be worth playing my frustrated smoker's card another night.

The bartender places my drink in front of me and I toy absently with the celery, swirling it around the thick, gloopy blood. Steeling myself, I take a gulp, then lick my lips as if in delight. It's not an easy expression to pull off. Next, I pull out a battered pack of cigarettes from my pocket. If nothing else, the taste of nicotine will mask that of the cocktail, although I also need the regular patrons to believe I smoke regularly if my plan is going to work. Checking the room again, I make a decision. Tonight's not the night. Besides, I've been coming here for less than a fortnight. If I want to gain the trust of a Medici minion, I need to be more patient. For credibility's sake, I rummage around in my other pocket and find my lighter. Then I lean back, taking my time and doing what I can to appear relaxed.

CHAPTER 7

TURNING POINT

When I get back home after stopping via the office and checking in with Matt, who has little to report, and Connor, who remains willing to open his veins for me, I head straight for the refrigerator and carefully remove X's little vial of blood.

I hold it in the palm of my hand and stare at it then, taking a deep breath, unscrew the top and inhale. Just like on the other occasions when I've done this, my nostrils are assailed by both salt and spice. Kakos daemon blood isn't like any other kind. In fact, rather than being repulsed by it, my stomach rumbles. Red blood cells only last for forty-two days, so I'm running out of time.

I still have no reason to trust X's word that drinking it will allow me to revert back to human but, even if there's only a slim chance it'll work, I'm still filled with burning desire to take it. It would be a wholly selfish decision, with vast repercussions for every vampire – not only in London, but across the world. Given the current climate, it would be a reckless move. That's not to mention the fact that it would stymie any chance I have to bring down Medici and would slam a huge rusty, tetanus-inducing nail into the coffin of the relationship between me and Michael.

I put the lid back on, making sure it's tightly shut, then close my fingers over the vial and squeeze it. I still have a few weeks left.

Kimchi pads up and whines. I rub his head in reassurance then smack my forehead in self-disgust as I remember I need to get him some food. Cursing, I replace the vial in its hiding spot and head downstairs. Dawn is too close; I'll have to prevail upon Connor's goodwill yet again. I don't deserve a friend like him.

I've barely closed the door behind me when I hear loud remonstrations and a familiar, disgusted voice coming from the New Order office. Frowning, I jog down the stairs. Foxworthy is standing over Connor, demanding to know where I am. Sensibly, Matt has vanished; even though Foxworthy is human, Matt would still be forced to do whatever was asked of him – including telling the good officer my whereabouts. I can do that myself.

I clear my throat, causing Foxworthy to spin round in mid-sentence. When he catches sight of me, he marches up, grabbing my t-shirt and throwing me against the wall. It doesn't hurt but I'm still pissed off.

'What the hell? What's wrong with you?'

'Like you don't know,' he snarls.

I scan his face. Fatigue is etched into every line and wrinkle of his weathered skin, but his eyes are alight with fury.

I'm more puzzled than anything. 'No,' I say softly, 'I don't.'

'Pleading ignorance isn't going to help. I should have stuck to my gut. You can't trust a bloodguzzler, no matter what pretty things they say.'

'Inspector, I still don't know what's wrong.'

'Here.' He thrusts a newspaper in my face. 'Evidence of your fucking handiwork.'

I focus on the headline. It's today's early edition. When the words sink in, my stomach drops and I close my eyes.

'You just couldn't keep your big trap shut, could you? You had to go blabbing.'

'It wasn't me.' I open my eyes and stare at the big man.

'Yeah? Who else knew this?' He waves the paper. '"Park Rape Vic Is Hooker". It even states that their source is someone from one of the Families.'

If Foxworthy had a gun, he'd probably shoot me. He's blindingly angry. I don't blame him. 'I'm telling you, it wasn't me,' I insist.

'Nobody else outside the investigating team knew she was a prostitute. And I can damn well tell you the leak didn't come from us.' His face moves down to mine, until it's so close that I can feel his breath on my skin. 'I told you we'd release the info that the bloodguzzlers weren't involved. The press conference is scheduled for ten. You couldn't even wait a few fucking hours?'

My whole body is tense but I make myself stay where I am. I don't want Foxworthy to be my enemy; we need a friend in the police. I meet his angry stare. 'Even if it was a vampire who leaked, it says the source is the Families. I'm not part of a Family. You know that. It couldn't have been me.'

'Do you think that makes a difference? If you didn't speak to the paper, then you spoke to someone from the Families who did. You're all the same.' He throws the newspaper in my face. 'Corinne Matheson has just gone from being a helpless rape victim to someone who can't be trusted and who was probably asking for it. Six hours ago there were a hundred officers working this case. Ninety per cent have been pulled off the case because public opinion rules everything we do. And public opinion will be that she's not worth it any more.' He lowers his tone but he's no less angry. 'She's a human being, a person who deserves justice. But now the entire investigation has been derailed and it's your fault. The guy who did this? He's not the type to do it once and then forget about it. He's going to try again. Next time he'll probably get lucky and kill whoever he abducts. Congratulations. You've just signed some poor girl's death warrant.' He gives me one last, disgusted look then stalks out.

Connor has backed away to the wall, his skin pale and his freckles standing out in sharp relief. 'Bo, you didn't do that, did you? Talk to the newspapers?'

I shake my head. 'No. I know who fucking did though.'

His eyes are wide. 'Who?'

'It's probably better for you if you don't know. Go home, Connor. Get some rest.'

He watches me for a second or two then nods. 'Okay. Will you be alright?'

For a moment, I'm so caught up in the maelstrom of my own thoughts that I don't respond.

'Bo?' he prompts.

I give him a smile. It's so forced that it's almost painful. Fortunately it's enough for Connor and he grabs his things and leaves. I wait until he's gone, then pick up the phone, not even bothering to wait for the receptionist to answer.

'Tell Lord Montserrat that Bo Blackman needs to see him at his earliest convenience,' I snap and slam down the receiver.

I'M LYING in bed with the duvet over my head, trying to catch some sleep, when I hear him enter. Michael Montserrat is a powerful vampire; usually if he doesn't want to be heard, he won't be. He wasn't counting on Kimchi, though, who barks enthusiastically at his arrival. The poor dog is probably hoping for food. After sending Connor on his way, I was forced to raid the office fridge for some cold cuts to feed Kimchi. I am no longer surprised that the dog is chewing everything in sight.

I flip back the cover and sit up just as Michael's muscular frame fills the doorway. I'm fully dressed: there is no way I'm going to have another confrontation in my pyjamas.

'Is everything alright?' he enquires solicitously.

A chink of daylight peeks out from under one of the blackout blinds but I really don't care. I stride over to him, in a fashion not unlike Foxworthy's. I don't try to push him against the wall, however; I simply slap him as hard as I can across his cheek. The sound cracks loudly across the small room.

He's more surprised than hurt. 'What the hell was that for?'

'Corinne Matheson.' I search his face. 'Why the fuck did you do it, Michael? Why did you go to the press?'

He doesn't even try to deny it. He draws himself up, shoulders straightening, and glares. 'I'm Lord of the Montserrat Family. I don't have to explain myself to you.'

Kimchi, sensing the tension, begins to growl from the other room.

'I represent New Order, remember? The agency designed to smooth out problems between the humans and the vampires. The one that *you* set up.' I put my hands on my hips. 'Or do you think you should be immune from anything we do? Because you're Lord Sodding Montserrat? Mr High and Mighty? Better than anyone else?'

'Bo, what on earth has gotten into you?' He seems baffled.

My lip curls. Fury snakes through my body and I realise I'm trembling. 'You're a bastard.'

He stares at me for a long moment then the corner of his mouth crooks upwards. 'You're pretty sexy when you're angry.'

I snarl and take a step backwards, jabbing a finger at his

chest. 'If you're treating this as some kind of booty call, then you are so mistaken.' I can't believe he's being so flippant.

His humour vanishes and he holds up his palms. 'If I've misjudged this situation I apologise but I've not done anything wrong.'

My voice drops to a whisper. 'You're not naïve. You've been around for long enough to know what'll happen to Corinne now everyone knows she's a prostitute.'

'Bo, I'm not responsible for how she chooses to live her life.'

'You didn't have to tell the world about it though.'

'Yes, I did.' He nods. 'You're right: I knew she'd be vilified. But she was lying. At a time when we need public opinion on our side, she was lying through her teeth and making us out to be villains.' He takes a step forward. 'Us, Bo. You're a vampire too.'

'She had her reasons,' I spit. 'Besides, the police had already established it wasn't a vampire who raped her. They were going to release a statement today.'

He shrugs. 'I wasn't to know that.'

'You could have spoken to me about it first.'

'I don't need your permission to act.'

'Because you're Lord Montserrat?' I sneer.

'Yes,' he replies. 'Because I am.'

I shake my head. 'Does being Lord Montserrat include having carte blanche to execute whoever gets in your way?'

Confusion clouds his face. 'What do you mean?'

Anger guides my actions. I turn my back and reach down to the bed, flipping over the mattress. The photo of him and Medici standing over the corpses and grinning is at the far corner. I yank it out and shove it in his face. 'This is you, isn't it?' I demand. 'The kind of person who beheads someone in the street and treats it like a big joke. Look at you! And since when was Medici your partner in crime?'

His face is white. He takes the photo from me and studies it for a moment. 'Where did you get this from?'

'Does it matter?'

His expression turns to granite. 'Tell me, Bo.'

'Or what?' I taunt. 'You'll go to the papers about me, too? Or perhaps you'll decide I'm too much of a thorn in your side so you'll…'

He grabs my shoulders, pulling me towards him. 'You go too far.'

I stare at him. 'Oh, I don't think I'm going far enough. I liked you, Michael. Even after you turned me when you knew it was last thing I wanted, I still liked you.' I burn my last bridge. 'Get out. And don't ever come near me again.'

He looks like he wants to say something but instead he turns on his heel and strides out, leaving nothing behind other than the lingering scent of his aftershave and a faint whine from Kimchi.

I remain where I am, standing alone, wondering if I've just made the biggest mistake of my life.

ONCE IT'S DARK AGAIN, I venture out. I don't bother checking in at the office on my way down and, even though the door is open and my grandfather and Arzo are in view, neither of them calls out to me. The walls around here are pretty thin. Chances are Arzo and Peter heard every single word between me and Michael and it's now common knowledge. Whatever the reason is for them leaving me in peace, I'm thankful for it. Even Kimchi, by my side on a makeshift lead made out of ribbon, is quiet.

I ignore the pitiful gaggle of protestors who are no doubt disappointed that I'm not still in police custody and sweep past as if they're invisible. I don't give them time to react to my appearance – which is just as well because I'm not sure my mood lends itself to responsible action.

The little shop at the end of the street is still open. Unfortunately, due to our proximity to the tourist hub of the area, it uses its spare shelf space for cheap London knick-knacks rather than anything useful like dog food. I heave a sigh and leave, heading for the supermarket a few blocks away. I walk with my head down, hoping, just for once, for a quiet life. It would probably be easier to manage if Kimchi didn't insist on sniffing every standing object and occasionally cocking his leg to mark his territory. At least he seems happy to be out, his tail wagging vigorously as we stroll along.

Once we reach the supermarket, I tie him to a lamppost. He immediately starts gnawing it. I'm watching him, idly wondering whether the council will be able trace the teeth marks in the metal and will send me a bill, when I catch something odd out of the corner of my eye. There's definitely a nip in the air but the weather is still unseasonably warm for October. Most people are wearing light jackets, so the figure shuffling along the far side of the street in the huge winter overcoat, furry hat and with a woollen scarf covering his face stands out like a sore thumb. I glance down at Kimchi, who is still fascinated by the lamppost. I'm not going to get distracted again. I'll get the dog food first.

I grab a basket and weave down the aisles until I reach the one I want. I grab several tins of 'Choice Venison Stew'. It's pricey but, given the rubbish I've fed Kimchi so far, the least I can do is treat him to a slap-up dinner. I throw in some bone-shaped chews and make my way to the checkout.

Mr Overcoat darts in, moving behind a display of Halloween-themed goodies. I'm tempted to confront him but I spot the besuited shop manager appearing beside the till as if to protect either the pimply teenager manning it – or the money inside it – from me. I'm betting it's the latter. I shrug and head over. The teen won't even look at me. His cheeks are a vivid shade of red and he mumbles the amount I owe. I hand over the money and he snatches it quickly, shoving it into the till. He holds out the receipt, his fingers shaking.

I put him out of his misery and politely decline it. I do, however, glance up at the manager. 'Thanks! Your store is great. I need to check on my dog outside but it would be great if you could remind my friend over there to pick up some pepper too.' I wink. 'It really makes the blood taste so much better.'

To give the manager his due, he answers steadily, 'Where's your friend?'

I point vaguely towards the Halloween display. 'He's over there somewhere. You can't miss him – he's bundled up like it's a winter's day.' I beam sunnily then stroll out, whistling.

Less than thirty seconds later, a figure is propelled out at warp speed. I wait.

'Bo!' The whine is familiar. 'That wasn't funny!'

I squint. 'O'Shea?'

He pulls down his scarf and grins. 'Of course! I'm in disguise.'

'Not a very good one,' I grunt, bending down to free Kimchi. The dog pants then, without warning, leaps at the daemon.

O'Shea laughs nervously and backs away. 'Dog saliva brings me out in hives,' he complains.

I regard him speculatively. 'Either that or you're afraid of tubby dogs.'

'He does have a bit of belly, doesn't he?'

I raise my eyebrows. 'That'll be all the daemon meat.' O'Shea takes another step back. 'I'm joking,' I say, exasperated. 'Why are you hiding from me, O'Shea? I'm not really in the mood for your shenanigans.'

'Oh, I'm not hiding from you.' He waves an airy hand in front of his face.

Against my better nature, I take the bait. 'Then who are you hiding from?'

'From us,' a gruff voice says. I look across, just in time to see one of two sharply dressed Agathos daemons raise a gun in my direction.

CHAPTER 8

UNDERGROUND ACTION

For a split second, time freezes. The bright, welcoming lights of the supermarket dim and the cars on the road appear to slow. Then I spring into action.

I grab the man's wrist, forcing the gun upwards just as he squeezes the trigger. The bullet scrapes past my cheek and the gun falls onto the pavement with a clatter. His partner, despite wearing a tight-fitting skirt, lunges at O'Shea with more speed than I would have thought possible. O'Shea blocks the move. Kimchi barks wildly, jaws snapping. The woman reaches inside her jacket to a shoulder holster and starts to pull out another shiny gun, while the man slams his hand into my nose, connecting with a painful crack. My head jerks backwards and lights dance in front of my eyes. Shit. These guys are good. I kick blindly upwards, aiming for the man's groin but he flips backwards just in the nick of time.

I wipe my streaming eyes as Kimchi leaps in front of me, using his body as a shield between me and my attacker. The woman tries to get off a shot but O'Shea crashes into her, knocking her off balance. I blink several times while Kimchi snaps and bites, preventing the daemon from reaching down to retrieve the gun. From behind me, in the relative safety of the supermarket, I can hear someone yelling to call 999.

I sidestep left until I'm closer to the gun than the male daemon. Although he's being kept back by Kimchi and he's concentrating on using his fists to prevent the dog coming any closer, he is still aware of me and knows exactly what I'm trying to do. He kicks the weapon out of reach under a nearby parked car. Or so he thinks. Kimchi's muscles are bunched up and taut: he's had enough and is about to spring forward. I wait for the moment when I think he's going to leap and do the same, jumping onto the car roof and somersaulting to the other side. Fur and skin collide as I slide underneath the chassis and curl my fingers round the gun's muzzle. I push forward, a sudden whine from the dog propelling me even faster, then grab the man's ankles and pull them towards me as hard as I can.

He slams forward onto the hard pavement so swiftly that he doesn't have time to put out his hands to break his fall. He lands on top of Kimchi but the dog pulls himself free, leaping onto the man's back and snapping at his head every time he tries to get up.

I slide free from the car, beckoning Kimchi to my side. I grab the man's shirt and heave him upwards, pushing the gun in his face. I glance over at O'Shea and realise with a sudden sinking feeling that the woman is doing exactly the same to him. Impasse.

'We're not interested in you, vampire,' she hisses. 'Walk away.'

O'Shea's orange eyes turn to me. His expression is calm. I press the gun into the man's cheek and he winces.

'Now,' I say, 'why would I want to do that, when we're just getting acquainted?'

'Don't think I won't shoot him.'

I shrug. 'I'll do the same.'

I can hear sirens in the distance, no doubt heading this way. From the opposite side of the street, a cowering figure holds out a phone in our direction, recording the action. I wonder how this will play out in tomorrow's papers. It's certainly not going to do me any good.

I try to calm things down. 'The police are on their way,' I say softly. 'Nobody's going to win here.'

She exchanges a look with her partner. I sense that neither of them is willing to back down. Trying not to think about what O'Shea has done to land us in this situation, I take a deep breath. 'Why don't we both put down the guns?' I suggest.

She eyes me. 'Alright then. On a count of three?'

'Why not? One, two...' I tense my muscles. 'Three.'

Neither of us moves. 'You didn't put it down,' she murmurs.

'You didn't either.'

The sirens are getting louder. I don't need the hassle of being hauled off to the nearest jail cell. Given that Family vampires are technically above human law, I can probably get myself out of it but it won't look good and it won't help O'Shea. I don't doubt that he's done something to merit this attention but I don't want to see his innards smeared across the street. I make a decision.

'Well,' I drawl, 'in that case...' I bend my knees, grab the handle of my shopping bag and fling it upwards in her direction with every ounce of muscle I can muster. The heavy tins of dog food slam into the side of her face, allowing O'Shea to lunge for the barrel of her gun. I throw a fist into the man's bloodied face and yank my free hand to the right, making sure O'Shea takes note. Then the three of us – daemon, dog and vampire – sprint away.

I speed up and pull away from them then glance backwards.

The flashing lights of a panda car pull into view but the two daemons have already vanished. I notice the fear etched on the faces of the pedestrians and realise I'm still clutching the gun in one hand and the shopping bag in the other. Unwilling to toss the weapon in the trash where anyone could scoop it up, I shove it into my waistband and veer right.

There's an underground station ahead so I shout to O'Shea and make a beeline for it, running down the stairs. A station guard strides forward, no doubt to inform me that only guide dogs are permitted. Kimchi barks with delight. The guard takes one look at the blood streaming from my face and the hard look in my eyes and changes his mind. I vault over the turnstiles. The other two copy my movements and we dash to the nearest plat-form just as a train pulls in. We clamber aboard.

The carriage is packed with commuters who, almost to a man, pull away from us. One have-a-go hero stands up, ready for confrontation, but I snarl at him and he backs down.

'This way.' I lead O'Shea and Kimchi towards the back of the train, just as the doors start to close. We reach the final carriage as the train trundles through the darkness to the next stop.

'We need to hide,' O'Shea says. 'They'll come after us.'

I nod, moving to the last set of doors and taking the time to check Kimchi over. He seems unharmed, although I'm sure the daemon managed to land a few hits. I crouch down. 'You're a bloody brave dog.'

He wags his tail and gives me a great big lick, lapping up some of the blood still dripping from my nose. His tail wags harder. I stare at him suspiciously. Is he enjoying the taste of the blood?

'Bo...' O'Shea begins.

I hold up my palm. 'Not yet.' The train's brakes whine as we pull into the next station. 'Tunnel,' I grunt.

He swallows in nervous agreement, takes off his hat and

ridiculous coat and folds them neatly over the handrail. I glance at the bunched-up passengers at the other end of the carriage. 'Don't worry,' I call out. Several shrink away. Damn it.

The train halts and the tinny voice of the announcer comes over the tannoy, informing us politely to mind the gap. As soon as the doors hiss open, we belt out and round the back, jumping down to the tracks.

'Avoid the middle track,' I shout to O'Shea, keeping a firm hold on Kimchi's collar.

'Why?'

'You'll be electrocuted!'

I don't wait for his reaction but run down into the darkness, ignoring the scuttling pair of rats heading in the opposite direction. We have barely minutes to get out of the way of the next train.

Fortunately my eyes do better in darkness these days than they used to and I pierce through the gloom easily enough to find what I'm looking for. Set into the side of the tunnel, less a few hundred metres away, is a service entrance door.

I run towards it. I'm nervous about how Kimchi will cope in such a small space, so I scoop him up in my arms. He lands another wet lick on my cheek and I shift his body so I can see round him. I should have bought diet dog food.

'Can you see the door?' I yell to O'Shea.

'Yeah!'

We run, just as the roar of another train fills the tunnel. I grab the door handle and pull. It's locked. Cursing under my breath, I pass Kimchi to O'Shea, who staggers momentarily under the dog's weight. I take a few steps backwards and launch a kick. The door splinters in just the right place, falling open with a rusty groan. I push O'Shea through it then follow him in, just as there's a rush of air and the next train flies past.

Once I know we're safe, I breathe deeply and regroup. Then I look around. This is obviously a fairly well-used entrance: it's well lit, with fluorescent strips overhead. Old-fashioned, albeit remarkably well-maintained, tiling covers the walls.

'Come on,' I say. 'Let's find our way out of here. The sooner we get back to fresh air the better.'

O'Shea seems alarmed. 'We can't. They must have a tracking spell on me, Bo. They could have placed it on me when they came earlier today. I had on a disguise – there's no way they could have found me otherwise.'

I raise my eyebrows. Considering how ineffective his disguise was, I'm not convinced. But if I had the means, I'd be using a spell to find my quarry too.

'We can't stay down here forever,' I tell him.

'Actually, I know which way to go,' he says. 'You just have to trust me.'

'Trusting you nearly got my head blown off. What have you done this time?'

'I'll explain later,' he mutters. 'We need to keep moving.'

I follow him down the corridor but, when we reach a small intersection, instead of continuing straight ahead O'Shea turns right, away from the lights and into the darkness.

'Are you sure about this?' I ask doubtfully.

'I told you, I know which way to go.'

'How?'

'These tunnels are a good way to move about the city without being detected.'

I open my mouth to ask him why on earth he'd need to hide in a subterranean maze then think better of it. I don't need to know.

O'Shea explains anyway. 'I used to run bootleg alcohol to various triber clubs in my youth.'

'Moonshine? London is hardly a prohibition city.'

'Not for normal spirits. Mine were,' he pauses, 'special.'

I dread to think. 'You don't do that any more, do you?' Despite having taken part in a gun battle in open view, I need to keep my nose clean for the sake of New Order.

'Nah, I was young and foolish back then.'

'Of course, now you're old and wise,' I mutter sarcastically. He doesn't answer.

We walk for several minutes. Kimchi trots beside me, seemingly undisturbed by our environment. At least he's not a nervous dog. I can't imagine Brinkish being too impressed if he found out where I'm taking his pet, though. I use spittle to wet the corner of my cuff and wipe away the worst of the blood on my face. It hurts like hell but I can already feel the healing process kicking in. It's not that long since I drank so I'll recover easily.

I'm satisfied that I've cleaned off as much as I can when I look up and realise there's a brick wall ahead of us. 'It's a dead end,' I hiss. 'We'll have to turn back.'

'Look closer,' O'Shea says.

I squint, scanning the wall, confident that we've taken a wrong turn. Then I spot the fallen bricks. Several in the far corner have been knocked out to create a hole leading into a gap of absolute blackness. I thought we were already fumbling around in the dark; I hadn't appreciated how much darker things could get.

'You're kidding, right?'

'I told you, Bo,' O'Shea says with renewed good humour. 'You need to trust me.' He gives me a tiny push. 'Ladies first.'

I grimace. Out of all the bad ideas in the world, crawling

through a dark hole far underground with a daemon and a dog seems about the worst. I have the strange sensation that I'm in one of those horror movies where the audience shouts at the dim-witted girl who's about to be eviscerated that she shouldn't open the damn door. Then again, in those sorts of films the dog always survives so as long as I stick close to Kimchi, I'll be fine.

I step forward carefully and eye the gap. I'm pretty darn petite but even so it's going to be a tight squeeze. I inhale then jump up, bracing my body with my palms. I start to wiggle through.

Although it's as black as tar on the other side, my eyes can pierce through enough to see that it's just another tunnel. Silently thanking whoever built this daft barricade for not making it more than one brick deep, I inch through. My jeans snag around my hips but I scoot through to the other side easily enough.

O'Shea lifts up Kimchi. I receive one enthusiastic lick across my mouth before I grab hold of his furry shoulders and help him through. Gallingly, despite the dog's podgy belly, he makes it with very little trouble; I wonder whether I've put weight on recently. I've been existing on a diet of little more than blood and chocolate but, considering how much money I've dropped into Cadbury's coffers, perhaps it's not surprising.

For some reason, O'Shea decides to scramble through feet first. I leave him to it and, keeping a tight hold of Kimchi, walk into the deep, dark unknown. 'Why was this bricked up?' I ask. My voice echoes.

Kimchi, who is quivering with excitement, barks once. When his woof returns tenfold, he barks again in delight. I wince. This could get tiring very, very quickly.

O'Shea joins me, dusting off his trousers. 'To stop people

from sneaking in and doing themselves harm, I guess. It's completely disused. If you go one way, you'll come across old platforms, still with their signs and stairs. They're pretty eerie. If you go the other way, you'll find the old bomb shelters.'

I shake my head. 'I never knew all this existed.'

He takes my hand and deepens his voice. 'There are many things I can teach you, little girl.'

I thump him. 'Piss off.'

He laughs. 'Come on. We're going to Down Street. It won't take us long.'

'That's next to Hyde Park,' I say grumpily. And Hyde Park is next to the Montserrat mansion.

O'Shea doesn't seem to twig my meaning. 'Yeah. It was closed in the 1930s but it's not as grubby as you'd think ' cos Churchill used it for war cabinet meetings back in the day.'

'You're a fount of knowledge.'

For a second he doesn't speak, then he says quietly, 'You know me as a petty criminal who steals from corpses, sucks at cards and was responsible for almost bringing down the five Families. There's more to me than that.'

'What happened with the Families wasn't your fault. Although...'

'What?'

'Maybe now would be a good time to improve my understanding of you as a person. Tell me why two goons with guns tried to kill you and why we're now hiding from them in a subterranean wilderness.' I trip over an uneven floor tile, adding weight to my words.

'That's your trouble, Bo. You're all work and no play. You need to loosen up sometimes.'

'O'Shea,' I warn. 'Don't test my patience.'

He sighs. 'Fine. A couple of nights ago, I happened to be down the East End. It started raining so I ducked into a nearby pub. I'd just ordered a beer when I saw the man of my dreams. A little rough around the edges but sexy as hell. We got chatting and he invited me back to his place. You wouldn't believe the size of his...'

'I don't need to know every detail, O'Shea.'

'Television,' he finishes triumphantly.

I roll my eyes. My expression is wasted on him, however, as it's too dark for him to notice.

'He eventually fell asleep and I decided I'd head home.'

'The walk of shame from the "man of your dreams"?'

'Let's just say he wasn't as impressive in the naked flesh.'

'You're so shallow,' I tut.

'Darling, if you saw his equipment, you'd be tempted to run too. Anyhow,' he continues, 'on my way out, I spotted the most gorgeous velvet jacket. You know, one of those old-fashioned smoking ones that make you feel like the lord of the manor.'

I wrinkle my nose. 'You stole his coat?'

'Nah. It didn't fit me. But I did try it on and check myself out in the mirror. A few twirls, that kind of thing.'

'Okay,' I say slowly, not sure where he's going with this.

'I put the lapels up but that looked kind of silly. So I tried it with my hands in the pockets. That's when I found it.' He lapses into silence. All I can hear are our footsteps and the trickle of water from somewhere in the distance.

'Come on, O'Shea, don't leave me hanging. Found what?'

'A little jewellery box containing an ear.'

I blink. 'A what?'

'An ear. The perfectly formed and neatly severed ear of an Agathos daemon.'

I swallow. 'Jesus. How could you tell?'

'I've been around a while, Bo,' O'Shea says drily. 'I know what ears look like.'

'No, I mean, how could you tell it belonged to an Agathos

daemon?' I like to think I'm pretty adept at discerning different tribers but, as far as I'm aware, an ear is an ear is an ear.

'I can just tell. But that's not the really interesting part. You see, it was pierced.' He pauses. 'With a ruby.'

'Shit in a hell basket,' I breathe, utterly stunned.

'And then some,' he agrees.

CHAPTER 9

IT HAPPENED ONE NIGHT

The world is full of crazy unsolved mysteries. The humans have them in abundance with things like the *Marie Celeste*, Lord Lucan and the grassy knoll. The Families have them with the second Lady Stuart and Jack the Ripper. The witches have Moll Dyer and Alex Sanders. Kakos daemons, well, they're enough of a mystery themselves without any extra help. But the Agathos daemons have Tobias Renfrew. He might just top them all.

It's said that Renfrew was conceived the night the *Titanic* went down. His mother, a young Agathos noblewoman, scandalously was travelling alone on the ill-fated ship to make a new life for herself across the Pond. She certainly did that, although given that it's been suggested it was a highly placed crew member who she was making that new life with, it's possible that hundreds of other lives were also lost in the process. Renfrew's alleged father had been on duty the night they hit the iceberg; he was mysteriously absent during the initial collision, however, and reportedly unkempt and dishevelled when he finally did appear - with Toby's mother in tow. Still, even if it had been his negligence that had contributed to the disaster, and he went down with the ship himself, he did manage to see his lover safely onto a lifeboat, saving the tiny embryo that was to become Tobias Renfrew in the process.

Devastated by what happened, and with a growing belly, she holed up in a corner of Brooklyn and sent tearful letters back to her family in England. Not long before Tobias was born, her father turned up on her doorstep and dragged her back home. I'm not sure whether he actually had to drag her, though; it can't have been a lot of fun being single, pregnant and penniless. Unfortunately for her, things didn't really improve back on home soil. She was hidden away in some godforsaken corner of the country to preserve the family honour. When she finally went into labour, the midwife wasn't called until it was too late. Little Toby was breech and was eventually cut from his mother's womb, apparently wide-eyed but entirely silent. She, meanwhile, bled out.

It would be safe to say that the Renfrew family suffered Tobias's childhood rather than enjoyed it. He was, after all, a bastard son. There were whispered tales of savage beatings and bloodstained dungeons. I suspect the truth is that he was simply ignored. Whatever, by the time he was a teenager, he had been incriminated in a number of local crimes and had run away at least three times from his spartan boarding school. His one champion was his aunt Molly, who tried her best to do right by him. But she was only a female daemon and the worse Tobias's behaviour, the more her pleas to help him fell on deaf ears. Eventually the rest of his relatives had had enough. Tobias was thrown out with only five pounds to give him a head start. Molly, in a fit of desperation, gave him her favourite ruby earrings, thinking that he could pawn them. He never did.

He joined the army, signing up just in time to get involved in the civil war in Afghanistan. He rose quickly through the ranks, even though daemons were viewed with as much suspicion in those days as any human who wasn't white skinned, God-fearing and male. He tripped from conflict to conflict, growing more bloodthirsty with each one until, inexplicably, he bowed out not long before the advent of the Second World War. He got involved in munitions manufacturing instead.

Whether it was from ill-gotten gains during his time fighting around the world, or from black market sales in the weapons' trade, by the time the 1950s rolled around, Tobias Renfrew had enough money to buy his ancestral home. He did to his relatives what they'd done to him: tossed them out with a barely civil farewell. Molly was long dead, killed during the Blitz and, despite his wealth, Tobias was still completely alone.

Instead of warmongering, he filled his days with politics. He schmoozed all the right people and feathered all the right pockets. His coffers grew and his sticky fingers dabbled in all manner of pots. And he did it all while wearing Molly's ruby earrings. If anyone ever teased him for such a girlish affectation, there is no record of it. He was not the kind of man you wanted to insult. Indeed, it was said that if he ever came across another daemon wearing similar jewellery, even if it was for reasons of flattery via imitation, he ripped it from their flesh no matter who they were.

At one point, Tobias seemed to take on a veneer of respectability. He started withdrawing from his more dodgy – as well as lucrative – dealings. My grandfather met him briefly during this time; unsurprisingly he dismissed him as a 'rough amongst diamonds'. It's been whispered Tobias was on course to become the first daemon Prime Minister. But that was before one cold night in January, 1963.

Tobias flung open the doors of his mansion to all and sundry. He didn't just invite politicians: there were film stars, powerful witches and the five Family Heads – apparently one of whom was the reigning Lord Gully. Champagne flowed, opium abounded and everyone had a merry old time. Despite his history, Tobias was a congenial host. His family had taught him how to hobnob with the rich and he'd taught himself how to mix with everyone else. Prior to a breathtakingly expensive fireworks' display, he gave a speech. There's an old recording of it somewhere that has been pored over by historians and conspiracy theorists for years. He made reference to 'hidden wealth' and 'mysterious saboteurs'. Then, just as he invited the entire gathering to raise their glasses and toast their own health, there was a flash of light and he disappeared.

His guests were amused, believing it to be some kind of clever trick – until someone went searching and discovered several body parts in an upstairs bathroom, along with copious amounts of blood. They came from at least five different corpses: one human, two witches, one vampire and one Agathos daemon. Tobias Renfrew was never seen again.

In the absence of any other suspects, he was indicted for murder. His surviving family members, all of whom had fallen on hard times, demanded that his wealth and properties revert to them. As a suspected, albeit not confirmed, murderer, the state and the increasingly powerful Agathos court wanted to confiscate everything for themselves. Tobias's will, meanwhile, left everything to a defunct children's charity. However, a very clever lawyer argued that in the absence of a body, his death could not be confirmed.

No traces of him were left behind. Because he was an Agathos daemon, Tobias's disappearance couldn't be explained away by him being turned into a vampire. The public nature of his departure also suggests that he wasn't attacked by a Kakos daemon. (There are, of course, those who suspect that in a fit of Sleeping Beauty-esque jealousy at not being invited to the lavish party, a Kakos *was* involved but then there are always conspiracy theorists.) The witches were equally discounted, as invisibility spells are nigh on impossible to maintain. Furthermore, to add to the mystery, to this day not even the more talkative ghosts will discuss it.

So, to all legal intents and purposes Tobias Renfrew is still alive. Nobody gets his money: not the descendants of his fickle family, nor the charity, nor the government. Every so often, another legal challenge is made and thanks to the intricacies of daemon law and the bitter greed of the parties involved, it always fails. It doesn't help that each interested party advertises large rewards for information regarding Tobias's whereabouts. They're each determined to get the jump on the other.

If he is still alive, Tobias would be well over a hundred years old – not unheard of for a daemon but not all that likely either. His wealth continues to grow and estate managers continue to be hired. The Agathos community, by some strange unspoken agreement, never wear rubies in their ears. Whether it's out of deference or fear, I don't know, but it's one of those weird foibles that people have that continues to linger.

'FINDING an ear in a pocket may be one of the most disgusting things I've ever heard of,' I say, 'but it doesn't necessarily belong to Tobias Renfrew. Anyone could shove in a ruby.'

'Sure,' O'Shea says. 'Anyone could. But why would they be so keen to come after me now that I know of its existence?'

'Last time I checked, no law allows for ear hacking. Perhaps you've just stumbled across a normal murder.' A normal murder? I wince at how casual I sound. 'Or it's an abduction. Or simple extortion.'

'Bo, these guys mean business. I was in disguise because this wasn't the first time they tried to grab me. There's more to it than a run-of-the-mill ear slice.'

'How do they know you saw the ear?' For a moment, O'Shea doesn't answer. 'You took it, didn't you? You took the damned ear.'

'You'd have done the same.'

I think about it. I probably would. It still makes my stomach turn. 'Where is it now?'

'Stuffed down my jeans. Wanna see it?'

'O'Shea! Ewwww! No!'

'It's still in the box. It's not like the ear itself is right against my skin.'

I feel nauseous. 'I can't believe you're carrying it around.'

'Well, I had a plan. I was going to give it to you. You were going to give it to them. They were going to leave me alone. I knew they meant business when they came to my house this morning. It's a miracle I got away. I thought you could deal with them and make things better.' He blows air out from his cheeks. 'They might not be so keen to talk to you now, though.'

I shake my head. 'It'll never work. They weren't trying to grab you just to get the ear back, they wanted to kill you. In fact, it looks to me as if they cared less about finding out where the ear is and more about simply shutting you up. So maybe it's a fake after all.'

'Either way,' he says mournfully, 'it's not looking good for Devlin O'Shea.'

'When is it ever?' I mutter. 'Look, there's a simple solution to all this.'

'I knew you'd come up with the goods! You're my hero, Bo. The wind beneath my wings. The custard to my apple pie. The...'

'Enough. Please.'

'So what do I do?'

I shrug. 'Easy. Take it to the Agathos' authorities and let them deal with it.'

'You're crazy! I can't do that.'

'There's a tracking spell on you. There's virtually nowhere you can go. Even if you stay down here, that couple will find you sooner or later. The only way to stop them from putting a bullet in your brain is to hand it over so it's no longer in your possession. And the whole world will know about it so there's no point in killing you to keep you quiet.'

'Bo,' O'Shea says patiently, 'there is an outstanding warrant on my name. I can't just turn up to the court and demand to speak to some Agathos bigwig. I'll be slapped in irons.'

Why am I not surprised? 'What is the warrant for?'

'Illegal magic possession, of course. A certain little enhancement spell that screwed you over. Some people seem to think all those bloodguzzlers going wacko was my fault.'

'Well, if you hadn't created the spell in the first place...'

'That's not helping.'

'You're going to have to face the music sooner or later. They're not going to forget about it.' O'Shea doesn't respond. I sigh. 'That's what you were hoping for, wasn't it? That the Agathos court would be absentminded enough to forget your involvement. It's not much of a strategy.'

'Some of those judges are getting on a bit. It's not easy to remember stuff when you're old.'

'Somehow I don't think that all the information about Agathos criminals is stored inside the brains of a few decrepit judges. Besides, Devlin,' I say, trying to impress upon him the gravity of the situation, 'you can't hide from your problems. Face up to them. Be proactive. Right now, you don't have a whole lot of other options.'

'I don't want to go to jail.'

I purse my lips. 'I know a lawyer who may be able to help you out.'

'That floppy-haired dude that dreamy Michael Montserrat dislikes so much?'

'That's the one,' I answer shortly.

'How is the hunky vampire Lord?'

'Don't ask me,' I say.

'Ha! I knew you were looking sad and depressed when I saw you in the street. Lover's tiff?'

'We're hardly lovers.' I'm relieved to finally spy some light ahead of us. I pick up speed. Maybe the prospect of escape from this underworld will encourage O'Shea to stop talking.

'Come on, Bo. Fill me in on all the juicy goss. I need to fulfil my dreams of him vicariously through you.'

'You'll need to find another hapless idiot for that. And stop trying to change the subject.'

'Bo,' he says, his voice dropping as he senses my evasion. 'What did you do?'

'What did *I* do? Says the daemon who's carrying around a severed ear in his sodding pants,' I scoff.

'Tell Uncle Devlin.'

I give in. Perhaps it'll be cathartic. Leaving out no detail, I explain what happened with both Corinne Matheson and the photo. By the time I've finished, the tunnel has widened out. We turn a corner and suddenly there are dim, flickering bulbs lighting our way. Thank goodness.

'The woman did lie, Bo.'

'Only because she had to. The police would scarcely bother to ask her any questions if she hadn't. Not that it makes any difference now. They've pulled almost all the manpower from the investigation.' If I sound bitter, it's because I am.

'She's just one person. With all the Families combined, Lord Michael is protecting 2,500 vampires. He'll do what he can to minimise any further damage to their reputation. That's what being a leader is about, making hard decisions.'

I remain stubborn. 'It doesn't make it right. What about the photo?'

'You don't know what happened. You weren't there. Why didn't you ask him about it sensibly instead of throwing it in his face?'

'I was angry.' I know it sounds feeble.

'You've had it for three weeks. You could have spoken to him about it on any number of occasions. Why didn't you? You're the one who's been telling me to face up to my problems and be proactive.'

'That's because it's a hell of a lot easier to dole out advice than to take it.' I rub my forehead. 'I was afraid of the answer. And,' I sigh, 'I didn't know the context.'

'And you still don't,' O'Shea points out.

'What about the way he disposed of that Medici bloodguzzler I had a showdown with? The time-honoured tradition of body disposal? What the hell was that all about?'

'That's easy. Kakos daemons.'

My mind immediately flies to X. 'Wh–what?' I stammer.

'All the Families do it. Someone dies under suspicious circumstances, you remove the body and blame the Kakos daemons. It averts further bloodshed.'

'That's awful!'

'Why?' he asks, bemused. 'It doesn't make a difference to the Kakos.'

'If people pin murders and disappearances on them when they haven't done them, maybe they're not actually as evil as we all think.'

'Trust me, mate,' he drawls, 'they're worse.'

I lapse into my own thoughts as we ascend a staircase to the surface. I'm too frightened to consider whether he's right about Kakos daemons because I'm already torn about X's supposed cure for vampirism. Unfortunately, I have to admit that O'Shea might be right about Michael. Maybe Michael was only doing what he had to under the circumstances. I've broken my own rules and focused on black and white instead of shades of grey.

Then I remember the bandages and bruises on Corinne's body.

We traipse up to the top of the staircase and arrive at a dusty landing and a set of chained double doors. I reckon I can snap the chains easily enough but O'Shea doesn't want to leave too many traces of our presence and digs around in his pockets, eventually producing a lock pick. He squeezes his hand through the gap in the doors but his fingers fumble. I tap him on the shoulder and, surprised, he hands me the pick.

'I am a private investigator, remember?'

'Who breaks the law from time to time if it suits her,' O'Shea says. 'Just like I do. Just like a certain young hacker who enjoys words does. Maybe the standard you're expecting from Michael Montserrat is unreasonably high.'

I stretch my hands to find the padlock. It takes me less than twenty seconds to click it open and loosen the chain. Kimchi barks several times as if sensing how close he is to fresh air and freedom. I turn to the daemon. 'Shouldn't people in positions of power be held to a higher standard? They choose to be there.'

'It's not because he's Lord Montserrat that you want him to be perfect,' O'Shea says wisely. 'It's because you think he might be The One.'

I meet his eyes then pass back the lock pick, without letting him see how much his comment has affected me. 'It's barely gone nine. The Agathos court is open for another hour yet. Shall we go? I can call Matt and get him to pick Kimchi up.'

O'Shea doesn't break eye contact but he speaks so quietly that he is almost inaudible. 'Sure.'

∽

THE AGATHOS COURT is rather more complicated than the human version because it combines lawmaking, policing and justice. Nevertheless, many of its structures and operations resemble those of the human court since that was the only way that the Agathos were given permission to run their own system back in the eighteenth century. They do eschew human opening hours, preferring to work late into the night, but their barristers and judges still wear those ridiculous white wigs. Until you've seen a fully blown daemon with orange eyes, olive skin and tightly curled white horsehair falling to its shoulders, you haven't lived.

D'Argneau meets us at the entrance, suited and booted as per usual. 'Bo!' he exclaims. 'How fabulous to see you again.' As he reaches over to peck me on the cheek, I note that his accent has suddenly become considerably more posh.

'Hi, Harry.' I introduce him to O'Shea, who surprises me by suddenly going all shy.

D'Argneau looks him over. 'So you're the one.'

O'Shea's chin lifts sharply. 'The one what?'

'The one who's caused so many problems for the Families. You know, you're lucky they've not taken action against you. They'd be well within their rights.'

'It wasn't really his fault,' I say. For all of O'Shea's bluster and my previous words to him on the subject, I know that deep down he feels the repercussions of his virility enhancement spell far more than anyone realises.

D'Argneau waves a hand in the air. 'Regardless, it's good you've decided to hand yourself in. I can probably bring the charges down to a minor misdemeanour. That is,' he adds, speculatively, 'if it's your first offence.'

O'Shea glances away. I check that no one is near us and lower my voice. 'Actually, we'd like to make a deal.'

D'Argneau raises his eyebrows. 'We?'

'It's just possible that O'Shea has proof of Toby Renfrew's continued existence.'

The lawyer's mouth drops open. He stares first at me then at O'Shea. It doesn't take long for a calculating and greedy expression to appear in his eyes. I can almost see the wheels turning in his brain. Being at the centre of the first real clue about the infamous daemon's fate is a lawyer's dream. It'll open up all sorts of triber doors.

'What sort of proof are we talking about?'

I'm getting nervous about still being out in the open. It would be suicide for the daemons to attack inside the court complex but out here is a different matter. With the tracking spell in play, it won't take them long to work out where we are. Of course we want them to find us but it would be better if we were tucked away and surrounded by the might of the law-abiding Agathos world first.

'Let's go inside,' I say firmly.

O'Shea shifts from foot to foot. 'We don't have to. Maybe if I just throw the ear away...'

D'Argneau's expression is a mixture of disgust and delight. 'Ear?'

I hear the screech of car tyres and turn to see a sedan with tinted windows bearing down on us. 'Get him inside now,' I say through gritted teeth.

O'Shea turns, spotting the car. His skin pales, changing to a sallow colour.

'Run!' I hiss.

They don't need any further prompting. D'Argneau and the daemon take off up the marble steps towards the glass doors that lead into the court. I brace myself, facing the oncoming vehicle. I ignore the hammer of my heart and paste on a grim 'don't fuck with me' expression.

The driver flicks his headlights to full beam so I'm nearly

blinded then accelerates. The wheels clunk as the car veers onto the pavement on a direct collision course with me. I hold my ground, waiting until the very last second to make my move. In the moment before the car reaches me I leap up, somersaulting over the vehicle and pulling out my phone. I execute a near-perfect landing and snap a photo of the number plate as the car speeds away.

I look around. Sadly, no one is around to notice my agile cat-like gymnastics. Vaguely irritated, I head inside after O'Shea and D'Argneau.

CHAPTER 10
ANOTHER BRICK IN THE WALL

The woman at the front desk eyes our motley group warily. She has heavy-set features with bushy brows which add to the disapproval emanating in our direction. No wonder O'Shea wasn't keen to hand himself in.

'Yes?'

'Good evening, Meg darling. You're looking particularly gorgeous today.'

If anything, D'Argneau's oily obsequiousness riles the glowering Meg even further. 'What do you want, Harold?' she sneers.

He doesn't miss a beat as he leans over her desk. 'We want to see the duty officer.'

'She's busy.'

'Darling, everyone is busy. Just tell her I'm here with a client who she won't want to miss.'

Meg flicks me a suspicious glance; surely she doesn't think *I'm* the client? I'm not even a sodding daemon. Despite his nervousness, O'Shea manages a choked guffaw. Still, Meg does as she's asked and clicks a button, mumbling into the intercom.

'She has a few minutes. I take it you can find your own way there?'

'Of course.' D'Argneau nods to us and we follow him through the building.

I've been here many times. It was often necessary to show up to various court cases or liaise with different officers when I was working at Dire Straits. I've never had cause to speak to the duty officer, though: that privilege is generally reserved for the criminals themselves.

I have a worrying suspicion that I know who is on duty tonight, however. 'You know this officer we're going to see?' I ask.

D'Argneau taps his temple. 'Darling, I have the schedules of every officer who works here ingrained into my skull. I am good at my job.' He throws me a look. 'You wouldn't have called me otherwise.'

'Good or not, don't bloody well call me darling,' I say.

'You can call me darling,' O'Shea interjects.

D'Argneau looks repelled but I'm relieved to see that O'Shea is regaining his sense of humour.

'What's her name?'

'Nisha Patel.'

I wince. Her reputation precedes her. I hope this isn't going to turn out to be a huge mistake.

We wander down numerous corridors, most of which are still busy. Hunkered down on the floor outside one closed door is a young daemon with a miserable face. He reminds me of Rogu3, and I'm tempted to reach down and give him a hug. Then I notice the gang tattoo on his knuckles and change my mind. As we walk past another office, a couple are arguing loudly. I peer inside, registering a daemon woman and a human man. They seem to be fighting over the custody of their child –

not because they both want him but because neither of them do. I shiver. I'd forgotten how depressing some people can be.

Eventually we stop outside a large office near the far end of the building. Typical bureaucracy, I decide, putting the person who needs to be at the forefront of the action as far away from it as possible. D'Argneau knocks on the door and it opens almost immediately to reveal a small Indian woman, peering over horn-rimmed spectacles. I'm gratified to see that she's not much taller than I am. Perhaps we'll form a certain kinsman-ship – short women of the world unite!

She doesn't even look at me; all her attention is on D'Argneau. 'Ambulance chasing again, are we?'

'Nisha, Nisha. I'm beyond such things. This is far more important than your average walk-in. You're going to be glad you were on duty tonight,' he promises.

'I doubt that,' she says. 'I'm missing my brother's wedding.'

D'Argneau's face falls. 'Oh. Sorry. You must be close.'

'Don't be ridiculous. The man is an idiot. But the food is something not to be missed.' She turns to O'Shea. 'Devlin O'Shea? You're the one who created that stupid enhancement spell, aren't you?' She doesn't wait for him to answer but just looks over at me. 'And Bo Blackman. The only person in history to escape the self-imposed slavery of newly fledged vampires.'

'That's some party trick,' I say. 'Or were you checking us out on the security cameras as we came here?'

She allows herself a tiny grin. 'No, I've read about you both. I've got an eidetic memory. Most of the time it's useful. Unless you're trying to pretend you don't recognise the ex-boyfriend who dumped you for the school bimbo back when you were fifteen.'

I try not to laugh, deciding I like Nisha Patel rather a lot. She's smart, quick-witted and very pretty. No wonder her repu-tation sucks.

'So,' she continues, 'I suppose you'd better come in.'

The office is cosy, with large leather-bound legal books on one side and a scratched mahogany desk in the middle. It's not without its homely touches; I admire the brightly coloured painting on one wall. It looks like expensive modern art. Nisha catches my gaze and smirks. 'My five-year-old nephew's handiwork.'

'Really?'

Her smile widens. 'I guess you'll never know.'

We take our seats then Nisha leans forward, knitting her fingers together. 'So I'm guessing, Mr O'Shea, that you are here to admit yourself into our custody.'

He swallows. 'Not exactly.'

D'Argneau shushes him. 'Let me do the talking. Devlin here has something in his possession that you'll want to see. It pertains to Tobias Renfrew.' He crosses his legs nonchalantly and waits for Nisha's reaction. If he's expecting fireworks, he's sadly disappointed.

'Really,' she murmurs sceptically. 'You do realise we get one of those a month? Even now.' She shakes her head. 'When it comes to money, some people will do anything. In fact, I've heard that of you, Mr O'Shea.'

'I don't want any money,' he asserts. 'I've had enough of people trying to kill me. I only came across the thing a couple of days ago and...'

'Hold on.' Nisha frowns, raising her palm in the air. 'Was Ms Blackman with you when you found this object?'

O'Shea is puzzled. 'No.'

'So why is she here?'

'Moral support,' I interject.

'You're a vampire,' she says.

'So?'

'Bloodguzzlers, in my experience, don't go in for much

support where daemons are concerned. Anything told to me here needs to be in confidence. Unless you've gained a law degree in the last week, Ms Blackman, and you're representing Mr O'Shea alongside Harry here, then you need to leave.'

O'Shea starts to protest but I shake my head. He doesn't need the extra hassle. 'She's right. I'll wait outside.'

Nisha nods approvingly. I walk out, leaving them to it.

With no chair to perch on, I lean against the wall and pull out my phone. It's time to make some amends. I call three times, waiting for Rogu3 to pick up. When he eventually does, his voice is uncharacteristically surly. 'What is it, Bo?'

'You shouldn't have run out like that,' I say. I have next to no experience dealing with hormonal teenagers so I decide to treat him like an adult.

'You're always asking me for stuff. The one time I come to you...' His usual self-possession has entirely vanished.

'Rogu3, you know I'd help you if I could. I'm not sure that lying is the way to go though. You don't want to start a relationship like that.'

He snorts. 'There is no relationship. Don't you get it, Bo? You think this is just some stupid crush. It's not. It's more than that.'

'And if it's more than that,' I say softly, 'treat her with more respect than some elaborate role-play to make her think you're a badass vampire killer.'

There's a moment of silence. 'You know I wouldn't have killed you, right?' he says finally.

I don't laugh. 'I know, Rogu3.' I tighten my fingers around the phone and try to remember what it was like to be that young. 'You know what will really impress her?'

'What?'

'Confidence. You don't need to be the best-looking guy in

the room. You don't need to be the smartest – although you probably are. Look, I'm pretty short, right?'

'You're a dwarf.'

I do my best not to take offence. 'But does my lack of height make me appear less than a person?'

'I guess not.'

'Exactly,' I say, satisfied. 'Fake it until you can make it. Think about your posture. Shoulders back, chin up and look people in the eye. Not just her – what's her name again?'

'Natasha.'

'Okay, don't just act that way around Natasha. Do it all the time, when you're walking down the street, sitting in class, whatever. Smile as often as you can. You know, you're pretty cute when you smile. And don't spend too much time inside your own head. You can over-analyse stuff.' I think of my epic blow-out with Michael. I really should learn to take my own advice. 'Don't wait for the right moment. *Make* the right moment.'

'I suppose.' Rogu3 sounds grudging but I think I'm finally getting through.

'Why don't you come by again tomorrow? We can practise.'

'Really?' The hope in his voice is heartbreaking.

'Sure. Come around five, right before dusk.'

'Thanks, Bo Peep.' He waits a beat, then adds, 'I'm sorry.'

'Don't be.' I almost add that I do remember what it was like to be his age, even if it's a struggle. Then I realise that would be patronising.

'Were the files I gave you any use?' he asks.

'They were just what I needed.' If nothing else, they confirm what Corinne's occupation is and make it clear that there is little in her history to suggest it was a targeted attack. I doubt she'd be impressed if I told her that she beat the statistics by not knowing her rapist, however. I reckon she was nothing more than very unlucky.

'Can I help with anything else?'

I bite my lip. I'd been going to pass the photo I'd snapped of the Agathos goons' number plate to Nisha but if the car was stolen, Rogu3 will have a better chance of tracking down information about it than either the court or the police. But I don't want him to think that's the only reason I'm calling him. It's not.

'Only if you've got time,' I say finally. 'I can pass it along to someone else easily enough.'

'What?' he shrieks. I wince and hold the phone away from ear. 'You can't go to someone else! Do you have another hacker? Is that it?'

I smile. Professional pride. 'No. But I'm at the Agathos court right now. I can pass it over to someone here.'

'They're completely fucking incompetent. Don't bother.'

'Don't swear.'

He laughs. 'Yeah, yeah. What is it?'

'I have a photo of a car that tried to run me over about half an hour ago. It was probably driven by a couple of Agathos daemons. Anything you can find out...'

'Send me it immediately,' he interrupts. 'I'll do more in five minutes than those idiots could in five hours.'

He's probably right. I say goodbye then hang up so I can forward the photo. It whooshes away just as I feel the tell-tale hackles rise on the back of my neck. Someone is watching me. I glance up and my eyes immediately meet X's black ones. He is standing in his glamorous human form at the other side of the corridor. I stiffen as he raises his hand in friendly greeting. My heart starts to race. He walks towards me unhurriedly. I know I can't escape. Even if I could outrun a Kakos daemon, my feet are rooted to the spot in terror.

'Ms Blackman,' he drawls. 'What a pleasure.'

I swallow, taking in his appearance. His tattoos aren't visible but his eyes still possess the menacing glitter I'd expect from one of his kind. His skin is so blemish free that he looks airbrushed. He leans in towards me. 'I exfoliate.'

I swallow again. 'What are you doing here?' I ask, congratulating myself on managing not to stammer.

The corner of his mouth quirks up. 'Streets of Fire has just gained the contract to run all of the Agathos court's computer systems. I was signing on the dotted line.'

Sweet Jesus. He's just infiltrated the entire court system – and he's getting paid for it. 'They're daemons, too,' I whisper. 'How can they not tell what you are?'

He shrugs elegantly. 'People think we're like witches. Two sides of the same coin. The truth is far more complicated. As you appear to be. Tell me, why haven't you taken the blood yet? I gave you your heart's desire, yet you are holding out. It would be disappointing to think you are enjoying the vampire lifestyle more than you expected.'

My eyes narrow. 'Piss off.' As soon as the words are out of my mouth, I realise what I've said. Fortunately, he doesn't take offence. 'Taking the cure doesn't affect just me.'

'Ah, I see,' he nods thoughtfully. 'If the world discovers there's a cure for vampirism, you're worried everyone will be after it.' He smirks. 'My blood won't last forever and this is a onetime deal. You won't get any more. You need to make a decision soon. Will you be selfish or selfless? I will wait with bated breath to see the result.' He grins. I can only stare at him. 'Well, toodle pip,' he says genially. 'You should have a look at the Wall on your way out. You never know what you might find.' His eyes gleam. 'I'll see you around, Ms Blackman.'

He turns on his heel and strides back the way he came, just as O'Shea and D'Argneau emerge from Nisha's office.

O'Shea frowns. 'Who was that?'

I cough. 'No one.'

He looks at me curiously look but thankfully doesn't pursue it. 'The good news is she's not going to lock me up.'

'You might be safer in a cell.'

'I'll take my chances.'

'Don't get too cocky,' D'Argneau warns. 'You're not going to get off scot-free.'

Given that this is the third time in the few months I've known him that someone has wanted to kill O'Shea, I agree. 'What about the ear?' I ask. 'And Renfrew?'

'Nisha is sending it to the lab. They'll get the DNA results back in a day or two. Until they know either way, they're not going to make a move. She's going to email several departments about it, though. The news will leak within the hour.'

Good. The only way O'Shea will be safe from further attacks is if there's no longer any reason to kill him. I nod briskly and start marching down the corridor.

'What's the hurry?' D'Argneau calls out.

'I want to see the Wall.'

'Why?'

My phone beeps with a text message, saving me from answering. I pull it out. It's Rogu3; that was fast work. I guess he really was determined to prove he was better than anything the Agathos court could offer.

Car stolen 2 days ago. Will scan thru CCTV 4 backtrack & email with news.

I ROLL my eyes at the emoticon. For someone who has an expansive vocabulary, it seems to be an unnecessary addition. I'm glad it's a smile, though, rather than anything else.

ALTHOUGH I'M irritated at following X's suggestion as if I'm little more than a trained seal, I can't let a potential tip slide by. The court is about to close and we'll all be turfed out soon, so I move quickly with both O'Shea and D'Argneau trotting behind me.

I know where the Wall is; it stretches the length of the building. I frequently scoured it during my Dire Straits days. As the name suggests, it is a wall. It's covered in missing persons' posters, wanted mugshots and requests for help. If you're a private investigator, it's a goldmine. If you're anyone else, it's a depressing comment on the dangers of living in today's society.

I don't have time to look over everything carefully, so I scan it all as quickly as possible.

'What are you looking for?' O'Shea asks.

'I have no idea. I just, um, have a feeling there might be something useful here.'

'About Renfrew?'

I purse my lips. I guess. What else could it be? I shuffle along as I read. It would be one thing if the Wall were reserved for violent criminals but it's more than that. I pass an entire section, at least three metres wide, filled with pleas from spouses – usually female daemons although not exclusively – searching for their errant partners who owe child support. There are also far too many parents desperately seeking their runaway children. I pause at one, tracing over the cherubic cheeks of Alice Goldman, whose unsolved disappearance resulted in my initial meeting with Rogu3. My chest is tight. I might be a damn vampire but it still feels like I have a human soul.

O'Shea whistles. 'There's a woman here who's embezzled more than three million by turning up to the homes of the elderly and telling them she'll daemon proof their houses.' He tuts. 'Even I wouldn't stoop that low.'

'Bo, the court will be open tomorrow. Why don't we go for a drink instead?' D'Argneau says.

I don't look but I catch him gesturing to O'Shea out of the corner of my eye. 'What?' the daemon asks plaintively. 'I don't understand.'

D'Argneau sighs melodramatically. 'After all that running around in the sewers…'

'Underground. Not sewers. Do I smell like shit to you?'

I do my best to ignore them and keep searching.

'Whatever,' D'Argneau says dismissively. 'You should probably go home and get some rest anyway.'

'Maybe I'd like to come out for a drink with you and Bo.'

I run my index finger down a line of alleged bank robbers. It's like looking for a needle in a haystack, except I don't even know what a needle looks like. I bet that somewhere X is laughing his sodding head off. D'Argneau and O'Shea continue bickering.

'You look too tired.'

'Oh yeah? Well, I think you look tired. And wrinkly.' O'Shea sniffs. 'Maybe you should go home. I can come with you and give you a massage to soothe those aching muscles. Do you have any scented oil?'

Annoyed, I turn towards them. 'Guys, will you cut it out?'

'Ooooh. Touchy much?'

I roll my eyes at O'Shea. 'This is a waste of time,' I say to myself. 'I need to get back to New Order and do some real work.'

'It's time you three left.' Meg, the unfriendliest receptionist in the world, is standing at the far end of the Wall, tapping her wrist. It's not as if she's wearing a watch. She must have some spooky powers because I could swear she appeared out of nowhere.

'We're going,' I mutter. Then my eyes fall on an old Crime-watch poster. I hear D'Argneau say something to placate Meg but I don't register the words. Instead I move forward. The paper is yellowing, with faded typeset appealing for information about the brutal rape of a young Agathos girl. Her attack took place four years ago on the other side of the city. What interests me is the one bloodcurdling detail at the bottom. Whoever the bastard was, he used stakes through her palms to stop her running away. I rip the poster from the wall while Meg protests loudly. I look up and give her my ultimate death stare. She falls silent.

'I'm taking this,' I announce, as if daring Meg to disagree.

Corinne Matheson wasn't the first.

CHAPTER 11

A MAN'S BEST FRIEND

As I sprint breathlessly into New Order, I realise from the sudden hush that everyone is talking about me. Not only that, every single person is in the office. That's not normal.

'Ah, Bo,' my grandfather says. 'I'm glad you could join us.'

I look from face to face. 'What's wrong?'

'We were going to ask you that,' Arzo says gently. 'The argument you had with Lord Montserrat was … loud.'

'That was ages ago. We've got much more important things to worry about.'

He raises his eyebrows. 'Bo, you effectively told the Lord of the most powerful vampire Family to fuck off. Have you been going to your counselling sessions?'

'Yes,' I say through gritted teeth.

'They can help a lot, Bo,' Peter says, not looking me directly in the eye.

I stare at Matt. 'Don't you have something to add?'

'You are a kind of Montserrat vampire,' he says awkwardly. 'I mean, you're not, but you are. If you see what I mean.'

I look at Kimchi who merely wags his tail. At least someone

is pleased to see me although he does seem to have gnawed off half a chair leg in the brief time he's been here. Tiny splinters of wood are lying in a pile on the floor. I drag my attention away from them as Connor approaches. 'Do you need some blood?' he asks.

I nod. As everyone is staring at me, I point towards the small room at the back. I don't need a sodding audience. 'Look,' I say, exasperated. 'It is possible I may have been too hasty in what I said to Michael. But it's between me and him. It's got nothing to do with New Order.'

'I beg to differ, my dear,' my grandfather says. 'He's responsible for setting up New Order. If we fail in our endeavours, he will go down with the ship, so to speak. It's imperative we maintain good relations.' He looks at me disapprovingly. 'And really, it's in incredibly bad taste to have a shouting match when one is in earshot of others.'

I grit my teeth. 'I get what you're saying and I will make amends. Right now, however, we need to find this Crimewatch video.' I wave the poster in the air.

Arzo scan it. 'Stakes? Bo, you don't think…'

'It's incredibly rare for cross-species attacks to occur,' my grandfather chimes in.

I soften my voice. 'Please, just find the video. We need to see it.' I follow Connor and close the door firmly behind me.

'Are you okay, Bo?'

I smile at him reassuringly. 'I am.' The etched furrow of concern on his forehead doesn't go away. 'I promise.'

He holds out his wrist and I check his eyes carefully. 'If you don't want to do this, Connor, I understand. You can say no whenever you want.'

He smiles faintly. 'I think you're still hoping I will say no. It'll get easier, Bo. Other vampires don't feel like this, so I'm sure your aversion to blood will go away soon.'

'Why do you do this?' I ask for the umpteenth time. I know he's answered me before but I'm still not satisfied. 'Is it because you want to be recruited and you think this is a way in?'

'Nah. I don't want to be a bloodguzzler. I thought about it for a while but seeing you...' He wrinkles his nose. 'It's not for me. I want a long life, though. I have other plans to achieve that longevity.'

'Eating your greens?'

He laughs. 'No. There's a company called Time Lapse that's doing cool things. You know how some rich dead people have their bodies cryogenically frozen so that when we solve the mysteries of death, they can be brought back to life? Well, Time Lapse have discovered there are these things called time bubbles. They're pretty rare and they don't have much reach but they can be used to preserve time. Maybe even to go back in time.'

I gaze at him incredulously. 'Time travel? That's your big plan to cheat death?'

'Don't scoff,' he says earnestly. 'They're a long way from success right now but I'm young. They'll figure it out.' He points to leaflet on a nearby shelf. There's a picture of an orb with blue swirls floating around inside and the words *Cheat Death* underneath.

I decide he's even crazier than I thought. He's probably in good company. He points to his neck and smiles at me so, for the sake of a quiet life, I bob my head. My fangs lengthen so I can sink them into his soft flesh. For a brief moment I gag before the sustenance his blood offers takes over.

Once we're finished, we re-enter the office. The others are crowded round a computer screen.

'We found it!' Matt says cheerfully. At my glance, his expression falls. 'Sorry,' he mumbles, subduing his tone. 'I mean, we found it.'

I join them, although with my lack of height I can't see anything. Connor manages fine. I cough delicately.

'Sorry, Bo,' Arzo says, moving out of the way. 'Always forget you are so short.'

'You're cruising for a bruising.' I give him my death stare that so effectively silenced Meg. Unfortunately, Arzo doesn't even notice.

The photo of the young daemon on the poster appears on the screen as the presenter details the circumstances of the crime.

'Park,' Peter mutters. 'Just like the other one.'

'That one's much more secluded though. You couldn't get more public than bloody Jubilee Park.'

'Shhh!' I hiss, pulling out my notepad and watching carefully.

The victim's name is Rebecca Small. I'm surprised that her identity is revealed so carelessly but the presenter says she has waived her right to confidentiality in the hope that her attacker will be brought to justice swiftly. I'm guessing that didn't happen then. She was barely seventeen when it happened and living with her parents; that probably rules out her being a prostitute like Corinne. Fresh-faced and very, very young – not to mention a daemon. They couldn't be further removed from each other.

I feel a flash of pain in my hands and realise that I've drawn blood with my fingernails. I try to release the tension in my body but it's not easy. Apparently, Rebecca was walking home from school when she was dragged off the street in broad daylight. The park she was taken to was quiet and rarely used at that time of year. The manner of her abduction suggests the perpetrator didn't worry about being seen. He was wearing a balaclava the entire time so there's no photofit to match with Corinne's. But, like Corinne, Rachel was staked to the ground and brutally raped. He didn't try to kill her though. Once he was done, he merely stood up, zipped his trousers and left.

'They have to be the same person,' Arzo says, once the video is finished. 'Even though the victims are worlds apart.'

'He's escalating though. He used to wear a balaclava; now he doesn't. He used to hide his crimes; now he doesn't. And,' I add quietly, 'he used to let his victims go. He'd have killed Corinne Matheson if he could.'

'He almost did,' my grandfather says grimly. 'Bo, you need to pass this information to the police. They can deal with it.' He shakes his head. 'This is why we need greater cooperation between different triber groups and the humans. The similarities between the two crimes should have been spotted earlier.'

I take a deep breath. 'There can't be just two. There's no way this prick left a four-year gap between Rebecca and Corinne. What was he doing in between? Going to work? Watching the soaps? Doing his laundry? No,' I shake my head. 'There are others.'

Peter's voice is so quiet I have to strain to hear him. 'Are we sure it's not a vampire who did this?'

'Yes. Whoever it is has a gold tooth.' I turn and glance at Kimchi for a moment. 'Have we heard from the vet yet?'

Connor nods. 'The dog is not a vampire.'

'Surprise, surprise,' I say drily.

'He is sensitive to light though. Photophobia. And he has pigmentation in his irises. That's why he's got the red in his eyes. Other than that, he's perfectly healthy.'

'It's almost a shame,' Arzo comments. 'With those symptoms, he'd make a perfect pet for a vampire like you.'

I look at Kimchi fondly until I realise that in the space of about three seconds he's managed to get hold of a suspiciously familiar looking pair of knickers. He couldn't have gone upstairs to the flat and brought them down here so he must have taken them earlier and hidden them somewhere like he was guarding a bone. Eurgh. I quickly retrieve the ripped and saliva-soaked underwear and stuff it in my pocket. Peter, Connor and Matt are gracious enough to look away; Arzo appears amused and my grandfather is horrified.

'I'm going to take him back to his owner,' I mutter. 'It's late but I've got a question or two that Mr Brinkish might help us with.'

'About these girls? How? Bo, it's not a vampire matter. Leave it for the police.'

I put my hands on my hips. 'Why? Because we're so run off our feet here that we can't spare the time? You didn't see her. You didn't see what he did to her.'

'Who'll talk to the police then?'

'Matt. He can speak to Foxworthy.'

Matt grins and nods, obviously happy to be useful. He's also probably relieved to not have to go back to Brinkish's place and be asked again to take off his shoes.

I give the little gathering a hard look. 'The rest of you should go home and get some rest. Tomorrow you'll need to start looking for evidence of similar rapes.' I pause. 'Or worse.'

BEFORE I LEAVE, my grandfather beckons me into his office and carefully closes the door. 'You should leave this to the police,' he growls.

'That's not what you really want to say. Spit it out. Tell me off again for arguing with Michael.' I fold my arms. I'm a big girl; I can deal with it.

'From what I heard, you had some reason to be angry.' I blink in shock. Is he agreeing with me? 'And,' he continues, 'I'm pleased to see you're standing up for yourself as far as he's concerned. It's certainly better than fawning all over him like a lovesick puppy.'

'I wasn't doing that!' I protest.

He ignores me. 'But I meant what I said before. You should apologise for the sake of propriety. And, for heaven's sake, Bo, next time either go somewhere you won't be overheard or keep your voice down. Airing your dirty laundry in public is such a lower class thing to do.'

I cannot believe he just said that. 'Well,' I say, 'there's nothing like a spot of bigoted snobbery to start the conversation off.'

He throws me a disparaging look. 'Have you made any progress with Medici yet?'

'I'd have told you if I had.'

'There's no need to get snippy.'

I throw my hands up in exasperation. 'As you said, it's taking a lot of time. At the rate I'm going, he'll be chucking a fully brainwashed Dahlia in Arzo's face before I've managed to reach the heady heights of small talk. And he's fully aware that I'm regularly turning up at his club.'

'Good. We want him to think he knows everything that's going on.'

'He *does* know everything that's going on,' I point out.

'For the moment,' my grandfather says. 'It won't last.'

'Are you going to let me in on the plans?'

'I'm still finessing the details. Patience, Bo. Patience. You can chase a butterfly all over a field and then, the moment you sit quietly in the grass, it'll land on your shoulder.'

'Medici is hardly a butterfly. He's more like the snake in the grass that'll come up and bite you in the arse when you're not looking.'

'Except we are looking. We are looking very hard.'

I bite my tongue. As far as the Lord of the Medici Family is concerned, I don't think we're doing nearly enough. On this matter at least, however, I've promised to adhere to my grandfather's wishes. He is the spymaster amongst us, after all.

I change the subject. 'The police have still got my bike. Anyway it's not practical to drive it when I'm with Kimchi. Can I borrow your car?'

'Absolutely not. I won't have my vehicle stinking of dog.'

He doesn't seem to mind it reeking of cat, I think sourly. Then I realise I've not seen his stupid moggy today. I look round the room suspiciously, wondering if it's eyeing me up somewhere and waiting for the right moment to pounce. Bloody thing.

'Peter's heading in that direction,' he continues. 'You can catch a lift with him.'

'How do I get back?'

'For goodness' sake, Bo. Do I have to think of everything?'

I swear, if he wasn't elderly I'd slap him around a few times. Then I notice the corner of his mouth twitching. Well, at least one of us is having some fun.

THE JOURNEY TO Brinkish's house is almost silent. I try to make conversation a few times with Peter but his answers are monosyllabic. Eventually, I give in so the only sound in the car is Kimchi panting. The dog takes great joy in squeezing from the back seat to my lap, where he sits happily for five minutes, then returns through the narrow gap between the front passenger seats for another five minutes.

I'm tempted to fiddle with the radio but I sense that Peter wouldn't appreciate it. When he drops the pair of us outside the house, he looks relieved. I wave a friendly goodbye but Peter barely notices before he speeds away. I chew my lip as he disappears round the corner. He doesn't seem to enjoy being Sanguine any more than he enjoyed being human or a vampire recruit. I don't mean to feel bitter – it's not his fault I didn't make it to Sanguine – but I can't quite avoid it.

Sighing, I walk up the path to Brinkish's front door. I'm halfway there when I realise Kimchi isn't following. I turn back. He's lying down on the pavement, his large brown eyes watching me. He lets out a small whine. 'Come on, Kimchi,' I say. He doesn't budge. I try again. 'Kimchi! Here boy!'

Slowly, as if it's a great effort, he drags himself up and lumbers over to join me. He looks at me as if to say that I'm betraying our friendship by bringing him back here. Then I wonder if I'm merely projecting my own thoughts.

I ring the doorbell and wait. After a few minutes the door opens a crack and a bleary-eyed woman peers out. She's wearing a brightly coloured floral nightgown that hangs around her large figure like a tent. This must be Mrs Brinkish.

'Hello!' I say cheerily. 'I'm bringing Kimchi home.'

Her gaze flicks from me to the dog, then back again. 'You're the vampire.'

I nod. 'Yes. We've had the results from the vet and I can confirm that the dog's definitely not a vampire. Truthfully,' I say confidentially, 'there's really no such thing.'

'You're not coming in. I'm not going to invite you.'

It's probably wise not to mention that her husband has already done that deed. If I wanted to offend my eyes again with their clashing home interior, I could. 'No problem.' I keep my smile fixed to my face and gently push Kimchi forward. 'Off you go.'

He whines again but does as he's told for once. Mrs Brinkish holds up her hand and he stops in his tracks. 'Barry!' she yells. Then, 'Get your arse down here. It's the bloodguzzler.'

She turns round, disappearing into the back of the house

but leaving the door wide open. When Brinkish appears, he's wearing pyjamas made out of the same material as his wife's nightgown. It's an arresting sight.

He frowns at me. 'Oh, it's you. You do realise it's the middle of the night?'

'I'm a vampire, Mr Brinkish.' I shrug amiably. 'I can't help it.'

He grunts. Kimchi thumps his tail and starts forward. Brinkish scratch his head, then suddenly withdraws his hand as he thinks better of it. 'So?' he asks.

'Kimchi is one hundred per cent dog.'

'Oh.' He seems slightly disappointed.

'He has photophobia, which is probably why he doesn't like going out during the day. The red in his eyes is nothing more than pigmentation.'

'You can keep him.'

I keep my expression blank. I was afraid this was going to happen. 'He's your dog, Mr Brinkish.'

'The wife wants a cat.'

'All the same, I don't live the sort of lifestyle that's conducive to having a dog.' Actually, despite the destruction of my belongings and the slobber, I'd quite like to keep Kimchi. He's a great dog. That would, however, make it too easy on the couple, especially considering they now want to get another animal. If you want to be a pet owner, you can't change your mind a few years down the line. It's a lifetime commitment. 'You can't just dump him, Mr Brinkish. He's your responsibility.'

He starts to say something but the expression on my face changes his mind and he backtracks. 'Fine,' he snaps. 'Get in here,' he says to the dog.

Kimchi gives me one last forlorn look and pads inside.

'Three months,' I tell him. 'Keep Kimchi for another three months. Try to remember why you got him in the first place.'

I'm not about to let the poor dog be ignored or thrown into the nearest shelter. 'If you can't manage that, then I'll take him.' My eyes harden. 'In the meantime, if you don't look after him properly we will talk again.'

To remind him that I can enter his property now whenever I wish, I step into the porch. I'm barely an inch inside but my point is made. Brinkish swallows.

'There's one other thing,' I say.

He glares at me. 'What?'

'Your tooth. Where did you get it done?'

For a second, he looks confused then he touches his gold molar. In one swift movement he yanks at it and it comes off. He holds it out to me in the palm of his hand. 'Go on,' he smirks. 'You can touch it if you want to.'

I look at the tooth, then at his mouth. There's no missing tooth: it is nothing more than a removable gold cap. Shit. I'd no idea such things existed. If Corinne hadn't confessed that her attacker was human, he could have been a bloodguzzler after all. It would be a pain in the arse to keep taking a gold cap on and off, but it would be possible. What Brinkish has is nothing more than jewellery.

'Where did you get it from?'

'Shipped from the States. I bought it via a local distributor.'

'Can you give me their name?'

'Some internet company." A flicker of pride crosses his eyes. "They custom made it to fit my tooth exactly.'

'How lovely,' I murmur. And what a waste of time. Both his, in getting the damn thing made in the first place, and mine for thinking he could help us track down the serial rapist. I didn't need to trek all this way, I could have gone downstairs and spoken to Drechlin. He'd no doubt have told me how easy it is to get hold of such things.

I try to recover. 'Thank you. And remember, three months,

Mr Brinkish. You need to treat Kimchi like a king or there will be consequences.'

I step backwards, keeping my gaze fixed on him. He mutters something under his breath and slams the door shut. I cross my fingers and hope I've done the right thing.

It's late by the time I get back to my flat. I'd been forced to piggy back on a delivery van heading into the city in order to make it home before sun up. I'm tired and grouchy, so when I reach the top of the stairs and realise my door is wide open, my mood doesn't improve. I tense and crouch low, ready to face the idiot who has decided to break in. I needn't have bothered; he's already heard me coming.

Michael steps out of the doorway and my stomach drops. I genuinely intended to offer my apologies to him for going over-board with my accusations, but I wanted to be prepared first. Instead, I'm covered in dirt and dust from the delivery van and my hair is sticking up as if searching for a satellite signal. Michael is wearing an immaculate, midnight-blue, v-necked t-shirt that clings in all the right places. He doesn't have a single hair out of place; the only suggestion that he is tense is the hooded expression in his eyes.

'Bo,' he murmurs. It sounds like an invitation.

I keep my voice steady but my reaction to his presence is clear from my words. 'How the fuck did you get into my apart-ment?' As soon as I've spoken, I berate myself. It's hardly the cautious opener I should have aimed for.

'You left your window open,' he responds smoothly. 'I wouldn't have used it normally but you weren't in. I figured you'd prefer if it I was inside rather than hanging around in the corridor where your colleagues might see me.'

I think of the anxious faces I'd dealt with earlier. He's probably right.

'I'm going to be optimistic,' he continues, 'and think that your words about me never coming near you again were spoken in the heat of the moment. After all, it will be difficult for me to avoid New Order for the rest of time.' He dips his head and I get the impression he's suddenly nervous.

'Um, yes.' I shuffle my feet.

He throws me something that glints in the air and I shoot my hand up to catch it. I open up my palm and look. It's a tarnished badge with the words Metropolitan Police inscribed around the outside. Puzzled, I look up at him.

'Medici and I were in the police together.' He says it stiffly, as if he's uncomfortable. 'We worked undercover. Chinese immigration was at its height and there were concerns about some of the more,' he pauses, 'criminal elements. Not to mention the long reach of the Kuomintang. We infiltrated their network and established ourselves as bootleggers. To prove our allegiance, we were asked to witness some executions. The smiles you see are part of our cover.' His mouth curves upwards, entirely without humour. 'Of course, I have no proof of this beyond the badge. The records are hidden away in some long-forgotten vault.' He runs a hand through his hair. 'Do the press have the photo too?'

I'm confused then I realise what he's getting at. 'No. I got it from O'Connell, the ex-CEO of Magix. I burned everything else. There aren't going to be any tabloid shocks.' I look away. 'At least not unless Magix does something with the originals. Their new CEO…'

'I know him. I'll sort something out.'

'Okay.'

'Do you believe me? About the photo?'

'Does it matter?'

He bunches his fists up. 'Yes,' he says quietly. 'It does.'

'I met Cheung. He's...'

'One of the Triad leaders.'

'He was afraid of you, Michael.'

'Our covers were blown. Mine and Medici's. It's the reason we both ended up being recruited as vampires – it was the only place left to hide. When the gangs realised they couldn't get to us, they took their revenge elsewhere.' Bitter anger flashes across his face. All this may have happened more than ninety years ago but I realise that, for Michael, it's as if it were yesterday. 'When I was strong enough, I went after them in return.' He meets my eyes. 'It's not something I'm proud of. But some people have long memories and pass warnings along to subsequent generations.'

I take a deep breath. 'Okay.' Whatever he did was no doubt bloody and brutal. I don't need to know the gory details.

Michael lifts his chin. 'I'm not going to apologise for what happened with the prostitute. I had to do what was best for us. For the Families.'

I nod my head. 'I understand. I don't agree with it, but I understand. I should have thought more about your obligations before I laid into you.'

He moves closer until he's barely a foot away. 'Is that an apology?' he asks softly.

I shake my head. 'No. But it is a peace offering.'

His eyes rake over me and a shiver runs down my spine. 'I can live with that.'

'Look at us,' I say, trying to sound light-hearted, 'all chatty and polite and getting along.'

He doesn't smile. 'Do you trust me, Bo?'

I can no longer meet his eyes. I'm not going to lie, though. 'No,' I eventually answer in a small voice.

He reaches out and brushes my bottom lip very gently with the base of his thumb. 'I can be a patient man.'

'I don't think this is going to work, Michael.' I take a deep breath. 'You're in a different place to me. We're different people. The mutual attraction is just because you bit me. Or this is just that recruit rebound thing you were talking about before.'

I see a tiny flash of rage in his face. 'Is this the part where you tell me you only want to be friends?'

I stare at him. I'm not sure we can just be friends but anything else simply won't work. Not if I can't bring myself to trust him. 'Friends sounds good,' I say eventually.

He watches me. I wish I knew what he was thinking. 'Friends then,' he agrees. 'With benefits.'

I gape. 'Um ... I don't think...'

'Benefits of working together to achieve the same goals,' he interrupts. 'Peace across the Families.' He gives me a wolfish smile. 'Why, what did you think I meant?'

'Nothing! Working together is good. Peace, yes.' I nod, aware that I'm starting to babble. 'Those kinds of benefits.'

He leans in. 'Fucking friends,' he mutters. Then he grabs my shoulders and pulls me towards him. His mouth descends in a hard kiss. Despite my better judgment, lust uncurls through my body and I squirm. The moment I yield and respond he breaks away, breathing hard. 'For old times' sake,' he breathes. 'It won't happen again. Not now that we're friends.' He emphasises the last word so that I'm not sure whether he's laughing at me or not. Then, before I can respond, he whirls past me and disappears in a flash.

I touch my bruised lips, suddenly no longer sure of anything at all.

CHAPTER 12

PRACTICE MAKES PERFECT

'So,' Rogu3 says, sitting on my small sofa, 'I've been through as many images as I can pull. Your guys stole the car from here.' He shows me the first photo. It's definitely the same two goons who tried to shoot me and O'Shea. 'It was at a car park near Brent Cross shopping centre. It's supposed to be one of those theft-proof cars. They had a hand-held computer and were inside in about twenty seconds flat.' He sounds impressed.

I purse my lips. 'So they have some skills.'

'Mad skills. You see the way they're keeping their heads down? They knew where the cameras were and where to avoid looking. But my skills are better.' He's smug in the way that only a teenager can be. 'I caught their reflection off this wing mirror, see? It was a simple matter to enhance it.'

I give him a quick round of applause but he holds up his index finger. 'Just wait, Bo Peep. I can do much better. I back-tracked through the other nearby CCTV and surveillance videos. London really is a godsend for this sort of stuff. I have them here,' he pulls out another photo, 'six minutes before they entered the car park. And here,' he points to another one, 'ten minutes before that.'

I squint. 'That looks like Hendon Central.'

'Well done. But they're not coming from the underground. Check this out. I got it from the camera inside Subway. Pretty impressive, huh?'

'Cooper Funeral Director's,' I read. 'They're coming out of the door.'

'Yup. And it's a tiny place. Even if they're not associated with it personally and they were visiting because they're both recently bereaved, they're going to be remembered.'

'Could you pull anything from surveillance inside?'

He shakes his head. 'Unfortunately not. These places tend not to use CCTV. You know, respect for the dead and all that.'

I stare at the two of them. They're wearing the same suits as when I met them face to face. And they have the same arrogant expressions on their faces. 'Does the funeral director's deal with Agathos daemons?'

Rogu3 grins. 'Exclusively. I tried calling. You know, pretended to be looking for the body of a friend of mine. The person I spoke to was male and had what sounded like an American accent.'

I scratch my head. 'That's not my guy. It's a huge help though, Rogu3.'

He beams. 'Told you I'd do a better job than the Agathos court could.'

'I had no doubt.' I write him a cheque not only for these services but also for the previous ones I still have on account. For a second, I think he's about to refuse it but when I frown he quickly pockets it.

He looks round my flat doubtfully. 'Are you sure you can afford me?'

'Don't worry about it.'

His eyes fall on the hand-drawn map I've tacked on the wall. I've only just started it but I've managed to draft out several key places already. 'Where's this?' he asks.

'London.'

'It doesn't look like London.'

'It's the underground,' I tell him. 'But not just the train lines. There are lots of tunnels and dead stations lurking down there.'

'Cool.' He points to an area I've shaded in red. 'What's that?'

'Fort Knox.' Rogu3 gives me a puzzled look but doesn't pursue it. 'It's your turn now,' I tell him. 'Stand up.'

He does as he's told. I look him over. His posture isn't too bad, but there's a lot of room for improvement. 'Pull your shoulders back a bit.' He makes a jerking movement and suddenly looks like a robot. I grin. 'No, like this.' I gently grab them and apply a bit of pressure. 'You need to look relaxed and comfortable to pull this off.'

'This position is not comfortable.'

'I said, *look* comfortable. There's a big difference. If I wanted you to be comfortable, I'd tell you to stay at home slumped in a chair.' I move round to the front of him and gently nudge his feet apart a few inches. 'Put your hands in your pockets. It can be hard to know what to do with your hands sometimes so if you have them resting there, you won't have to worry. Just, you know, don't go fiddling or fumbling or anything.'

Rogu3's face screws up. 'Bo! As if.'

I smile. 'Okay, let's try walking.'

Rogu3 takes a few steps. From behind his back, I wince. That's not going to work at all. It takes half an hour of practice before I'm satisfied he's got it right. 'We're going to try it in the real word,' I say finally.

He blanches. 'Shit.'

I cuff him round the ear. 'How many times...?'

He rolls his eyes. 'Yeah, yeah. You know what I think next week's word will be?'

'If it's a profanity,' I say primly, 'I'm going to call your parents.'

'Curmudgeon,' he tells me. 'That's what it'll be.'

I step back and stare at him. He blinks and looks away. 'Sorry,' he mumbles.

'See? That's the sort of look you want to create.'

'Like I'm about to bite someone and drain them of all their blood?'

'No,' I tut. 'That you're right and they're wrong. I told you – it's all about confidence.'

He nods. 'Like the painting guy.' I glance at him questioningly. 'Guy walks into a gallery in Liverpool. Wants to steal a painting. He tries to take it out of the frame so he can roll it up and hide it inside his jacket but it won't work. So he pulls it off the wall and just walks straight out with it under his arm. Not a single person stops him.'

'Um, yes, like that guy. Just don't go stealing anything.'

'Well, he did get caught about five feet from the gallery.'

I give him a look as if to say 'I told you so'. 'Come on. There's a café nearby, we'll try that. It's dark now, so there shouldn't be a problem.'

Rogu3 shakes his head. 'I have a better idea.'

We wander downstairs. I can see Arzo inside the office, craning his neck to see who my visitor is. Even O'Shea, who knows of Rogu3, has no idea who he really is. For the teenager's sake, I keep him to myself. I glance in through the glass at Drechlin's on the way out. The dentist is sitting in a large comfortable chair. My grandfather's cat is on his lap, looking for all the world like it belongs there. Its eyes are closed and

Drechlin is murmuring something to it. Then, as I watch, one yellow slitted eye slowly opens and stares at me malevolently. I stick out my tongue childishly. Unfortunately, Drechlin thinks I'm doing it to him and scowls at me. Oops.

The protestors outside are very audible. They seem better organised today and are chanting in a more synchronised fashion. 'Blood is for life, not for dinner! Blood is for life, not for dinner!' It's one of their more inspired offerings, I suppose. They could still do better.

'Rogu3, this might not be a good idea,' I say. 'I don't want you to get hurt.'

'Blame the teacher, not the student,' he grins. He pushes open the door and walks out with me at his heels, ready to launch myself at anyone who so much as gives him a funny look. Bloodguzzers' reputation be damned.

Rogu3 strides forward, using the gait I just taught him. I hang back as the protestors target me rather than him. The people standing in his path actually move out of his way. He stops, puts his hands in pockets and smiles. I admit that it is a rather disarming grin.

One by one, like participants in an odd Mexican wave, the protestors fall silent. A few look puzzled. An older gentleman at the back appears angry and tries to get the chanting going again but when the others don't join in, he falters. I keep my eyes on him anyway. Rogu3's smile widens.

'Thank you so much,' he says softly to the small crowd. 'You are very loud and my ears were starting to hurt.' Then he walks through the centre of the group and they part like the Red Sea.

He ruins the effect somewhat by spinning round and giving me a huge, cheesy thumbs-up once he's a few metres away from them. It's still a pretty awesome effort though.

I follow him but the crowd suddenly bunches up to stop me.

I'd try the same confidence trick but somehow I don't think it'll work. These people can't see past vampire.

'Spawn of Satan!' the man at the back yells. I give him a dirty look. I skirt round the group, keeping my distance in case they decide to rush me. I suppose I should be grateful that most of them are too afraid to try. At least Spitting Woman isn't here.

I catch up with Rogu3 and we amble towards the bus stop. He's so buoyed with success, he's almost bouncing along next to me. The streets are full of tourists, even though it's late in the year. I receive several wary looks, probably because I'm wandering along with a teenage human boy; for once, I choose to ignore them and instead search for a target.

I spy a girl about Rogu3's age perched on a wall. She's staring into space. Nearby, an older couple with similar features are busy snapping away with large expensive looking cameras, so I guess she's on holiday with her parents. They're having far more fun than she is.

I nudge Rogu3. 'Okay, you see the girl? With the long dark hair?'

His eyes widen. 'She's pretty.'

We draw closer and I spot a small badge on her jacket. The word 'fille' is written on it in large curly letters. Perfect. 'And she's here on holiday, probably from France, so there's no danger of any broken hearts – given that yours is already taken.'

'What do I do?' Rogu3 asks, suddenly nervous.

I glance at him from under my eyelashes. The closer we get to the girl, the more scared he seems. It's one thing to approach a vengeful group of adults with violence on their minds and quite another to say hello to a pretty girl.

'Exactly what we practised.' I give him a little nudge then cross to the other side of the road. There's only so much I'm willing to do to be his wing-man; he has to do this part solo.

He takes a deep breath and walks up to her. His gait verges

close to an arrogant strut but when he smiles I know it'll negate any bad vibes he might give off. Rogu3 looks the girl directly in the eyes and starts to speak. Her face softens and I swear I can see a red stain on her cheeks. He puts his hands in his pockets and relaxes, chatting to her and pointing something out. When the girl's parents look over – and the father frowns with overly-protective concern – I know Rogu3's succeeded.

When he rejoins me, I'm reminded of Kimchi and his ecstatically wagging tail.

'Did you see? Were you watching?'

I smile. 'I was.'

'Her name's Nicole and she's from Marseilles.' He drops his voice. 'She wanted to know where she could get some cigarettes.'

'She's far too young to smoke!'

'Bo, you don't get it. She thought I was cool enough to know that kind of thing. She put her hand on my arm!' He laughs with giddy excitement.

'Do you know where to get cigarettes from?'

He doesn't even hear my question. 'If I can act like that around Natasha then maybe she will notice me after all!'

He hugs me, squeezing me tight. It's galling to note that he has to bend down to reach me: there's something depressing about being shorter than a fourteen year old. I let the cigarettes' matter go; I'm sure he's too sensible for that. Just because I occasionally smoke to aid my investigations and provide useful conversation openers, doesn't mean I approve of anyone else doing it.

'I think you're ready,' I grin. 'When's the disco?'

Rogu3 gives me a funny look. 'Disco? Who are you? John Travolta?'

'Uh, party then.'

'It's a gig,' he tells me, witheringly. 'And it's on Friday so I've got two days to perfect my routine.'

'Don't overdo it,' I warn him. 'You want to be natural.'

He beams. 'You're my guru, Bo. You should hire out your services as a relationship consultant.'

I think of the mess I've made with Michael and my chest tightens. I'm pretty certain my skills lie in other directions but I'm glad that Rogu3 is feeling better about himself. 'Call me once it's finished,' I order. 'I want to hear all the details. And not just "it was fine". I want to know *everything*.'

'I will,' he promises. A bus comes towards us. 'I'd better go. Thank you, Bo. I don't need to be the geek hiding in his parents' garage any more. I can do anything!'

He dashes across the road, hailing the bus just in time. I wave goodbye, wishing everything in life were so easy.

I LEAVE a voice message for Nisha Patel, telling her what Rogu3 uncovered about the funeral directors. Tempted as I am to visit it, it's not my gig. I'll just have to tamp down my curiosity about Tobias Renfrew and whether he is really out there or not. The Agathos court is more than capable of sorting it out without my fumbling help and I can read about in the newspapers along with everyone else.

Instead, I want to do something to erase the haunted look in Corinne Matheson's eyes. I can't turn back time but I can try to find the bastard that did this to her and goodness knows how many others. Foxworthy may not want me to interfere but I'm not backing out now. I'm pleased to see that I'm not the only one – as soon as I walk into the office, I spot a brand-spanking-new whiteboard. There are numerous notes, a detailed timeline and several photos. My colleagues have been busy.

I'm about to move forward when there's a blur of move-ment at my feet and I feel a sharp pain in my calf. A deep, loud purr reaches my ears. I scowl down at the cat then, before Arzo can begin to quiz me on Rogu3's identity, I stride up to the board.. 'This is impressive.'

Arzo nods. 'Frankly, it's scary what we've managed to uncover.' He points to the timeline. 'Thirteen possible victims.'

I feel sick as I stare at the names. 'Thirteen? How could no one have noticed this before?'

'They weren't looking,' he says grimly. 'Obviously we already know about Rebecca Small and Corinne Matheson. The first one we've found is here.' He taps the board. 'We don't have a name for her but she was abducted just outside her home, taken to a local park and tied up.'

'No stakes? No rape?'

'No. But the nature of her kidnapping and the way her wrists her bound are similar enough to the others. And it was reported in the news at the time that her assailant had a gold tooth.'

I suck in a breath. 'So he didn't start using the stakes until here?' I point at another name. 'Girl three?'

'Yes. Her name was released. Barbara Fenwick. Twenty-two years old. Daemon.'

'But he didn't rape her,' I muse. 'That didn't happen until the fourth victim. Why's her name in green?'

'The green ones are daemons, the blue ones are human, the yellows are witches.'

I close my eyes briefly. 'Then who are the reds?'

Arzo's voice is quiet. 'Vampires.'

I step back. 'You're kidding me.'

'I'm afraid not.'

'Corinne Matheson's attacker was human. There's no human on this planet that could overpower a vampire on their own. It's hard enough to believe that witches and daemons have been victims.'

Peter joins us. 'What about the cuffs?'

'You mean the ones Magix created?'

He nods. 'They inhibit vampires.'

'They're brand new. They've only just come on the market.'

'How long have they been in development though? Did O'Connell tell you?'

I try to remember. 'No. He didn't say.'

'It's a possibility, Bo.'

I stare at the colours. 'Human. Witch. Daemon. Vampire. Human. Witch. Daemon. Vampire. Human. Witch. Daemon. Vampire. Human.'

'It doesn't take a genius to work out the pattern, does it?'

'His next victim will be a witch,' I say flatly. 'By switching between different tribers, no one noticed until now that the crimes are linked.' I slam my fist down onto the desk.

'By his sixth victim, he'd escalated to murder. But,' Arzo taps each name, 'none of the bodies were found. We're presuming it's the same guy because of the pattern. Plus, they were either snatched in broad daylight or trace evidence was found in nearby public parks.'

I'm troubled. 'That doesn't make sense. We know that this prick enjoys dancing with danger and making his attacks as public as possible. Why hide the bodies afterwards?'

'Maybe he eats them.'

'What, every part? Really? He's human, not a Kakos daemon.' Although as soon as I say it, I realise that X's glamour is so strong, it could be possible. I can't see a Kakos daemon escalating crimes in this manner, however: he'd start at full throttle and continue that way.

'We don't have an answer for that,' Peter says. 'But look at the time frame. There was almost a year between the first and second victims. Then months. The gap between each attack has been lessening. From the disappearance of this vampire to Corinne Matheson, there were only...'

'Three weeks,' I breathe. I look at them both. 'We need to talk to Foxworthy. Now.'

There's a meow and the damn cat appears again, jumping onto Peter's desk and facing the whiteboard. Its eyes stare unblinkingly at the multi-coloured scribbles.

'The inspector is on his way,' my grandfather says.

I meet his eyes. 'This is bad.'

'I know. And considering that vampires are now involved, it falls under New Order's remit.'

'I guess no one expected them to be victims instead of perpetrators.' I shake my head. 'This is so fucked up. All this time and no one bothered to connect the dots.'

'I hope you're not blaming us, Ms Blackman.'

I turn and see Foxworthy standing in the door. Despite his large frame, he seems diminished somehow. There are heavy circles under his eyes. For one brief angry moment, I don't care. Then I manage to dampen down my bitterness. It's the bastard who's doing this that I'm really angry with.

'Someone is to blame,' I say. 'We should all have picked up on this earlier.'

Foxworthy rubs his forehead. 'Yeah, I suppose so.' He stares at the board. The dratted cat jumps off the table and winds around his legs as he takes out a notebook. 'May I?'

I nod. 'I'm not the one who leaked the information about Corinne. We need to work together on this if we're to succeed.'

His jaw tightens. For a moment, I think he's going to dismiss all of us as nothing more than a mouthpiece for the Families, a two-bit investigation firm that can't scratch the surface of what the police can offer. He surprises me. 'If that's what it takes, then I'm prepared to do it,' he grunts. 'And I know it wasn't you. Michael Montserrat paid me a visit.'

'Lord Montserrat went to see you?' Arzo raises an eyebrow. 'In person?'

I look away. I know Michael probably did it to appease me. I'm not sure whether that makes his confession better or worse.

Foxworthy reaches into the top pocket of his wrinkled suit and pulls out a small, well-chewed pencil. It's so short that I'm amazed he can grip it in his large hands. He glances at his own notes and up to the board.

'Did you know about the others?' I ask.

'We were already onto them but the vampire you sent helped direct our inquiries,' he admits. 'We hadn't considered that tribers might be involved too. Although what happened to Ms Matheson was too brutal for it be the perp's first time.' I like that he doesn't just call her the victim. She's a real person to him. 'We unearthed all the human victims. You have one missing though.' He points the end of his pencil at the whiteboard. 'Lacey Anderson. A nineteen-year-old nurse.'

'When?'

'She went missing a month before Ms Matheson.'

'Human?'

He nods as Peter grabs a blue pen and adds her name to our timeline.

I frown. 'That messes up the pattern. Two humans in a row.'

'We didn't have any of the vampires,' Foxworthy continues. I'm surprised at his honesty. 'And we only knew of Rebecca Small as far as the daemons are involved. Thanks to you.' His lip curls. 'The Agathos court is not responding to our inquiry for information with much haste.'

'Bureaucracy,' I say. We share a look of understanding.

Arzo nods. 'It's a matter of who you know with the

daemons.' He looks at the board. 'Maybe we've missed some victims.'

'Or maybe the pattern was just too pat to be real. It could just be a coincidence.'

My grandfather shakes his head. 'No,' he says. 'There's no such thing as coincidence, not where this kind of crime is concerned.' He points at Lacey's name then at Corinne's. 'There's only a month between these two. Our rapist broke his own rules either for Lacey or for Corinne. He made his first mistake with one of them.'

'He's not a rapist,' I correct. 'He's a murderer. A fucking serial killer.' I chew my lip. 'Look, Corinne is older than the others. And here. We've got a student, a teacher, and a nurse amongst the humans. The witches and the daemons are similar. Why break the mould and suddenly go for an older prostitute? She's the one. Something happened that caused him to go after Corinne instead of a witch. We need to talk to her again.'

'And his first victim too,' Arzo adds. 'She was probably close to him. He'd start with someone familiar.'

A shadow crosses Foxworthy's face. 'That's a no-go, I'm afraid. She died in a hit and run three years ago.'

Bloody hell. She escaped being brutally raped and battered to death because the perp hadn't worked himself up to that point yet. In a sense she'd been lucky but fate apparently had other plans for her. Poor girl. 'She's still worth looking into. She may have left diaries or there could be friends around who she talked to.'

'I'll send Nicholls tomorrow.'

'And Arzo.' I point at him. He's not really an investigator these days but I want to make sure we get the same leads the police. Just because Foxworthy is suddenly being helpful doesn't mean rest of them will be.

Foxworthy looks at me, obviously mulling it over. 'Okay,' he agrees finally. 'But we're going to need more information about the bloodguzzlers. Which Families they're from and what their roles were before they vanished.'

I look at my grandfather. 'They're all from one Family,' he says. My heart sinks. He nods at me. 'Medici.'

Nobody speaks. Foxworthy seems baffled as he glances from one tense face to another.

'There's no such thing as a coincidence,' I mutter.

CHAPTER 13

A HIGH PRICE

The walls of Marsh Prison loom high. In case anyone is in any doubt about the purpose of the vast complex, they are the dull colour of cement and ringed at the top with lethal-looking barbed wire. The sharp spikes gleam as they catch the light from the lampposts on the pavement. The wire seems pointless to me; Marsh Prison is used to punish tribers, not humans, and the security system focuses more on magic than the mundane. I suppose that the walls' real purpose is to make it appear secure to worried humans. And maybe knowing the walls are there makes the experience of being in prison more real for the inmates – although the tiny cells, plastic spoons and frowning guards probably have that covered in spades.

Foxworthy has called ahead. It's handy having him around; there's no way I'd get inside the prison as a vampire. In fact, even if I were still human, I'd never gain access at this time of night. I imagine the inspector had to call in numerous favours, despite the fact that we're trying to hunt down a serial killer. Prison rules and regulations tend to run independently of the world outside.

Despite being forewarned of our arrival, we're still forced to cool our heels in the visitors' ante-room. Nondescript chairs are laid out in depressing rows, as if to force outsiders into becoming part of the institution. Scratched graffiti is visible on several of the breeze-block walls. I guess a lot of people have spent a lot of time waiting around here. Just as I'm tempted to take out my keys and add my name to the rest, the door opens and a well-dressed woman with a dark tattoo signifying black witch strolls in. She has patent-leather high heels, a knee-length skirt and hair pulled back in a tight bun. I recognise that we're in the presence of someone who is more than a guard; she gives off the air of dominatrix. Maybe that's inevitable in her line of work.

'Inspector Foxworthy.' Her voice is cool and she reaches out to shake his hand briskly. She doesn't look at me.

He inclines his head. 'Ma'am.'

'You realise how unorthodox this is.'

He doesn't miss a beat. 'The crimes we're investigating are equally unorthodox.'

'Permitting entry to a bloodguzzler does not sit well with me.' She still refuses to flick so much as a disdainful glance in my direction. I'm obviously not worthy enough to be addressed directly.

'Ms Blackman has a previous relationship with the inmate. We believe he will be more amenable to answering our questions if she is present.'

'Is that the royal we?'

'No.'

'Tell me,' she asks, 'how does the law deal with bloodguzzlers who don't claim allegiance to a Family?'

'It's not for me to say, ma'am.'

I curl my fingers into my palms but otherwise try not to tense up visibly.

'I met her grandfather once. You know he's not as posh as he likes to make out.'

Foxworthy's expression remains bland. 'I am sure you are correct.'

I decide to stop feeling annoyed at being ignored and focus instead on what I can learn from the policeman's attitude. If ever there was an opportunity to learn how to deal with self-important bureaucrats, this is it. Foxworthy panders to her comments without making any of his own, seeming to agree without being overly sycophantic. I take careful note. I used to pride myself on being able to deal with people from different walks of life but it's more difficult now I'm a vampire and I face so much open hostility and wilful ignorance. I'll take all the tips I can get.

'I'll have someone escort you to the visiting room,' the woman says. 'Just keep that damn guzzler on a leash.'

Foxworthy shoots me a nervous look but I bow my head obediently. 'You can put the cuffs on if it makes you feel better.' I hold out my wrists. I hate the damn things but if this is what it takes then I'll do it. Though I dread to think what the expression on O'Connell's face will be when he sees me wearing his damned creation.

'I didn't bring them with me,' the inspector says smoothly. I know he's lying although I can't fathom out why. I spotted the tell-tale bulge in his pocket when we got out of his car.

She sniffs and spins on her heel, leaving us alone. I raise my eyebrows questioningly but Foxworthy shakes his head, jerking his thumb up to the ceiling where the security camera stares down. I doubt he's suddenly decided to trust me; it must be something about the warden that has him acting like my best friend.

It's another twenty minutes before the door opens again. Foxworthy and I spend the time in silence. I try to appear calm, sitting down and crossing my legs to appear as benign as possible. The effect is somewhat ruined when there's a distant, bloodcurdling scream that makes me leap to my feet just as a fresh-faced prison officer appears. He looks at me nervously.

'Sorry,' I mumble. 'I heard a scream.'

'It's a triber prison,' Foxworthy reminds me. 'There are always screams.'

It's hard not to dwell on that comment. I lapse into silence as we trail after the officer. Posters line the walls, detailing the many contraband items that cannot be brought inside and the severe penalties for anyone who attempts a spell. I can't imagine that any of the prisoners is stupid enough to try.

We stop in front of a large steel door. 'I have to pat you down,' the officer says, not looking me in the eye.

I step forward and hold up my arms. Thankfully his movements are swift and perfunctory – but I'm still annoyed when he doesn't search Foxworthy, even though the burly policeman assumes the required position.

Satisfied, the prison officer unlocks the door. He fumbles with the keys, revealing his fear at having me at his back. Considering he spends his days overseeing all manner of triber criminals, his worry about one tiny vampire seems misplaced. Even with our name cleared in relation to the Jubilee rape, the fingers of terror regarding the Families are stretching further and further across society.

The prison officer directs us inside and quickly departs. The walls of the room are beige breeze-block and the floor is scuffed lino. It is almost bare: the only furniture is a table and three chairs. At least this room is camera-free so our conversation will be private.

I sit down at the table, with Foxworthy by my side. There's barely enough time to get comfortable when the door opposite opens and O'Connell shuffles in with two prison guards.

They're patently not taking any chances; his hands and his feet are shackled together with rings of steel. The ex-CEO, however, appears none the worse for wear, despite being forced to lose the magical gloss he had during his tenure at Magix. He gives me a bright smile as if we're meeting in a bar for drinks.

'Ms Blackman!' he says, as he sits opposite us. 'What a delightful surprise. I hoped you'd visit.'

'Why is that?'

'You outplayed me. That doesn't happen very often. You have a lot of potential, you know.' He glances at Foxworthy. 'You should stop hanging around with humans though. You'll appear meaner if you avoid them altogether.'

I eye him warily. 'I'm not really going for mean.'

He smiles. 'You set me up for a crime I didn't commit. I'd say that was pretty mean.'

Foxworthy throws me a sidelong glance. 'I have no idea what you're referring to,' I say.

'Of course not. You're the picture of innocence.' He says this entirely without malice. 'You're just working to make the world a better place.'

I stiffen; that was the motive he gave for the actions that brought him here. Foxworthy, thankfully, fills the sudden, tense silence. 'The handcuffs,' he says, 'the ones you created for the bloodguzzlers. Tell me about them.'

'Who are you?' O'Connell asks. 'Ms Blackman's new sidekick?'

'Answer the question,' I tell him.

He leans back. 'No,' he says airily. 'I don't think I will.'

'Come on, O'Connell. You're one of the good guys, remember?'

His eyes gleam. 'Just like you.'

I dislike the suggestion that he and I are similar but I cling to what he's given me. His comments and his reactions provide just the leverage I need. O'Connell still refuses to believe that he did anything wrong. I can use that. 'We're hunting a rapist,' I say softly. 'Someone who maims and kills humans, daemons, vampires. This man is the scum of the earth. With your help, we can catch him.'

There's a flicker of interest in his eyes and I know I have him but he's still determined to dance around a bit first. 'Why should I care? I'm sure you and your,' he glances at Foxworthy, 'crack team will track him down sooner or later.'

'He's attacking witches too. If he sticks to his pattern, then his next victim will be a witch. Probably someone young and defenceless.'

The tattoos on both O'Connell's cheeks flare. 'He's a bad man, then.'

'He is.'

'Not like me.'

'Of course not.' I try not to choke on the words.

O'Connell leans back, his chains clinking. 'Go on. What exactly do you want to know?'

'He's human. He could never overpower a vampire without some help.'

'So you think he used my handcuffs?'

'We do.'

'They've only just come onto the market. Either your killer has done a lot of work in the last few weeks or he's used something else to subdue his victims.'

I keep my gaze steady. 'When did you have a working prototype?'

'Three and a half years ago.'

I think about it: that fits with the time frame we've established. Even if the first version of the handcuffs wasn't perfect, it could still have been enough. 'Who developed it?'

'If you think there's a single, mad scientist behind our products, you are sadly mistaken, Ms Blackman. There are large teams of people who work in development at Magix. No one person is responsible.'

'Do you have a list of who was on the team?'

He shrugs. 'I'm sure you'll get it if you subpoena the records. We're talking about dozens of people, though.'

'A male,' Foxworthy interjects. 'Probably in his twenties. Someone with a chip on his shoulder and a grudge against the world. No romantic relationship to speak of, despite him having an attractive physical appearance. In fact, he would be shy around women, possibly unable to look them in the eye. He might even stammer. He likes order and routine.'

I raise my eyebrows at the inspector and he catches my glance. 'I did a profiling course recently,' he explains. 'Some people think it's pseudo-science but you'd be surprised how accurate it can be.'

O'Connell clears his throat, demanding our attention. 'To be honest, that could be any one of our production specialists. They're single geeks by nature.'

'He might have a gold tooth,' I add.

He looks thoughtful. 'There is someone who might fit that description. He left the company a couple of years ago.'

Foxworthy and I sit up. O'Connell smirks. 'Well, that caught your interest, didn't it?'

'Who is he?' I keep my voice low. It's becoming harder and harder to avoid showing how much I despise him.

He throws back his head and laughs. 'If I tell you, then where's the fun? You know, I used to say the same thing to my employees: you have to work for what you want. Nothing is ever handed to you. Money doesn't just fall into your lap.' His eyes glitter. 'Suspects don't just spring out of nowhere.'

'What do you want?' Foxworthy growls.

'Please,' O'Connell scoffs. 'You think I merely want something to make my own life easier? A television set in my cell? A reduced sentence? My case has yet to go to trial. I'm not ready to bargain away my future just yet.'

'You realise how far the evidence is stacked against you?'

He holds my gaze. 'Perhaps. But I was set up. You know that.'

'You're still responsible for murder.'

'And what will you do, Ms Blackman, when you finally meet this rapist face to face? Slap him in chains so he can face a lengthy trial? You're not the sort; you've got a heady lust for blood pulsating through your body.' He licks his lips. 'I can taste it from here. You think you're better than me? We're just the same.'

I fold my arms. 'Except I'm the one who will walk out of here. What's your price, O'Connell? Stop beating around the bush.'

He looks at Foxworthy. 'Inspector, I'm thirsty. Why don't you fetch me a glass of water? Room temperature. And with a slice of lemon.'

The malevolence in Foxworthy's expression is frightening. 'Kitchen's closed,' he says sourly.

O'Connell shrugs and leans back. 'So be it.'

I look at Foxworthy and his eyes meet mine. 'Fine,' he snaps, standing up and pushing back his chair. It scrapes against the floor, making a noise like fingernails on a blackboard. A shudder runs down my spine; I'm not sure whether it's because of the noise or the prospect of being alone with O'Connell. Foxworthy stalks to the door and thumps it loudly. It's barely three seconds before it swings open. Our escort must have been standing outside with a glass to his ear.

O'Connell wags his finger. 'No listening in, mind. If I catch the slightest scent of your sour body odour, I'm not going to say another word.'

The guard's head turns to the left and he sniffs. I roll my eyes.

'Try anything,' Foxworthy warns, 'and I'll make sure a few extra charges are added on to your warrant sheet.' He slams the door shut with such force that the steel reverberates in the frame.

O'Connell knits his fingers together and smiles. 'Pleasant chap, isn't he?'

I lean forward. 'I'm getting tired of your games. What do you want?'

'I believe I may have told you this before, Ms Blackman, but knowledge is power. And you know something no one else does.'

I frown. I have absolutely no idea what he is referring to. I passed over all the information I uncovered about him when he was arrested. There's nothing else to tell.

He tuts. 'One thing I've discovered in my short time behind these walls is that you can learn a lot by watching people. It took me a while and I had to replay our conversations several times in my head to work it out, but I learnt something about you.'

'Really,' I say flatly. 'Do enlighten me.'

'You don't want to be a vampire.'

I raise my eyebrows. 'That's it? That's your big reveal? It's hardly headline news.'

He seems amused. 'No.' He runs his tongue over his teeth. 'I imagine it's not. However, what I can tell that others might miss is that although you despise yourself, you're not as upset about it as you should be.'

'You're talking in tongues. And I don't despise myself. I just don't want to be a bloodguzzler.'

'There you go again,' he whispers. 'There's no desperation

in your words. There's not even resignation.' He tilts his head. 'There's hope. You, Ms Blackman, have a cure.'

I stare at him. The lie springs to my lips. 'There's no such thing as a cure.'

'Now I know you're lying.' He sounds satisfied. 'Who else knows about it?'

I look away. I'm under strict instructions from X not to reveal the truth to anyone. If I do, he'll rip them apart. I have no idea whether he has the capabilities or reach to get inside a triber prison – but this might play into my hands after all.

I take a deep breath. 'No one,' I answer truthfully. 'Only the person who gave it to me. And you should know that he made it clear he'd kill anyone else I told. Don't think you're safe just because you're behind bars.'

'I have a lot of friends. Even here. I think I'm safe.'

'So that's it?' I ask. 'I tell you about the cure and you'll give me the name?'

'That's it. As easy as pie.'

'What difference does it make to you?'

'Imagine what we could do with such a thing! We could wipe out this country's vampire problem in one fell swoop. I'll be the hero that saved the world from the undead. They'll give me a fucking parade instead of a sham trial.'

Now it's my turn to laugh. 'Vampires aren't undead. And somehow I don't think you'll be able to manufacture – or find – enough to turn even one itty-bitty little vampire back into a human.'

'Oh, you'd be surprised what the technicians at Magix are capable of. I might be behind bars but don't think I'm not still in charge.'

'Then give me the name and I'll tell you what you want to know.'

He shakes his head. 'You first. Time is ticking, Ms Blackman. The next victim may already be in danger.'

No way. He'll realise his mistake when I tell him what the cure really is then he'll clam up and I'll get nothing. This is my only chance. 'No deal, O'Connell. You go first or I'll find another patsy. It'll take a bit longer to shake down your other Magix employees but I'll get there in the end.'

He realises that I'm not bluffing and snarls, 'Give me your word.'

'The word of a mere bloodguzzler?' I ask.

'Give it.'

I meet his eyes. 'You have my word.'

'Terence Miller. You won't find him under that surname any more though.'

'Why not?'

'He told me he was leaving to join the Medici Family. He didn't return so I'm assuming he succeeded.'

I hiss involuntarily. 'You're lying. Or wrong. The man I'm looking for is human.'

'Don't be so naïve. Do you really think it would be hard for a bloodguzzler to pass themselves off as something different? Especially a bloodguzzler who used to work for me?'

I have the sinking feeling that he's telling the truth. But Corinne was also telling the truth in that hospital room: she thought her attacker was human. He may have tried to fool her but it made no sense for him to bother because he was planning to kill her. Why would he care what she thought he was? I mull it over. The perp may still be linked with O'Connell's bloodguzzler. It would make sense, given that all the victims are from the Medici Family. Perhaps it's a bit of quid pro quo: in return for help in dispatching some more victims, the ex-Magix employee gets to name who will be next. It's a theory. A very shitty one if it's true, of course. It had been nice to think that the vampires were in the clear.

'The wheels are turning, I see,' O'Connell says, tapping his forehead. 'Now give me what I asked for.'

'I meant what I said. If I tell you this, you'll be dead.'

'I'll take my chances. I still have a few tricks up my sleeve.'

'It's your funeral.' He can't say I didn't warn him. 'The cure is simple. No chemistry. No magic. No sacrificial lambs.'

'The suspense is killing me. Spit it out.'

'You need the blood of a Kakos daemon. Not much. A mouthful will suffice. And,' I add casually, 'the Kakos daemon who gave me that information promised he'd kill anyone I told.' I watch as the colour drains from O'Connell's face. 'Do you still think those tricks will help you now?' I ask softly.

'I was right about one thing, Ms Blackman,' O'Connell says quietly, obviously struggling with the news.

I raise my eyebrows. 'What's that?'

'You really do lust for blood, whether you make the killer-blow or someone else does.'

I shake my head. 'You're mistaking my apathy about your future for something entirely different.'

I stand up and walk to the door, banging loudly to be let out. I'm grateful that this time it takes longer to swing open; this would not have been a good time for eavesdropping. Then, without another word, I leave the ex-CEO slumped in his chair.

CHAPTER 14

THE LION'S DEN

'So now you're telling me that this fucking bastard is a bloodguzzler after all?' Foxworthy says as we pull away from the prison.

'No. O'Connell may have been lying. Or the man he's thinking of – this Terence Miller – may have nothing to do with it.'

'There's another possibility,' he says grimly. 'That this Miller is helping the attacker.'

I nod. I'm glad he's arrived at the same theory as I did. 'That crossed my mind too,' I admit.

'Regardless of anything, we know that the Medici Family is involved. Whether it's because some of their number are victims or it's something more sinister, it's clear where we need to go next.'

I'd been afraid of this. I shake my head. 'I'm sorry,' I say. 'You can't.'

His eyes narrow. 'Why the hell not?'

'Because,' I remind him patiently, 'Lord Medici isn't particularly impressed at the other Families' newfound openness. He doesn't want anything to do with it. As far he's concerned the old ways are the only ways. There's no way he'll talk to a human.'

Foxworthy's knuckles whiten around the steering wheel. I can't say I blame him. 'I thought you bloodguzzlers were changing.'

'We are but it's going to take the Medici Family a little longer than everyone else.'

'If what you're telling me is true, he'll be no more likely to talk to you than to me. You represent the new guard.'

'If I can get face to face with him, I think I can persuade him.'

'And how exactly are you going to manage that? Considering it will be dawn in less than an hour and you're in for barbecue time.'

'I have an idea.'

Foxworthy accelerates to beat a red light. He's getting more and more upset. I suddenly appreciate how frustrating it is for the human police to be left on the sidelines whenever the Families are involved in criminal activity. The Families have been above human law for so long that I never really questioned it, even before I turned. Medici aside, they are trying to open up and be more honest about their dealings; now I wonder whether it might be time to change more than just a willingness to tell the truth. Adapting their legal position could do the world a whole lot of good. I doubt I'd have much chance of persuading any vampires of that, however. At least any who can make a difference anyway.

'What did you give him?'

'Mmm?' I'm so lost in my own thoughts that I almost miss the question.

'O'Connell. What did you give him to make him talk?'

'It doesn't matter.' Then I look at him anxiously. 'You didn't hear anything, did you?'

Foxworthy snorts. 'You tribers may not have much honour but I do. Besides, I thought that as we're working together, you'd tell me later. I guess I was wrong. It didn't take you long to stop cooperating.'

I sigh heavily. 'What I told him had nothing to do with you and nothing to do with this case. And O'Connell's regretting it now,' I add under my breath.

'What's that supposed to mean?'

'Nothing. Look,' I say, in a bid to appease him, 'I told you what he said, that a vampire might be involved. I wouldn't have done that if I wasn't trying to cooperate.' Foxworthy doesn't reply but I can tell he realises I'm speaking the truth. 'The only way Medici will talk is if another bloodguzzler faces him. I'll do what I can and call you as soon as I'm done. I promise.'

Foxworthy is silent for a moment then he says, 'I've never heard another bloodguzzler refer to themselves that way.'

'Pardon?'

'Bloodguzzler. Your lot always just use "vampire".'

'Yeah, well, perhaps everything's not as clear-cut as you think,' I inform him. 'And why didn't you put the damn cuffs on me? I know you had them with you.'

'That woman winds me up.'

'The warden?'

'Yeah. And I was starting to think you maybe weren't so bad.' He says it quickly as if he's hoping I won't hear.

'Was?'

'I'll reserve judgment until you tell me what Lord fucking Medici has to say.'

Fair enough. 'Drop me here,' I tell him.

He glances out the window at the darkened underground station. 'The trains won't be running yet. It's not far back to your place.'

'I'm going straight to Medici. I'm just not travelling conventionally, that's all.' I wink at the inspector and grin to myself. My little adventure in the tunnels with O'Shea has opened up a whole new world of possibilities.

I watch Foxworthy drive away. I know he's still pissed off that I'm not letting him join me but he's smart enough to recognise it's the only way we can approach Medici.

I'm not completely stupid: I'm not about to broach the lion's den without a back-up plan. Normally, I'd text O'Shea or even D'Argneau, but they probably still have their hands full with the Tobias Renfrew mess. Matt, unfortunately, is too vulnerable. I only know one person who can gain admittance to the Medici headquarters without a prior invitation. It's time to test that friends' theory. I type the words in quickly and press send before I can change my mind. At least he can't text back; there won't be any signal where I'm going.

The station entrance is barred. I tug the steel gate to test it but it's shut firmly. As a vampire I probably have enough brute strength to break it open but the law-abiding part of me doesn't want to cause more damage than I need to. Besides, I remember O'Shea's eagerness to use a lock pick rather than leave a trail. If I want to use these tunnels regularly as a way to cross the city during daylight hours, I need to be circumspect or the council will get wise and start putting bloodguzzler inhibiting spells on the night-time security gates.

With that in mind, I skirt round to the back of the station. It's a low-lying building so it's easy to wing myself up to the roof. There's an access door at the top. It's locked, of course, but I'm skilled enough to pick it and I pry it open in record time. Once inside, I dart down the stairs and emerge in a small staffroom. The health and safety posters pinned to the wall blare warnings at me in the gloom. As the last thing I need to worry about is what to do in the event of platform overcrowding, I ignore them and slip out to the main passenger area.

Little in the world is more eerie than a train station in the dead of night. The closed booth that sells newspapers, chocolate and fizzy drinks, together with the silent turnstiles and dark corridors, give the place a ghostly feel. For some reason the station is spookier than the abandoned tunnels O'Shea and I ventured down a couple of days ago. Despite my sense of unease, I make my way to the platform and jump down next to the rails. At least there are no trains to dodge this time. I glance up and down the tunnel to get my bearings and then start jogging. I hope this is going to work.

I duck inside the first service door I come across. I know I'm close to the Medici den; I just need to find the right exit. Ignoring all the tunnels that branch off, I count my footsteps. Once I've gone about eighty metres, I stop and look around.

There's a door to my right. I hold my breath and carefully turn the doorknob, easing it open. I wrinkle my nose at the stale air. As quietly as I can, I tiptoe down another corridor. Unlike the previous one, the walls here are tiled only three-quarters of the way up. I knock gently along the old tiles, listening for the right note. When I finally I hear a dull thud, suggesting some sort of hollow chamber, I stop.

Even though I can see a long way through the darkness, I can't detect any other entrance. I chew my lip. I'd been afraid it would come to this. So much for tiptoeing.

I take off my jacket and wrap it around my right fist. I'm glad I'm not wearing my trusty leather jacket, it's been damaged enough in the name of vampire escapades. I tighten my fingers, clenching hard, leap forward and smash my fist into the wall. I succeed in knocking off several tiles. They fall to the ground with a loud clatter and I freeze, listening hard. When

I'm sure I'm still alone, I use my other hand to pull away more tiles so I have a bigger gap to work with. I step backwards and try again. Chunks of plaster break off and I start coughing as I'm assailed by a cloud of dust. I wave at the air to clear it. Satisfyingly, I can see several cracks. Perhaps this won't be so hard after all.

I back away to the opposite wall and focus on the largest crack. Steeling myself, I inhale and jump, feet flying out in front of me like a kung-fu master. The wall is thin and my strike is powerful enough that my foot goes straight through it. Rather embarrassingly, however, it also sticks fast. I tug at my leg, trying to pull it free. More plaster comes away. It takes several twists and one difficult shimmy to extricate my foot. Still, I reckon I can now knock off enough plaster around the small hole with my fingers.

Most of the plaster around the foot-shaped hole is old and crumbling. To be fair, I got lucky. If this entrance had been bricked up as well, I'd have had no chance without a few tools to help me. When I've done enough, I step back and eye my handiwork. It'll have to do. I pick up a small chunk of plaster and shove it into my pocket before squeezing through to the other side.

Dusting myself off, I look around. I'm in a large room full of empty crates and shelves. I spot a barrel date-stamped 1772. I hope I got my bearings right and I'm in the right place; it'd piss me off to find that I'm in some ancient smugglers' den rather than where I want to be. I edge forward, old cobwebs brushing past my skin. To my left I hear a sudden scuttling, followed by a squeak. I grimace. Bloody rats get everywhere.

I think I've reached a dead end, when it suddenly occurs to me to look up. As soon as I do, I smile. I was right. A small trap-door has been placed into the ceiling.

I roll a barrel underneath it. Being this short really is a pain in the arse sometimes. Even the barrel isn't tall enough so I grab a box and put it on top. The effect is like an upside-down wedding cake. I clamber up, praying to the powers that be that it will be high enough. Fortunately, I can place my palms flat against the rough wood of the trapdoor.

I push upwards, hoping it's not locked. It's heavy and there is something lying over it, but I create enough of a gap to wedge in my fingers and pull myself up. I use my head to open the trapdoor more fully, push aside the rug that was lying over the trapdoor, drag up the rest of my body and roll onto my back, panting. That was bloody hard work; it had better be worth it.

'Fort Knox, baby,' I whisper to myself.

My long shot has paid off. I've not had much time to research the Medici headquarters – not that I'd have gleaned much from the internet even if I'd had weeks to spare. I'm aware that for once Lady Luck is on my side. Now I'll just have to hope that my luck continues.

I scramble to my feet and straighten out the rug. It's Persian and probably an antique but it's also very threadbare. I'm defi-nitely not in a main Medici thoroughfare. From what I know of the vampire Lord, he surrounds himself with beautiful things. I bet he spends very little time in this part of his house.

Looking around, I decide I'm in the basement. It reminds me of the room under the kitchen at the Montserrat mansion where the vampire records are kept. Other than the faded rug, however, there's nothing down here apart from some old boxes. There's a door at the far end, stripped of its varnish, that adds to my belief that this is nothing more than a spare room that is rarely used.

I crack my neck and perform a few perfunctory stretches. My aim is to catch Lord Medici off guard; it's the only way he's likely to be honest with me. That means I need to locate him when he's alone – and avoid everyone else into the bargain. Piece of cake.

I walk to the door and open it cautiously. When I'm satisfied that the corridor beyond is empty, I venture out. So far I think I'm safe but I keep a close eye out for security cameras. The Montserrat mansion only uses them at the front of the house – and those were only installed recently after the burning cross incident.

Vampires are expected to be completely loyal to their Families so watching them suggests a degree of distrust. In my experience, when people are given high expectations to meet, they rise to them. When they're treated like cattle, they act as such. It doesn't always work like that; executions have taken place when bloodguzzlers stepped out of line – and it's impossible to forget what Nikki did. But when you have a bunch of ex-criminals under your wing and you want to prove you're serious about wiping their slate clean, you need to put your money where your mouth is. Having said that, if you're going to break the most sacrosanct Family rule and turn people like Arzo's ex, Dahlia, who don't want to be turned, then you have a different set of problems to worry about. That's why I'm not taking any chances.

I pass a small table with a vase on it. Hanging above it is a pretty seascape in a gilt frame. I'm three steps beyond it when I twist back, remembering what Rogu3 told me about the art thief. I grin and hoist the painting away from the wall. Carrying it awkwardly in front of me so it obscures my face, I continue.

At the far end of the corridor there's a staircase that I start to climb. It's not long before I hear voices coming towards me. Trying not to panic, I keep moving.

'So,' a female voice says, 'I told him that if he thought he could take on a vampire, then I was game. I suggested that the best part of his body to sink my fangs into would be where all his blood rushes.' She pauses. 'And expands.'

'No!' Her friend laughs.

'He was a bit confused. I undid the zip on his trousers and showed him my fangs.'

'Then?'

'Then he ran a mile. I didn't think humans could move so fast.'

She brushes past me as they continue their descent. Neither of them even looks at me. When they're out of earshot, I exhale loudly. I didn't even realise I was holding my breath.

I reach the top of the stairs and peer round the picture frame. I have two choices. I reckon I'm at the north end of the building, probably on the ground floor. Lord Medici no doubt lives in the nicest part of the house, which probably means the south-facing side. I chew my lip. The sun must be coming up by now and, unless the Medici Family uses the same UV-filtering glass panes as the Montserrat Family, I'm in danger of getting fried. I need to avoid any windows just in case.

I turn left, making my way south while shifting the painting slightly. When I hear another set of footsteps coming towards me, I stop. 'Hey!' I call out from behind the canvas. 'I'm taking this over to the Lord's office but I can't see a damn thing. Tell me I'm heading in the right direction, will you? If I put it down, I might damage it.'

It's a flimsy excuse but I'm counting on apathy from whoever I'm speaking to. Sadly, things don't work out that way. 'I'll help you with it.' The speaker has a deep Welsh burr.

Sodding hell. I'd been hoping all the Medici bloodguzzlers would be as arrogant as their Lord. A polite offer of help is the last thing I need. I can't expose my face; given that I'm the only vampire to leave a Family in living history, my days of travelling incognito are long over.

'No, no,' I say, as cheerily as I can. 'I have direct orders and it's probably better if I carry them out on my own.'

'It's no trouble.' He starts to take the picture from me.

My fingers tighten round the edge. 'Really, I can manage. I just need to know I'm going the right way.'

'Don't be ridiculous.' He continues to pull the frame. Cursing inwardly, I let go. When he catches sight of my face, his eyes widen in recognition. I clench my fists and slam them into his face in quick succession. He staggers back.

'Sorry,' I mutter. 'I guess it's hard being a gentleman in this day and age.' I crash both my hands onto the top of his skull. He collapses.

I bend down to check he's not dead. When I'm satisfied that he'll suffer from nothing more than a sore head, I grab his feet and drag him into a nearby empty room. I close the door and return to the corridor, picking up the stupid painting again. So much for that idea.

The good Samaritan, with his preternatural vampiric healing abilities, won't be unconscious for long. I probably have less than ten minutes to find Lord Medici before the alarm is raised. The smart thing to do would have been to kill him outright. Despite O'Connell's belief in my lust for blood, however, I'm no cold-blooded murderer. Instead I pick up speed, walking briskly in what I hope is the right direction. I wonder briefly if I'll bang into the unfortunate Dahlia and whether she'll help me if I do.

I round a corner, catching the deep tang of fresh blood. I must be close to where the Medici vampettes hang out. That won't help. Lord Medici will have his willing victims delivered to him personally; he won't demean himself by coming here to drink alongside his minions. Perhaps all is not lost after all.

I follow my nose until I locate a group of humans clustered

together. Less concerned about them than I would be about a fellow bloodguzzler, I let the painting fall a few inches.

'Hey!' I keep my voice hard, hoping the edge of intimidation will stop them looking at me too closely. 'Lord Medici wants to see you.'

A willowy blonde extricates herself from the group. I note a few grimaces from the others. She must be one of his favourites. That's good – it means she'll know the way.

I raise my eyebrows. 'Don't keep him waiting. He's not in a good mood.'

She lifts an elegant shoulder as if she doesn't care, but her expression flickers, and she strides off quickly. I frown at the others, baring my teeth, and they all flinch. Then I follow the blonde. Her high heels click on the mahogany floors so it's easy to keep my distance. When she finally stops and speaks to someone, I know I've found my mark.

A business-like woman seated at a desk is peering at the human over half-moon spectacles. Even from this distance I can see that the lenses are only glass; Lord Medici's secretary wants to look like Miss Moneypenny. Or perhaps he wants her to look like that. I smile at the thought of the portly vampire Lord fancying himself as James Bond before digging in my pocket and taking out the chunk of plaster.

'What do you want?'

'I was told Lord Medici wanted me.'

I heft the plaster in my fingers and move back a few steps then I let it fly. It smashes into the light bulb at the opposite end of the corridor. Miss Moneypenny and the blonde fall silent. I count to three as they both move towards the shattered glass, drop the painting as quietly as I can and dart forward, managing to sneak behind the pair of them and into what can only be Medici's office.

CHAPTER 15
A LITTLE SNACK

The room is smaller and darker than I expected; it's more like a windowless tomb than the grand space a Family Head would boast about. Medici is bowed over a desk scribbling away at something. I reach behind, sliding shut the old-fashioned lock on the door just as he glances up. His reaction is fast; he's on his feet and leaping over the desk within a fraction of a second. I'm better prepared than he is, however, and whip my hand forward ready to smash the base of my palm into his face. I stop a whisker's breadth before I connect and smile broadly.

'Lord Medici, if I could beg a moment of your time?'

His bottom lip curls. 'Blackman. What do you want? If you're here to take me down, know that you'll fail. You can't manage it in my club and you can't manage it here. You're still nothing more than a fledgling, no matter what you and that Montserrat idiot think.'

I'm reminded how, according to Michael, they used to work together. 'I'm not here to challenge you, my Lord. I'm working undercover.'

His eyes narrow suspiciously as he tries to decide whether I just made a throwaway comment or I know more than I should. 'I will rip your throat out for daring to come here,' he tells me.

I hold my ground. He doesn't scare me – not much anyway. 'Before you do, you should hear me out.' I rock back on my heels, counting on his curiosity to get the better of him. I'm not disappointed.

'About what?'

'About *whom* is what you should be asking.'

He folds his arms and glares at me. 'Go on.'

'Terence Miller.'

His nose wrinkles. 'I have no idea who that is.'

'He left his old job to be recruited into your Family.' I lean forward. 'And he might be a serial killer.'

Medici stares at me. 'There are no killers in my Family.'

'Oh, he's not just a killer. He likes to rape as well. To pin his victims to the ground with stakes. To beat them to a raw bloody pulp. Either that or he's helping the real killer.'

'You're referring to Jubilee Park.'

I nod. 'I am.'

'The police cleared the Families of that. Perhaps you missed it. Besides, that woman was nothing more than a whore.'

I grit my teeth. 'That woman was not the only victim. There have been four vampires as well.' I meet his eyes. 'All Medici.'

'Impossible,' he says dismissively. I catch the glimmer of doubt, however.

'Jane. Linda. Bella. Letitia.' I tick their names off on my fingers. 'What happened to them?' He doesn't answer. He knows exactly who they were. 'They disappeared, didn't they? Four powerful vampire women who vanished in broad daylight. Don't you care what happens to your underlings?'

'If a Kakos daemon didn't get them, then it was one of the other Families,' he snarls. 'Trying to undermine me.'

I shake my head. 'Unlike you, the other Families have been

cooperating with us. It wasn't them. We've checked the dates and the pattern. The Jubilee Park attacker abducted your vampires. Look into my eyes. Am I lying?'

His face twists. 'And did this attacker also abduct and rape Andrew?'

My brow furrows. 'Who?'

Medici's voice drops. 'He disappeared in the middle of a street near Covent Garden a month ago. Not too far from where your pitiful office is located, I believe.'

I know who he's referring to; I knocked Andrew unconscious and Michael disposed of him. It's been a point of contention between us. I lift up my chin. 'No.' I want to add that Michael didn't abduct Dahlia and turn her into an unwilling bloodguzzler either but that would be giving away too much.

'I see the look in your eyes,' he hisses. 'You despise me. You think I'm weak.' He shakes his head. 'You're the one who's weak and you're bringing every other Family down with you. What do you think will happen when you start meeting the humans halfway? When the Families give up the power that they've fought for centuries? You're just a little girl, you have no idea what you're doing.' He towers over me. 'You'll bring us all down.'

'You can't live in the nineteenth century forever. If you don't compromise, every vampire is doomed.'

'Compromise? We're the most powerful beings on this planet. We don't compromise.'

I think of X. 'Vampires aren't the most powerful and you know it. But I'm not here to discuss that. Terence Miller,' I remind him. 'Where is he?'

'I don't fucking know.'

There's a muffled crash and a scream outside. The door behind me rattles and I leap out of the way as the lock splinters and it springs open. A thunderous looking Michael glares at us.

'Hi there!' I chirp. He's early. Why couldn't he have waited another five sodding minutes?

Moneypenny appears behind him. 'I'm sorry, my Lord. He wouldn't take no for an answer. He just barged in...'

Medici holds up his hand. 'It doesn't matter. Leave us.'

She squeaks out something that might have been 'as you wish' and disappears.

'I might have guessed,' he sneers. 'Where the dwarf goes, you won't be far behind, Montserrat. You should stop hanging onto her apron strings.'

'Let her go,' Michael growls.

I roll my eyes heavenward. 'I'm not his prisoner. We're having a conversation.' I look at Michael pointedly. 'Could you give us a few more minutes?'

'You asked me to come.'

'No,' I snap, 'I asked you to be around for back up. Not to smash your way in here like a battering ram. I'm not a damsel in distress, I'm trying to do my sodding job.'

'You should have spoken to me first.'

I sigh, exasperated. 'How many times do I have to say it? You're not my boss.'

Medici chuckles. Michael and I turn and stare at him. 'Look at you two,' he says. 'You should get a room, you know.'

'We're friends.'

Medici nods. 'Right. Of course you are.'

'Where is Terence Miller?' I ask again. With Michael's arrival, I feel my control of the situation slipping but I'm not going to leave without the information I came for.

My good Samaritan, now sporting a rather unsightly bruise, appears at the door, gasping for breath. 'My Lord, the Blackman woman. She's here. She...' His eyes fall on me and his voice falters. He also notices that the door is hanging off its hinges.

'Hey,' I say. 'Sorry about earlier. It wasn't personal.'

His eyes swing to Medici who appears vaguely irritated. 'Joseph, find out for me if we have a Terence née Miller, will you?'

'Yes, my Lord.'

I raise an eyebrow. He has them well trained. 'Thank you,' I say as poor Joseph departs to do his bidding.

'Let's get one thing straight, Blackman,' Medici says. 'You have broken into my house. You have defiled my Family name.' Michael opens his mouth to speak but Medici jabs a thumb in his direction. 'You are no better.' His eyes harden. 'We are not friends. I have no wish to do you any favours. If what you say is true, I shall deal with this Terence myself.'

'Actually, if you have him, it would be better if you handed him over.'

'The law hasn't changed while we've been talking, has it? We still maintain Family rights?'

I curse inwardly. Foxworthy will kill me if Miller is the perp and we don't get to speak to him. 'Yes,' I say through gritted teeth, 'but...'

'Then there are no buts.' Medici strokes his chin. 'How did you get in here with no one noticing?'

I press my lips together. He'll find the trapdoor and the wall I bulldozed my way through easily enough. It doesn't mean I need to spell it out for him, though.

'You're a very irksome child,' he tells me.

I shrug. 'You wouldn't have talked to me if I'd tried to make an appointment.'

'You are probably right.' He looks at Michael. 'You should keep better control of your people.'

'She doesn't belong to me,' Michael replies. I almost stagger back in exaggerated shock. 'Anyway, my people don't go around raping and killing defenceless women.'

'My vampires are not defenceless,' Medici spits.

Maybe I should tell them that it might not have been the vampires' fault if they became victims. If Miller had O'Connell's special handcuffs, as I suspect, they couldn't have guarded themselves against him. But at that moment Joseph returns, awkwardly clearing his throat.

'Well?' Medici demands. 'Is he one of ours?'

'He applied, my Lord. At the last minute the recruiter decided he wasn't suitable. There was too much,' Joseph swallows, 'anger inside him.'

Medici looks at us, satisfied. 'Our recruitment policy holds true. Better than I can say for yours, Montserrat. That stupid girl you took on caused all these problems between us.'

I'm about to respond that no one could have foreseen Nikki's actions but Michael jabs me in the ribs. 'Do you have an address for him? Terence Miller?' he asks.

Medici speaks before Joseph can breathe a word. 'Don't give it to them. I will deal with this Miller myself. He will learn what it means to cross the Medici Family.'

Shit. Shit. Shit. I'm not going to let that happen. Miller might not even be the perp; right now, he's only a suspect. I step back, angling myself appropriately. Just as it dawns on Joseph what I'm about to do and he tries to move away, I snatch the piece of paper he's holding. 23 Arton Road. I rip off the address and stuff it into my mouth, chewing until I can swallow the damn thing. Let him find it now.

Medici gives me an exasperated look. 'Joseph, print out another copy of that, will you?' My heart drops. I'm a total idiot. 'It's daylight, Ms Blackman, and you're barely three months old. How do you think you'll reach Miller before I do?'

I close my eyes briefly. The bloody vampire Lord has a point. '23 Arton Road,' I tell Michael. 'Phone Inspector Foxworthy.'

Michael watches me with hooded eyes. 'I will. What are you going to do?'

I reach up onto my tiptoes and peck him on the cheek. 'Run, of course,' I say. Then I push Joseph out of the way and sprint.

I KNOW where I'm going this time but, alerted to my presence either by the noise or Joseph and Miss Moneypenny, the corridors are now full of Medici bloodguzzlers. The first ones I reach are so surprised that I get past them without incident but when Medici roars, the others spring into action. One female vamp grabs hold of my sleeve. I pull away from her and run. A large, burly bloodguzzler steps into my path so I dive and slide through the gap between his legs. I curve my ankle round his leg once I'm through and catch him off balance; he crashes to the floor.

'The bigger they are, the harder they fall,' I mutter.

There's a stampede of feet as the others charge after me. I twist right, making it to the staircase. Instead of running down the stairs, I leap up, angle my toes forward and slide down the banister on my feet. Before I reach the end I jump off, gaining an extra couple of metres on my pursuers. I'll need them if I'm going to get the trapdoor open again.

I pick up speed as I hurtle down the corridor. I yank the small table and vase down behind me to make another barrier and fling myself into the last room, slamming the door shut behind me. There's no lock, but I grab one of the boxes and push it against the door. It won't hold more than a few seconds.

Ripping up the rug, I open the trapdoor, drop down and land next to my improvised ladder. Then I run to the hole in the wall. It's a good thing I'm petite; the hole won't be large enough for most of the Medici vampires to get through. I dive forward, hands outstretched so I can wriggle through as quickly as possible.

I've almost made it when I feel an iron grip around my boot. I pull frantically, trying to free myself, but my captor is too sodding strong. I'm still tugging, aware that I'm losing the tussle, when I feel the boot loosen. I reach back and unfasten the side zip. My foot is free. With one sock flapping, I run unevenly down the tunnel and back to the train line. I can hear shouts and curses behind me, together with falling plaster as the Medici vampires smash their way through the wall.

I crash into the door at the end, my palms sweaty as I twist the doorknob to pull it open. There's a rush of air as a train whizzes past. I brace myself then, the second the last carriage is upon me, I jump. I grab hold of the train's door in the nick of time, clinging on with all my might. The pale face of a commuter stares out at me in shock but I ignore him, twisting round as a horde of Medici vampires burst out of the door I just exited. Several of them run in the direction of the train, but they won't catch up with me now. I give them a wave, grinning as they're swallowed up by the darkness. Then I reach down and pull off my other boot. I'll run faster without it.

And if I'm going to get to Arton Road before Medici and his goons, I'm going to have to run fast.

CHAPTER 16

BURN

The train screeches to a halt as it arrives at the next station. I'm on the wrong line for Arton Road but I can change here. I can travel quickly using the underground network but it's rush hour and I've got hundreds of commuters against me. And I've no idea what on earth I'll do when I reach my destination. It's a good two or three hundred metres from the station entrance to Miller's house. In theory I can cover that distance in seconds but the sun is out and I'll self-combust almost immediately.

Concentrating on getting as close as I can, I vault onto the platform. It's densely packed with people and, while the majority wait patiently for other passengers to disembark before they push onto the train, many are none too impressed as I squeeze past them, banging into elbows and warm bodies. It doesn't take long for someone to spot that I'm not human and shout out; immediately others jump to the side and clear a path. They might be moving out of my way for the wrong reasons but it's damn helpful.

I abandon the escalator in favour of the stairs, taking the steps four at a time. I swerve round a woman who has her nose buried in her Kindle as she ambles slowly towards me and I reach the top quickly. Unfortunately, my timing is awful: another trainload of passengers is coming down the corridor and out into the waiting world. I have to fight another tidal surge of humanity to cross the station and get to the platform I require.

As I round the corner, more people flood in my direction. I curse loudly, ignoring the startled – then fearful – looks I receive in return. 'I'm a fucking bloodguzzler!' I yell. 'Get out of the way!'

This time it doesn't work. Instead, everyone who hears me freezes. Those with earphones don't and start colliding with others in a bizarre rendition of fairground dodgems. There are just too many damn people. I glance up, noting the fluorescent strip lights bolted to the ceiling. It'll slow me down and I may well end up arse over tit, but anything will be faster than continuing to push against the crowds. I take a deep breath and launch upwards, grabbing the long bulb with my hands. I shimmy along, ignoring the searing burn in my palms. When I reach the end of the first one, I swing my legs to gain enough momentum to leap to the next. My socks scuff heads and several people shriek; I'm not sure if it's because I'm ruining their city hairdos or because they're worried about what damage a vampire's feet will do to them.

I drop down as the crowds start to thin. The next staircase down to the platform is a few feet away. I hear the rumble of another train pulling in and I know I only have seconds. I pull my limbs back and fling my body forward. The second my toes touch the top step, I sail into the air and clear the first flight of stairs in one jump. I spring forward and do the same to the next, before pelting round the corner just as the train doors begin to close. I make it just in time, knocking down one poor man as I smash into his. The doors shut and the train slides off.

I help the man to his feet, apologising profusely. He blinks at me. 'You're a vampire.'

Out of the corner of my eye, I note the people around me flinch away. 'Yes,' I pant, trying to catch my breath. 'I am.'

He squints. 'You're Bo Blackman. The one who left her Family.'

Shit. 'That's me. A lone wolf. But,' I add hastily, 'I can still call on plenty of back up if I need it. In case you were thinking of trying anything.'

He laughs. 'No. But could you give me your autograph?'

I start. 'What?'

'Your autograph. You'll be on the cover of *Time* before you know it and I want to prove I met you in person.'

'Er...' I'm completely nonplussed. Unable to dredge up a good reason to refuse, I agree. 'Okay.'

He takes a pen out of his briefcase and hands it to me.

'Do you have some paper?' I ask.

He shakes his head and starts undoing his top button. 'No. I'd like you to sign here.' He points to his jugular.

'You're kidding, right?'

He winks at me. 'I'll never wash that spot again.'

Incredulous, I stretch up to scribble my signature onto his skin. He's quite tall and it's awkward to make it legible. In fact, my scrawl looks like a child has ham-fistedly attacked him with a felt-tip. I suppose it's a good thing he can't actually see it.

'Thanks!' He beams at me and moves towards the train door as the next station approaches. 'Would you like to meet up for a drink some time?'

I stare at him. 'Probably not a good idea,' I say finally.

'You're right. I'm not sure my company would be too keen if they knew they had a vampette working for them. Nice to meet you anyway, Bo.' The doors open and he exits. I watch him go, my mouth open. That's the first time a human has recognised me and I'm not sure I like it.

I hitch up my socks, glad that these aren't the ones with the holes in the toes. Nevertheless, a few passengers look at my feet, then away, then back again, as if they're not quite sure what they're seeing. I suppose it isn't every day you travel to work with a shoe-less, Z-list vampire celebrity. I ignore the stares and prepare myself. There are two more stops and only eight minutes to go. It's time to work out how in hell I'm going to get to number twenty-three without getting baked.

I grab my phone from my pocket, thinking I could call Rogu3 and see if he can pull up a sun-free route for me, but there's no signal and I don't have time to wait for one. I know that most umbrellas will block out a three-quarters of ultra-violet light from the sun so that could be an answer. Unfortunately, everyone on the train is apparently prepared for a beautiful sunny day and I can't see a soul with a brolly. A man towards the far end has a flat cap on but it would only cast a shadow over half my face. Hardly appropriate.

I'm well aware how ridiculous my situation is. I'm preparing to risk my own life for someone who may be a bloody serial killer. It's not going to help a soul if Medici slaughters him, though. What I need – what everyone needs – is to see him carted away in handcuffs. There's no place for vigilantes in the current climate. As long as I keep telling myself that, I may start to believe it.

I'm still out of ideas when the train arrives at my station. I know some shops line the road outside and they may have awnings I can duck under. It's a slim shot, but I have to try. I position myself at the doors, ready to spring out. The second they start to open, I force my way through and run again.

Obviously I entered the station without an Oyster card and now I don't have time to make explanations or to queue up and pay my way. Given how rich the vampires supposedly are, it won't look good if I jump over the turnstiles and do a runner but there's not really a choice between having a corpse on my hands or a bit more bad PR. I bounce over the barrier and don't look back when a guard shouts.

It's less than fifty steps to the station entrance and I can already see the sunshine. I rush forward, halting at the edge of the shadows where sunshine meets safety and gaze out, frustrated. I'm right about the shops but only one has an awning and it's some distance away. I'll never make it.

I howl. This can't be where the race ends. I cast around in desperation. There's a row of parked cars across the pavement – maybe I could slide under them. It'd be slow going though and they only continue halfway up the street. After that, I'm screwed.

There are some free newspapers in a display to my right. I could unfold one and hold it over me but if one inch of my skin catches the sun, the newspaper would go up in flames faster than I would. I clench my teeth. There has to be something.

A woman pushing a buggy is coming in my direction. The buggy has a handy sun shade covering her sleeping baby. I'm petite – but not the size of a child. Just then, the pram's wheels clunk as they hit something. I look down: a drain with a manhole cover. It's about the most distasteful thing I can imagine but it might work.

'I'm calling the police!' a grim voice calls from behind. 'You didn't pay!'

I waste no more time. I crouch down and curve my fingers under the rim of the metal cover. With one swift movement I flip it up, already aware of the blisters appearing on my hands and the back of my neck from the sun. The stench of burning hair reaches my nostrils. I jump down and land in stinking water. Then I roll out of the way of the shaft of sunlight that's still beaming down on me.

My body feels like it's seizing up. My skin is searing hot but my insides are frozen and nausea roils in my stomach. I was in the open air for barely two seconds and I feel like I'm dying. If I thought it'd do any good, I'd duck down into the water but not only is it dark brown and reeking of sewage, it's also unpleasantly warm. I'll get no relief from that quarter. I grit my teeth, doing what I can to ignore the pain then I start running again.

Water splashes up around my feet and several times I slip on the slime underfoot. The socks are a hindrance so I pull them off, battening down my disgust as my bare skin wades through raw sewage, old rainwater and polluted rubbish. I don't have time to be prissy. I throw myself forward, praying that my bearings are correct. I can bloody well do this. I force my legs to keep moving until I think I've gone far enough.

It's lighter than I expected down here in the sewers, probably because they are only just underground, unlike some of the deep tunnels I traversed beside the train lines. I locate another manhole cover that leads to the surface but it's well out of reach. I hunker down while my skin screams in agony, then use all the power I can garner from my legs to launch myself upwards. I punch a closed fist at the cover and it shoots up several inches before falling back down again. I fall too and land in a sprawled heap in the rank water.

I try again, this time scraping my knuckles forward so that the cover doesn't fall back into place. It works. I have a little gap to work with so, if I can jump up one more time and squeeze my fingers through, I should be able to haul myself up. But the gap is letting in more sunlight. I know my limitations: I'm not going to have the energy to leap up more than once. I stare at the murky water. This is going to be nasty.

Gingerly, I lie down and roll until I'm covered from head to foot in foul-smelling slime, retching all the while. Then I get back into position.

I swallow hard. I hope there's no one out for a stroll when I emerge. I look – and smell – like the swamp thing. I can also barely stand. But now this is about more than Terence Miller: it feels like a personal battle between me and Medici. One that I'm determined to win.

I brace myself, bouncing on my toes until I can wait no longer. Then I push off. Only one hand connects and I'm left swinging. Tears leak from the corner of my eyes and I grit my teeth. Muscles straining and fingertips bleeding, I just make it. I shove the cover off and pull my body through. Dripping wet and burning again in the sun's glare, I twist left into the shade of a large tree. It's not enough and I glance around in panic. Then I see it; the next house along is number twenty-three. At last.

I gather my last ounce of energy. The sun is so bright, my eyeballs feel like they're on fire. For all I know they actually are. I squeeze my eyelids shut and run, then I'm on Miller's porch, finally shaded from the sun and hammering on his door.

It takes an eternity to open. When it does, there's no mistaking the man standing there. Corinne Matheson did a good job describing her attacker's features to the police. This guy has a gold tooth and cold eyes and I know I'm looking at the face of the person responsible for all those deaths.

'Terence Miller,' I croak. It's a statement, not a question.

'What the hell are you?'

'I'm the creature from the black sodding lagoon and if you don't invite me in right now, you're a dead man.'

He takes a step backwards. 'Bloodguzzler.'

'That's right.'

'I'm not inviting you in.' He starts to close the door in my face.

'I know what you've done. I know what you are,' I shout. He pauses. 'Others are coming. If you don't let me in right now, I can't help you. There's nowhere to hide. Make a choice, Miller. Your freedom or your life. You can only have one.'

He looks at me disdainfully. 'Piss off, bitch.'

Suddenly there's a crack and something whizzes past my ear. A blossom of red appears in Miller's chest. For a moment he stares down at it, as if confused, then he slowly starts to fall forward. His hands flail and pull at my shirt. I watch as the light in his eyes flares and dies. I only just manage to step away before he lands headfirst at my feet. Slowly, I turn round.

Two Medici vampires wearing the tell-tale red of their Family grin at me. The one on the right lowers a gun. 'You can go in now if you want, Ms Blackman. You look like you could do with a bath.' They climb into a car, close the doors and ramp up the music. I can't be sure because of the dull thud in my ears that seems to mute everything around me but it sounds like 'Bat Out of Hell'.

I stare after them dumbly as they accelerate down the street before I stumble into Miller's house and head for the kitchen and the large chest freezer in the corner. Flipping up the lid, I clamber inside and close my eyes.

When I finally come to, two anxious faces are peering down at me. It takes me a moment to register who they are.

'Bo, you're turning blue. What happened? What did that bastard do?'

I blink at Michael. 'Sun,' I mumble.

A fleeting of look of horror crosses his face and he reaches down, putting his hands under my back.

'Don't!' He ignores me, scooping me up as if I weigh nothing. 'I smell bad,' I say pitifully.

'Shhh,' he replies, 'it's alright.'

I squint up at Foxworthy whose expression is grim. 'Sorry. I contaminated your crime scene again.'

He looks at me and then into the freezer. 'We still have to find the bodies.'

My stomach lurches. 'I wasn't … no, I couldn't have been … are they…?'

He shakes his head. 'Just peas and fish fingers, I think.'

I breathe again. Thank goodness. 'They got to Miller. Medici's people. They shot him before I could do anything.'

'We figured,' Michael says.

Foxworthy nods. 'At least we know they didn't shoot an innocent person. He's definitely the man who attacked Corinne Matheson. Did he say anything?'

Michael growls. 'This is not the time for questions.'

'No. Nothing useful,' I tell the inspector.

'I'm taking her home,' Michael says.

I try to protest but my efforts are feeble. I can hardly raise my head, let alone form a coherent sentence. I give up, resting against his broad chest. I sense him looking at Foxworthy over my head and nodding. Then he gently carries me out.

There are people everywhere. I recognise Ursus and he gives me a tiny smile before he covers me from head to toe in a solar blanket. I hear voices and sirens and even through the material, the sun still feels like it's scorching my skin. A car door opens and I'm bundled inside. The air-conditioning is a blessing beyond words. I pull the blanket off and glance around.

'This is your car,' I say.

'Yes.' Michael's tone is short and I wonder why he's so pissed off.

'Sorry,' I repeat. 'I'm covered in shit.' Literally.

'Go to sleep, Bo. It'll help you heal.'

'Medici won. Again.'

'Sleep,' he tells me again.

When the car glides to a stop and the door opens, I wake with a start. I realise with relief that he's brought me back to New Order – and to my own flat. He carefully arranges the blanket over me and picks me up again.

'I bet Drechlin's loving this,' I mutter.

'Hush, Bo.'

Michael takes me upstairs into my own home. It's not until we're in the small bathroom that he finally puts me down. He pulls back the shower curtain and turns on the water. 'Clothes off,' he says.

Alarmed, I shake my head. 'No. I'll do it. You go.'

'I'm not trying to get into your pants, Bo. This is what friends do for friends.'

I'm in too much pain to argue. He raises my arms, peels off my t-shirt and unclips my bra. Embarrassed, I cross my arms over my breasts although they're covered in so much gunk, they're hardly visible. Michael pays no attention, moving down and unbuttoning my jeans. He helps me take them off, his fingers gentle. When he hooks his fingers round my knickers, I finally stop him. 'I'll do these.'

He nods and turns his back to afford me some privacy. But he starts taking off his own clothes too.

'Michael…'

'I told you to be quiet.' His voice is low. 'One of these days, you're going to do what I tell you to.'

'Never,' I whisper.

Wearing only a pair of boxers, he turns around and helps me get into the shower. I try not to stare at his broad, tanned chest and the angel wings tattooed across it. Then a wave of dizziness hits me and the lust uncoiling inside me dissipates.

Michael picks up a sponge, squeezes on some shower gel and carefully wipes my skin. I should be embarrassed: I'm covered in sewage, completely naked and with the man I recently rejected. Whether it's a result of the pain or the events of the morning – or simply Michael himself – I don't feel at all self-conscious.

When I try to wash myself he stops me, so eventually I give up and let him clean away the dirt and the hurt and the shame. He takes particular care over the blisters and raw, red skin. I hiss in pain a couple of times and he pauses, checking that I'm alright before he continues. Finally he lathers up shampoo and washes my hair.

When we're done, he steps out of the shower and grabs a towel. He pats me down where my skin is undamaged then wraps me in it.

'Connor's waiting.'

I start to shake my head but he presses his finger against my lips. 'No argument. You need to drink and then you can sleep. When you wake up, you'll feel a lot better.' He brushes away a tendril of wet hair from my face. 'I shouldn't have let you go running after Miller. It was too dangerous.'

'You're not my boss,' I mutter. A ghost of a smile crosses his face.

There's a tentative knock on the door and a worried-looking Connor appears.

'Drink,' Michael tells me again. 'Then sleep.'

I nod dutifully. This much I can do.

CHAPTER 17

VICTIMS

Bless the darkness. I'd never fully appreciated how wonderful night time is before. I stretch out, promising myself that I will never venture out in daylight again while I remain a fledgling vampire.

I sit up and prod my face carefully. Most of the blisters have already subsided and new skin is forming. I'm aware I've been bloody lucky. I seek out some clean clothes and pad into the bathroom. It's spotless. I wonder if Michael grabbed a pair of Marigolds and scrubbed all the crap away. Marigolds and boxer shorts and nothing else... Maybe not the boxer shorts...

I slap myself round the face. 'No!' I mutter. 'Bad Bo.' Friends don't have sexual fantasies about other friends. Maybe if I keep telling myself that, sooner or later it'll be true.

I stare into the mirror. The effect of falling asleep with wet hair makes me wince. I tie it up, ignore my blotchy skin and head down to the office. Distasteful as it was, I'm glad I drank from Connor before crashing. I wouldn't say I feel invigorated but I'm not at death's door.

Arzo is waiting for me. He squeezes my arm. 'You did good,' he says quietly.

'Medici's boys got to Miller.'

'True. But the important thing is that he's not going to destroy any more lives.'

I nod. He's right. It's not about me versus Lord Medici, it's about Corinne Matheson – and countless others – sleeping more easily tonight.

Arzo's jaw tightens. 'Did you...?' He looks away. 'When you were in the Medici house, did you see Dahlia?'

'No. I'm sorry.'

'That's okay. It's good. It means that Medici is still trying to keep her hidden. He doesn't know that we know that he has her.'

I'm not sure whether he's trying to convince me or himself.

'Good grief, Bo,' my grandfather says, appearing in the doorway. 'You look like you've been dragged through a hedge backwards. Appearances are vital in our line of work. People trust what they see and when they see you, they'll think we're running a den of heroin abusers.'

I suppose it's a good thing that he didn't see me curled up inside a freezer and covered in sewage. He frowns and I sigh, stepping forward to kiss his cheek. 'Good evening to you too,' I murmur.

'You're damn lucky,' he whispers in my ear. 'Don't you dare put yourself in that kind of danger again.' From behind him, his cat meows. I peer round his shoulder and it glares at me. The bloody thing starts purring before starting to wash its face.

'So,' my grandfather says, returning to his normal voice, 'I think it's safe to say we've been successful. The streets are safe and vampires solved the problem. I've already released a statement to that effect. Whether Medici or you will be credited remains to be seen, but we can assume that the tabloids will reflect the sentiment that the bloodguzzlers saved the day. I hope we will also see a rise in clients.'

At that moment, the phone rings. My grandfather smiles in satisfaction, as if to say that this is no doubt one of our many new customers. Peter answers it and looks in my direction. 'It's for you. Some lawyer.'

I take it from him, puzzled. 'D'Argneau? Either you're calling to congratulate me or the results are back on the ear.'

'Neither, I'm afraid,' he says grimly.

I don't like the tone of his voice. 'What is it?'

'It appears that one of the barristers in my firm had your Terence Miller as a client.'

'He was not my Terence Miller,' I snap. 'He was a vicious killer.'

'Just so,' D'Argneau agrees. 'That's why this is rather unfortunate.'

Tentacles of icy dread lick at my veins. 'What?'

'Mr Miller apparently left strict instructions to be carried out in the event of his untimely death. In point of fact, a statement. Shall I read it out?'

I sit down heavily. 'Go on.'

D'Argneau clears his throat. '"I, Terence Timothy Miller, being of sound mind, make this final testament. Public opinion will no doubt place me on trial for my actions in participating in the deaths of several women. The truth is more complicated. I petitioned the Medici Family, asking to be recruited into their midst as a vampire. A condition of their acceptance was that I prove myself worthy by making a sacrifice. If I severed twenty souls, I would gain admittance. I am not proud of my actions but I was coerced into them. May God have mercy on my soul."'

I don't say anything.

'Bo? Are you there?'

'I'm here.' My voice is barely audible. 'D'Argneau, you can't release this.'

'We don't have any choice. We act for the deceased.'

'He's a fucking rapist and serial killer! You can't trust anything he says! You know this is bullshit, right? Even Medici wouldn't do this.' As soon as I say it, I know I'm right. The vampire Lord I confronted yesterday may have made an illegal move against Dahlia, but he'd never put his Family in jeopardy by asking a potential recruit to kill people. He wouldn't be so stupid, even if he were that bloodthirsty.

'It's not for us to say,' D'Argneau says. 'But, yes, you are probably correct.'

'You can't do this. Please, Harry.'

'I'm sorry, I can't prevent the statement being released. I shouldn't even tell you about it in advance. I thought it might help if you knew though.' There's a muffled sound from his end of the line. 'Look, I have to go. Nisha Patel is here to talk to me. I'm sorry, Bo.' He hangs up.

My shoulders slump. Arzo gazes at me with concern. 'What is it?'

Everyone is watching me. I give them the gist of Miller's statement. Matt's eyes widen. 'Would Medici really have done that?'

Arzo shakes his head. 'No. I've never heard of such a condition. We should send someone to speak to him to make sure but it's incredibly unlikely.' I open my mouth to speak but I don't get the chance. 'I don't think it would be a good idea if it were you, Bo.'

'I'll do it,' my grandfather says, surprising all of us. 'I want to meet him face to face. You can't get the true measure of a man until you look him in the eye. And he's not likely to try and manipulate me.'

As much as I hate to admit it, he's probably right. 'Terence Miller is somewhere in hell, laughing his bloody head off,' I say. 'He had no reason to do this other than to make life more difficult for the Families. Medici wouldn't take him in and he's getting his revenge.'

'Or it's an insurance policy he never had the chance to cash in,' Peter suggests.

'Either way, he's completely screwing us. We need to do something to mitigate the effects.' I think, then say, 'Nick.'

'Who?'

'He's the Bancroft bloodguzzler who was castrated when he was turned. We need him to tell his story to the press.'

Peter nods. 'I'll contact Lord Bancroft immediately.'

'Make sure he's coached first,' I warn. 'He has a big mouth and he likes to show off. He needs to be serious and make it clear that what happened to him was because he was a rapist when he was human. That behaviour like that isn't acceptable to any of the Families. If we can get his statement out ahead of Miller's, we might sway public opinion in our favour.'

Arzo raises his eyebrows. 'Our? That's the first time you've used that pronoun, Bo.'

I meet his gaze. 'I'm a vampire too.' To avoid further discussion on the subject, I stand up.

'Where are going?'

'Back to Miller's house,' I say grimly. 'I want to see what the police found and if there's anything we can use.'

'Are you sure you're up to it?'

I set my mouth into a thin line. 'Cooling on a slab or not, Terence Miller won't get the better of us.'

Arriving at Miller's place, I have a strange sense of déjà vu. The house is cordoned off and I recognise a few of the faces from the crime scene at Jubilee Park. This time, however, I don't hide my presence. I walk up to the outer cordon and duck underneath the tape.

'Hey! What do you think you're doing?' A young police-woman strides up to me.

'Is Foxworthy here?'

'You're a bloodguzzler,' she sneers.

Suddenly I'm tired of being treated like a second-class citizen. 'Yeah? What of it?'

'Let her in.' I look up and spot Nicholls hovering a few feet away.

'Thank you.'

Her face twists. 'Don't think we're best buds now or anything.' She jerks her thumb towards the house. 'Foxworthy's in there.' She throws a white suit and a pair of bootees at me. 'Put those on first.'

I bite back a reply at her supercilious tone and do as I'm told. The suit is about three sizes too large and, with the wind blowing behind me, I resemble the Michelin Man. I pad forward and go inside.

There are other white-suited people milling around. It's difficult to tell which one is Foxworthy because they all look exactly the same. I wander round, peering into faces. It's not until someone gestures at me from the door leading to the garden that I finally spot the inspector.

'I thought you'd show up sooner or later,' he grunts. 'Your bike is outside.' I'm surprised; I'd assumed I'd have to go through the rigmarole of paperwork and fines to release it from where it was impounded. 'Least I could do,' he grunts.

'Have you found anything?' I ask him.

The answering look in his eyes is enough. I glance beyond him to the garden and the large pit that now extends across what was the lawn. I step forward to take a look and gag. There are ten bodies lying next to one another with their hands clasped together. It reminds me sickeningly of the strings of paper cut-out dolls I used to make when I was a child. The corpses are in varying degrees of decomposition and the smell is horrific.

'Are they...?'

'Yes. All the missing women.'

I swallow hard and look away. I've never been confronted before with violent death on such a scale. It's not like it is on television.

'If you want to throw up, there's a bucket over there,' Foxworthy tells me. 'You won't be the first.'

At least he appreciates that just because I'm a bloodguzzler, I'm not immune to gore. I only just manage to keep hold of the contents of my stomach.

'We haven't found their clothes. There's no diary or notes or anything that suggests his motive. He was just a sick bastard who took pleasure in the suffering of others.'

I agree wholeheartedly but I can't help thinking that Miller remains one step ahead of us. He didn't fake the surprise in his face when I showed up at his door and he definitely wasn't expecting to be shot dead on his own porch. With what I now know about the statement he left with his lawyers, I can't shake the feeling that there's more to come. There's not a shred of evidence to support my uneasiness, though, so I don't share it.

'We're starting to inform the victims' families,' Foxworthy says. 'Although a lot of them probably already have a good idea. The press are all over this.'

What a horrible way to discover that your loved one has been brutally killed.

'Would you like to come with me?' he asks suddenly.

God, no. I can't think of anything worse but I also feel I should take some of the responsibility. And I might learn something. 'Okay,' I tell him.

'We've sent liaison officers to speak to the triber factions. They'll inform those families.'

'So you're doing the humans? Will they be happy about a vampire being there too?'

'If it wasn't for you, we'd still be chasing our tails on this one. They'll understand that.'

'He's left a statement with a lawyer. Miller, I mean. He must have done it ages ago. It says that the Medici Family forced him into it.'

Foxworthy snorts. 'Forced him into abduction, rape and murder? As if.'

Given the degree to which he despises the Families, I'm glad he dismisses the theory so easily. Maybe everyone else will do the same. Then he throws me a doubtful glance. 'Did they?' he asks.

Shit. 'No. We're double-checking just to be sure but it's unlikely.' I'm keen to change the subject. 'Have you found out much about Miller?'

'Very little. Both his parents are dead. He was bounced around foster families then had a string of dead end jobs. He doesn't seem to have many friends.'

'His neighbours?'

'Said he was polite and courteous but kept to himself.'

Many people do these days. 'Have you found any magic residue?' I ask as we make our way back out through the house.

'You're referring to the fact that he was able to attack the women in such public places?' I nod. 'No. We've not found a damn thing.'

I find it hard to believe that no one noticed what he was doing. 'It doesn't make any sense,' I say, frustrated.

'It often happens with cases like this. Sometimes there are questions that never get answered. By the way, the man we questioned at Marsh Prison – O'Connell?' I know what he's going to say. 'He was found dead this morning. His heart is missing.'

My stomach turns. I suppose I should be grateful that X didn't dispose of the entire body and force the police into a pointless manhunt. Then I wonder when I became so callous that I can shrug off an execution so easily.

'You don't seem surprised,' Foxworthy comments. 'Even though the mode of killing would suggest Kakos daemon, which makes no sense at all.'

I'm saved from answering by Nicholls. 'You're going?' she asks. 'And you're taking her with you?'

'If you have a problem with that, just say.'

'Nah.' She gives me a hard look. 'It's about time you blood-guzzlers realised how much the relatives of vanished victims suffer.'

Aware of what she's referring to, I mirror her stance. 'Anyone who chooses to turn does so of their own volition.' I think of Dahlia and myself and realise that's not entirely true. I'm also not sure why I'm suddenly defending the process.

'Your motorbike's there.' Foxworthy points, looking for a way to avoid further conflict between Nicholls and me.

There's a long scratch down the bodywork which definitely wasn't there before. If that's the worst of it, I suppose I got lucky. 'I'll follow you,' I tell him.

He turns to Nicholls. Realising by his body language that he wants some privacy, I leave them to it and walk over to the bike. As I start the engine a few words drift over – 'cooperation' and 'not as bad as you think'. That could be my tagline, I decide: 'Bo Blackman – she's not as bad as you think.' It's not very catchy, though.

〜

THE FIRST FAMILY isn't far away; in fact, they live less than a couple of miles from Miller's house. I wonder with a shiver whether they may have bumped into one another at the supermarket or the local library.

I park the bike behind Foxworthy's car and we walk up the path to the front door. We're barely halfway up when the door opens and a grey-haired woman appears. Her face is tear-streaked and drawn. I can see a small boy staring at us with wide eyes from behind her legs. She shoos him inside and steps out to meet us.

'It's her, isn't it? At that house? It's all over the news. It's my Tammy.' Her back is straight but her hands are trembling.

Foxworthy nods. 'We think so.' A moan escapes her and she steps backwards. 'We need to confirm the DNA matches but we are fairly certain it's Tammy.'

The woman gulps in air. I watch helplessly. Fury at Miller rises inside me again. It's not just those girls' lives that he destroyed – it's the lives of all the people around them too.

She looks at me. 'They're saying a vampire killed him. Was it you?'

I can barely bring myself to look her in the eye. 'No.'

'Did he suffer? Tell me that bastard suffered. He deserves it after what he did to my baby.'

I take a deep breath. 'There's nothing I could do that would make him suffer enough for what he did to your daughter. To those other women.'

She chokes slightly but composes herself enough to speak. 'Did he rape her?' For a moment neither Foxworthy nor I speak. 'Did he rape her?' she repeats, her voice rising.

'Yes, Mrs Lamb. He did.'

A spasm crosses her face. 'I hope he rots in hell.' She folds her arms tightly across her chest. Her pain is obvious but it's her stoicism that I find most heartbreaking. Even in the face of such soul-destroying news, she keeps it together. It occurs to me that women all over the world are like that; their strength and ability to absorb pain is far greater than someone like Miller could ever imagine. Through women like her, we've defeated him after all.

'Is there someone we can call, Mrs Lamb?'

She tilts up her chin. 'No.' She looks at me and Foxworthy in turn. 'Thank you.' Then she turns round, goes back into her house and closes the door. It doesn't slam. There's no shriek or wail or tearing of clothes. The ball of unshed tears expands in my chest and I push it down angrily. If she won't cry then I have no right to.

'Everyone's different,' Foxworthy says quietly. 'Everyone takes the news differently.'

I can't trust myself to speak so I acknowledge his words then walk stiffly back down the path.

The phone in my pocket starts ringing. I ignore it. I don't want to speak to anyone right now. Whoever is calling is insistent though. It rings and rings and rings until I give in and answer. 'This is Bo Blackman.'

'You said he wasn't a vampire! You said you'd done the tests!' His voice is barely audible over the loud, incessant barking.

I frown. 'Mr Brinkish?'

'He's going fucking nuts. I took him out for a walk and he tried to attack a daemon on the other side of the street for no damn reason. And now I've forced him to come inside the house, he's throwing himself at the door and he won't shut up. He's foaming at the mouth. He's crazy! The dog's crazy!'

There's an odd splintering sound. 'Mr Brinkish?' I ask in alarm. 'What's that?'

I hear a thud and then a scream. Kimchi is still barking and

Brinkish is saying something in background. 'No, no, no, no, no,' over and over again.

'Do you have a radio?' I shout at Foxworthy.

'Yes. What's wrong?'

I start running towards the bike, yelling Brinkish's address behind me. 'Get the police there now!'

'What's happening?'

'Get them there!' I leap on the bike and rev the engine. Then I accelerate as quickly as I can.

CHAPTER 18
THE SKY IS FALLING

The door to Brinkish's house is hanging off its hinges. I ignore the huddle of worried neighbours on the opposite side of the street and stride towards it. Fresh blood hangs in the air. I can't imagine that Kimchi caused this.

I step over the threshold and immediately see the foot sticking out of the living-room door. I bend down. It's Brinkish. His head is skewed at a terrible angle and his eyes stare glassily at me. I look up and see his wife, her blood staining the sofa barely visible against the garish pattern. There's a ragged wound in her throat that looks like it was caused by a bullet.

I sink to my knees. What in hell has happened? I thought I'd already seen more death today than I could ever imagine and now I'm confronted with yet another house of horrors.

There's a quiet whine behind me. I twist round and see Kimchi, lying on his side. His breathing is and shallow and his fur is matted with blood. There's a gaping wound in his belly. Despite this, his tail wags feebly when I approach.

'Good boy,' I whisper. My voice is as shaky as my limbs. 'Good dog.'

I pat his head and he whines again. I can't make sense of

what I'm seeing. The only light in the room comes from the pictures flickering across the television screen. Whoever did this might still be here. I stand up. I should investigate the rest of the house silently but, right now, I don't care. If the person who did this is still here, they're going to regret the day they were born.

I charge through the ground floor. Kitchen. Bathroom. I overturn a table and fling open cupboard doors. I run upstairs and into every bedroom. There's nothing.

Hearing the crackle of a radio and low voices, I start back down the stairs. Two uniformed officers stand there, staring at me.

'Don't move!' the first one yells.

Slowly, I put up my hands. 'My name is Bo Blackman,' I say, as clearly as I can. 'I'm the one who alerted you. Call Inspector Foxworthy. He'll tell you.'

They glare at me suspiciously. 'You're a vampire. How did you get in here without an invitation?'

His partner looks down at Brinkish's body. 'He's dead. That's how she got in. There are no living owners any more. What did you do?'

I grit my teeth. Logic is not their strong suit. 'Call Foxworthy. And a damn vet.' When they don't move, I bare my teeth and let my fangs grow. 'Now!'

Keeping his eyes trained on me, the nearest police officer grabs his radio and mutters into it.

'You need to get a vet,' I say desperately. 'The dog can still make it.' I hear pounding feet and Foxworthy appears. 'Tell these two I didn't do this,' I snarl.

He looks around, taking in the situation in one swift glance. 'She's okay,' he mutters.

Both policemen seem uncertain but they step back in deference to Foxworthy's rank. I rush back down the stairs to the dog and check on him. He's still alive. 'Come on, Kimchi. Hang on in there. Help is coming.'

'What happened here?' Foxworthy asks.

I shake my head. 'I have no idea.' I gesture at Brinkish's fallen body. 'He called me when we were outside Mrs Lamb's house. He said Kimchi, the dog, had gone crazy and attacked a man and when he brought him home, he got even worse.'

I can hear the question in Foxworthy's voice. 'He attacked a man? A human?'

I stroke Kimchi then freeze. 'Wait,' I say slowly. 'Not a human. A daemon. This dog spent three days with me. He growled a few times but he never tried to attack anyone – not unless he had a good reason.' And I may know what that reason was.

'Talk to me, Blackman.'

The Agathos daemons, the ones who threatened us in the street. They had a gun. My eyes drift to the bullet wound in Mrs Brinkish's throat. If one of them was outside and Kimchi recognised him, the dog would attack him. He'd consider it self-defence. But why would the daemons come here? How would they know to come here?

I replay our encounter on the pavement outside the supermarket. The male daemon fell on top of Kimchi before we fled. I grab hold of his collar and unclip it.

'Blackman! What is going on?' Foxworthy demands.

I don't reply. Instead I turn over the collar and stare at it. It's covered in blood but is there anything else? I lift it up and sniff. Magic. Whatever fucking tracking spell they had on O'Shea, they used it on Kimchi too. I know it in my bones. They must have thought that they'd find O'Shea and me by following the dog. I look at the dead couple. This is my fault: I led those daemons here. The Brinkishes just got caught up in the middle.

I show the collar to Foxworthy. 'A spell,' I say dully. 'A fucking spell.'

'Shit,' one of the policeman exclaims.

I look up at him, expecting his reaction to be a result of the bloodbath or my discovery about the use of magic, but he's not looking at the Brinkishes. He's staring at the television screen. Whatever programme was on has just been interrupted by a news broadcast. It's the Agathos Court building – and there's been an explosion.

I stare at the images. Fire licks the stone walls and the glass frontage has been smashed. There's a cloud of thick black smoke rolling heavily from the back of the building, right where Nisha Patel's office is.

'There are no coincidences,' I whisper into Kimchi's fur. Then I get to my feet.

Jabbing my finger at the horrified policeman who can't tear his eyes away from the television screen, I snarl, 'If the dog dies, then you'll regret it.'

His blue eyes dart to me, confusion and fear reflected in their watery depths.

'You know what this is about,' Foxworthy says quietly.

'I have a pretty damn good idea.'

'Blackman...'

I ignore him and stride out of the room. The policeman leaps out of my way, almost tripping over Brinkish's corpse.

Foxworthy tries again. 'Bo, help me out here.'

I turn and meet his gaze. 'I don't have time. I need to get to the courthouse. Stay here and sort out this mess. I meant what I said about the dog.' I realise belatedly that I'm giving him orders. I soften slightly. 'Please.'

He scans my face. 'Are these attacks linked? Is there going to be another one?'

O'Shea. I have no idea where he is right now. 'Possibly,' I grunt. 'And that's why I need to go.'

I whirl away, yanking my phone out of my pocket to call O'Shea. It doesn't even ring; it goes straight to voicemail. Cursing, I try D'Argneau and get the same response. I chew my lip and try Michael. He answers on the second ring. 'Bo, are you alright? Have you seen the news?'

'Just now. It's linked to O'Shea.'

Michael exhales loudly. 'That damn daemon. Why is he involved in everything?'

'Just sheer blind luck, I guess.' I climb onto my bike. 'I'm going to the courthouse. I don't know if O'Shea is there or not but I left him with D'Argneau.'

There's a moment of silence. 'The lawyer?' he asks finally.

I don't have time to play office politics. 'Yes,' I answer shortly. 'They both might be in trouble. I know it's a lot to ask but can you…'

'I'll get my people out looking for them now.'

'Thank you.'

'Bo, how are you? When I left yesterday…'

'I'm fine.'

'Are you sure?'

I turn on the engine. 'I'm a bit sore and tender but I'm fine. Find O'Shea.' I hang up and take one last look back at the Brinkish's house. The lone sock that was hanging on the washing line the first time I visited is still there. I watch it flap in the breeze. And then I'm gone.

THERE ARE roadblocks around the Agathos Court. Daemons and humans are everywhere, some dazed because they were close to the explosion and others merely gawking at the spectacle.

Acknowledging that I'm not going to get any closer with the bike, I park it and start running. I don't have time to waste explaining myself to the officials manning the roadblocks so I use a fire escape to clamber up a nearby building. Running lightly, I vault from roof to roof.

The fire brigade is already in attendance. There's a helicopter overhead but the sound of its rotor blades is drowned out by the screams and yells of the people below. Despite the firemen's best efforts – or perhaps because of them – I'm enveloped in a billowing cloud of smoke. My eyes stream, reducing my vision to virtually nil. With no choice, I drop back down to the street and sprint towards the front doors of the courthouse. Someone catches my arm and I rip it away, spinning around.

'I'm a vampire,' I yell at the daemon who grabbed me. She's wearing the uniform of an Agathos security guard. 'I can help. Are people still trapped inside?'

Her pupils are narrow slits, indicating her shock that someone dared to do this to the heart of the Agathos' justice system. 'I think so.'

'I can help them,' I repeat.

She nods uneasily and I sprint up the steps and inside. I know exactly where I'm going. I'm barely past the Wall and its hideous posters of misery, however, when I hear a cough. I look over and spy Meg, the Agathos gatekeeper, on all fours. She's almost obscured by the heavy front desk. Her leg is broken, her shin bone protruding from her ripped tights and pale skin. No wonder she can't stand up.

I hook her arm round my shoulders. 'Come on,' I tell her, 'I'm getting you out of here.'

'No,' she moans. 'There are still people inside. It's my job to get everyone out.'

'Right now, it isn't.'

She's easy to carry despite her heavy frame; another thing to thank my vampire blood for, I suppose. To speed up matters, I pick her up in a fireman's lift and place her carefully over my shoulder, then move outside as quickly as I can. As soon as the air hits me, hands reach out to help. I pass her over to a soldier wearing army fatigues and run back inside, skidding on the marble floor.

Away from the main lobby, the corridors are filled with smoke. I use the cuff of my jacket to cover my nose and mouth and duck down to stay low and retain as much visibility as I can. Pausing at every door, I listen for the sounds of anyone who is trapped but it seems as if everyone except Meg got out. I push forward. I need to get to Nisha's office.

From somewhere ahead, there's another booming explosion and the sound of breaking glass. The building trembles with the force and something hard and heavy lands on my head. I roll to the side, realising it's a gilt-framed painting. I shove it away from me, revealing in the process that it's a print of that bloody painting I used to hide myself in Medici's lair. Perhaps it's some kind of bizarre, inanimate revenge.

By this point my lungs are burning. The smoke is so thick that I'm forced to shut my eyes and grope my way forwards. When I feel a light breeze to my right, I change direction and head into a room at the side. I won't make it unless I can find something to protect myself with first. The room is smoky but it's clear enough for me to open my eyes and look around. Closing the door behind me, I search around the small office. The windows have been blown out and the curtains ripple in the light wind drifting in from outside. I spy a glass of water on the paper-strewn desk. That'll do.

I take a gulp to cool my insides then I move over to the curtains and yank the first set down, ripping off a foot of fabric. I douse it in water but, just as I'm about to wrap it around my head, the other set of curtains moves and I freeze. Someone's on the other side.

Keeping low, I step backwards, watching the window carefully. There's a flash of fabric and a leg appears. Whoever it is, they're not wearing a fireman's livery. The fingers of my right hand curl around a heavy bust on a shelf above me. The second I see a torso join the legs, I let the bust fly. It connects with the body and I hear a startled ooomph.

Sodding hell.

'Why didn't you say it was you?' I stride over and help Michael to his feet.

He glares at me. His face is streaked with soot, making his eyes stand out. And they're not happy. 'What?' he demands. 'On the off-chance that an idiot like you was hanging around? What's with the projectile weapon?'

'Sorry,' I mutter. I notice belatedly that he's wearing the Montserrat midnight blue. 'I thought you were one of them.'

'One of whom, Bo?'

'The fucking daemons who are attacking this place.'

'How do you know they're daemons?'

I sigh. This isn't the time for lengthy explanations. 'I just do.'

He gives me a hard look. 'You shouldn't be risking your life for a dodgy human lawyer and an even dodgier quarter-daemon.'

'Neither should you,' I shoot back.

'It's not them I'm here for.'

I fall silent. With extraordinarily bad timing, both for the building and for us, a sprinkler in the ceiling decides to turn itself on. Water rains down with surprising power. At least I got what I came for.

'Here,' I grunt, passing him over the piece of curtain. 'You'll need this.' I rip off another section, let the water soak it, then wrap it around my head.

'Do you know if they're still here?' Michael asks.

No longer able to see him, I shrug. 'I have to be sure.'

I edge back to the door and fling it open, then get down onto all fours. Taking a deep breath, I crawl towards the heat again. I keep my head down and continue moving, putting one hand in front of the other. It's not until something blocks my way that I stop. Pulling up the edge of the fabric, I peek out. As far as I can tell, part of the ceiling has collapsed. Exposed wires hang down but I think there's a big enough gap to squeeze through.

Michael tugs my ankle. 'There are three fire engines round this side. It's getting too dangerous, Bo. Leave it to the professionals.'

I'm about to reply when I hear a shout from the other side of the rubble. I throw him a look and he nods reluctantly.

'Don't you have minions to do this kind of thing for you?' I ask, trying to keep my tone light.

'None of them are stupid enough to run into a burning building,' he answers.

I pull my makeshift mask back down again and start climbing, pushing chunks of fallen plaster out of my way so I can enlarge the gap and make it wide enough for Michael to follow. Blinded as I am, it's not particularly easy, but with a little perseverance and sweat I make it through. I listen. I can't hear any more shouts.

'Hello!' I yell. 'O'Shea! Nisha! Harry!'

Panting slightly, Michael joins me. 'So he's Harry now, is he? When did that happen?' He pauses. 'Wait, let me guess. You're friends, right?'

I don't deign to answer. Instead, I lurch forward. 'Devlin!

Are you there?' I turn my head back. 'He's a friend too,' I sniff. 'That's why I'm here.'

There's an answering shout from up ahead. The smoke is getting thicker, if that's possible, and it seeps through the wet rag round my face. I plunge in deeper, arms out in front of me. I find the far wall and feel my way forward. That's when I realise I've found them.

Nisha's office door has buckled. My fingers brush a warm hand that's reaching out to me. I grab the fingers and squeeze tight.

'Bo? Is that you?'

O'Shea. Thank goodness. 'It's me!' I yell.

'We're trapped. The ceiling has caved in on the other side. We can't get to the window and we can't open the door.'

'Who's with you?' Michael asks calmly.

'Nisha.'

'Is D'Argneau there?'

'No, he'd already left.'

'Hardly the conquering hero, is he?' Michael mutters.

'Stand back,' I shout. 'We'll try to break the door down.'

'Be careful! I think it's the only thing holding up the wall right now.'

I nod grimly. I turn to Michael. 'Can you...?'

'I'm already there.' I sense him moving beside me and stretching up to hold the door frame.

'Are you strong enough to do this?' I ask.

'Are you suggesting I'm not?' he shoots back.

I take three steps back, brace my legs and launch forward, smacking my shoulder into the door. The wood splinters with a loud crack.

'Almost!' O'Shea calls. 'Do it again.'

I take a deep breath. 'Ready?' I ask Michael.

'Do it.'

I hold nothing back. I may be small but I've got both power and strength. This time, I hit the door in just the right place, forcing it open. There's an almighty creak from above and Michael grunts. 'Move fast.'

Nisha appears, blood streaking her face from a wound on her cheek. She's caked in dust and very shaken, but otherwise unhurt. O'Shea follows. 'We need to get out of here now!' he gasps.

'Go!' Michael yells.

I lead them back down to the mountain of rubble. 'Michael!' I scream.

'You first.' He still sounds calm and collected whereas I'm shrieking like a bloody banshee.

I spring up, my hands scrabbling over plaster and bits of stone. I throw myself over. 'Get ready to run,' I hear from behind.

There's another ear-splitting creak and I feel the floor vibrate. Then Michael's hands grab me as he pulls himself through. Together the four of us start sprinting as the walls and ceilings finally yield. There's a loud rumble and a crash. We swerve through the corridors; Nisha and O'Shea aren't moving fast enough and we won't make it in time.

I pull down the wet rag and exchange a look with Michael. He nods and lunges for O'Shea, throwing him onto his shoulder. I grab Nisha and do the same. My legs pump and my eyes stream. Nisha clings on to me for dear life. We twist left into the glass-covered lobby. There's another boom, although I can't tell whether it's more of the building collapsing or another explosion. I put my head down. Shards of glass fly up around my feet as I run towards the large front doors. Then we're out, running down the stairs and breathing in fresh air.

I finally come to a halt when I'm down the steps and onto the road. Gasping for breath, I put Nisha down. Her knees buckle and she collapses. A paramedic rushes over and fixes an oxygen mask round her face. Another paramedic gestures towards me but I wave him away and turn to look at the Agathos court. Although the fire brigade has extinguished most of the flames, the entire east side of the building is devastated.

O'Shea hacks out a long cough and doubles over.

'Do you need oxygen?' I ask

He waves me away and straightens up. His face is still pale and his orange eyes blink at me in shock and horror.

'What the hell happened?'

He shakes his head. 'I don't know. Maybe it was a bomb.'

'Is this about the ear?'

'If it is, then you need to run, Bo.'

Puzzled and alarmed, I look at him questioningly. Nisha pulls off the oxygen mask. 'The ear is a fake,' she gasps. 'It's not Renfrew.'

Michael starts. 'Tobias Renfrew? You're kidding me. That's what this is about?'

'Bo!' O'Shea begs. 'You have to run.'

He's not making any sense. 'Run where?'

'They're after everyone.'

I nod. 'I know. Kimchi and his owners...'

'No, you're not listening. A letter arrived by messenger just before the first explosion.' He thrusts a crumpled piece of paper at me. 'They're going after everyone who knows who they are.' He stares at me. 'How did you know about the funeral directors, Bo?'

I know what he's getting at instantly. 'Rogu3,' I whisper.

O'Shea closes his eyes. 'Run,' he repeats.

CHAPTER 19

FRIDAY NIGHT FRIGHTS

I don't even look at the piece of paper. I simply thrust it into my back pocket and do exactly as I'm told, taking off down the street. I'm vaguely aware of repeated flashes of bright light pointing in my direction and voices calling my name, but I focus on one thing and one thing only – getting to my bike and getting to Rogu3.

From the footsteps behind me, I can tell I'm not alone. 'What day is it?' I shout. My words are whipped away into the wind.

'Friday,' Michael answers. 'Who the fuck is Rogu3?'

'Friend.'

'Another one?'

I run faster. I leap over a cordon, ignoring the wide-eyed looks and smartphones held in the air. The bike is just ahead. I pivot round a group of Japanese tourists who goggle at me and vault onto the bike. Michael joins me, his arms linking round my waist. With a loud roar, the bike takes off, tires squealing.

'What time is?' I call back.

'Almost ten.'

I thought it was later. Rogu3 will probably still be at that gig. By blowing a hole in the goddamn Agathos court, the daemons have proved they don't care who gets hurt. So not only is Rogu3 in danger but so are all of his friends.

'My phone's in my pocket,' I yell to Michael. 'Take it out and call the third number in the contact list. Call it three times. Tell the person who answers to hide. Now.'

Thankfully, Michael doesn't ask any questions. He reaches into my pocket for the phone. I weave round waiting traffic, ignoring the red light up ahead. Cars sound their horns and a cacophony of hoots blares through the night. I narrowly avoid hitting a jogger and curse.

'There's no answer,' he shouts in my ear.

'Then keep calling!' Although if Rogu3 is round the back of the proverbial bike sheds with his Natasha, he'll never pick up. My heart pounds painfully. Michael senses my panic and tightens his grip round my waist. 'It'll be alright,' he says into my ear.

I shake my head. Not if they hurt Rogu3, it won't be.

Eleven and a half minutes later, I screech to a halt outside the school gates. They tower menacingly, as if the school is as much of a prison as Marsh. Still, at least the gates are open to allow for the steady influx of teenagers.

I jump off and start running again. There's a kid leaning against one wall, smoking; he holds the cigarette awkwardly as if he doesn't quite know what to do with it. I guess some things never change. I snatch the glowing end, throw it away and grab the lapels of his denim jacket.

'I'm looking for ...' Shit. I pause. I don't know Rogu3's real name. 'A teenager. Good with computers. He's about this tall,' I raise my hand, 'and has brown hair.'

The smoker shrugs. 'Lady, you just described about a hundred people.'

I lean my face in closer and bare my fangs. He flinches. 'Where's the gig?'

He points to his left with a shaking finger. I release him and launch myself in that direction. I look left and right. I can't see any daemons around – adult or teen. It doesn't mean they're not already here, though.

Michael catches up. 'Bo, this is a school.'

'I know.' I slam open a set of double doors and run down a corridor towards the thump of music. My shoes squeak on the floor and there's the distinct smell of chip oil in the air.

'Bo!' He grabs my arms, swinging me round and forcing me to stop. 'We're vampires. We can't be here. You can't go around threatening children.'

I yank myself free. 'Then go,' I snarl. 'Get out of here. I'm not leaving.'

I set off again. The music gets louder. I'm almost there. All of a sudden, I hear the tinkle of smashed glass and a fraction of a second later, there's a familiar piercing howl. I whirl round. Michael is standing beside a fire alarm set into the wall. I nod at him as kids pour out of a room at the far end. Virtually all of them are taller than I am. I moan in despair, shoving my way through the crowd, craning my neck upwards to find Rogu3's familiar face.

'Curmudgeon!' I yell as loudly as I can. 'The word of the week is curmudgeon!' Startled eyes flick in my direction. None of them are Rogu3's.

'Everyone, you know the drill. Just because it's night time, things don't change. Make your way calmly and quietly out to the field.' I look at the harassed teacher ushering the kids out and push my way towards her. 'Is everyone out?' I ask.

Her mouth drops open.

'I said,' I grit my teeth, 'is everyone out?'

She nods. I mutter a curse under my breath. 'Check the toilets,' I instruct Michael.

His face is an impassive mask. 'I don't know what I'm looking for.'

'Teenager. About this tall.' I indicate Rogu3's height. 'He has brown hair and he knows who I am. If you find him, phone me immediately. The daemons who attacked the Agathos court will be after him.'

'From what I can gather, they'll be after you too, Bo.'

'I can look after myself. He can't.' The teacher's eyes dart from me to Michael and back again. 'Go,' I growl.

Michael takes off while I turn back to the shaking woman. 'Do you know who I'm talking about?' I demand.

She blinks rapidly. 'That could be anyone.'

'He likes words,' I tell her. Her expression flickers and I know it's dawned on her who I mean. 'Where is he?'

'I don't know,' she stammers.

I take a step towards her. 'Yes, you do.' I try to soften my voice. 'I know I'm a bloodguzzler. I know you think I'm probably the devil incarnate. But if you don't tell me where he is, he will be killed. I can protect him.' My eyes implore her. I need her to understand I'm no threat to Rogu3. Right now, I'm all that's standing between him and certain death.

'My great-uncle is with the Stuart Family,' she says. 'I know what it means to be a vampire. Alistair left about twenty minutes ago with a girl.'

'Natasha?' She bites her lip and nods. 'Did you see where they went?'

'No. But it was probably the grandstand. That's where...' She swallows. 'That's where the kids normally go. It's beside the field where we muster for fire drills.'

She's telling the truth. 'Thank you,' I say.

I join the last of the teenagers bustling out of the door at the far end of the corridor. Elbowing my way through, I make it outside. There's already a fire engine in attendance: those guys move fast when children are threatened. I ignore the fire fighters jogging towards the school and follow the rest of the crowd. Most are ambling slowly towards the open space at the back of the buildings. They're too used to fire drills to take them seriously. Familiarity doesn't just breed contempt; it encourages apathy, as well.

Several of the kids whistle in my direction as I speed past them; they're more excited by the sudden presence of a vampire than adults would be. I weave in and out of the loners, the couples holding hands and the groups of friends. I can see the grandstand now, shadowed in darkness at the far end of the school field. There's at least one group of standing figures, none of whom seem to be fazed by the alarm pealing out from the buildings. And, for now, none of them are being attacked by vigilante Agathos daemons.

I'm halfway across the field when I spot Rogu3. He's halfway up the grandstand steps and there's a girl next to him, but she's edging away as four other kids further down take what appears to be a threatening stance. High school bullies. Like I say, some things never change. I fly towards them and grab Rogu3's arm.

'We're leaving,' I tell him. 'Now.'

'Bo?' He seems stunned.

The largest boy moves up a step. 'Who's this, Alistair? Your mum?' The group cackles.

I whirl round, baring my fangs. The boy blanches. The girl next to Rogu3, who I presume is Natasha, lets out a small shriek. 'A vampire? You're friends with a vampire?'

Rogu3 gives me a half smile, tinged with relief. 'Are we friends, Bo? Or do I have to fight you?'

I realise he thinks I'm here because of his original plea. I start pulling him away. 'We're leaving now.' I look at Natasha and the group of boys staring at us. For goodness' sake. 'I need you to help me with a vital Family matter.'

The ringleader finds his voice. 'Are you a vampette now, Alistair? Do you let this *thing* suck your blood?'

I step towards him and he jumps about three feet in the air. 'Get lost, little boy.'

'You can't hurt me,' he says, although there's a tremor in his voice. 'You wouldn't dare.'

I raise my eyebrows. 'Do you want to test that theory?'

He spits on the ground. 'Forget it. He's not worth it anyway.' He turns to go but I let go of Rogu3's arm and grab his instead. 'Bother my friend again,' I whisper, 'and I'll come after you.' I stroke his cheek. He shudders. 'I promise.'

He yanks his arm away and runs off with his cronies at his side.

'Bo, that was fantastic. I can't believe you...' As Rogu3 speaks, there's a sudden flash. I leap towards him, knocking him down just as I hear the crack of a bullet.

'Get down!' I snarl at Natasha. She does what she's told, pressing herself flat. I twist my head, searching for the source of the shot. I scan the huddled groups of teenagers, several of whom have recognised the sound and flung themselves to the ground. The rest are joining them. There are whimpers and a few screams. But, despite the shadowed field, I can't see any damn daemons.

Two fire fighters come running from the school entrance. They press themselves against a wall, looking for the same people as me. The shooters have got some fucking balls thinking they can storm a school. Then I remember they've just destroyed half of the Agathos court. They don't care.

I keep my breathing calm and continue to search. Finally I

spot a flicker of movement on the opposite roof. We're directly in their line of sight. I tug at Rogu3. 'We need to move. We're going to keep low and head right, okay?'

He doesn't answer. Instead of repeating my instructions, however, I'm forced into silence as I see the familiar Michael-shaped silhouette appear at the building's edge. He must have heard the shot. He springs upwards, not bothering to hide his approach. Two heads appear and the unmistakable shape of a long-barrelled gun swings in his direction. The daemons squeeze off three shots in quick succession.

I hold my breath, my heart in my mouth, but I needn't have worried. Michael's a far older and more powerful vampire than I am. He flies up into the air like Batman on speed. That's a nifty trick, being fast enough to dodge a bullet; I wonder if he can teach it to me. He lands beside the two shooters before they can fire again. In the blink of an eye he grabs the gun, flinging it over the edge of the building. Then he lifts them both by the scruff of their necks and dangles them over the side. I can see his mouth moving but he's too far away for me to hear the words or lip read. Satisfied that he has things under control, I turn back to Rogu3.

'We're going...' My voice falters as I take in his pale sweating skin and dilated pupils. I realise I'm soaked in blood – and it's definitely not mine.

Frantically, I search for the wound. I pull up his shirt and stare at the mess of blood. No, no, no, no, no.

'Stay with me, Rogu3,' I say, pulling out my phone. 'I'm going to get an ambulance.'

His eyes catch mine and I can sense the life draining from him. His lips move but there's no sound. I stare down at the ragged flesh in his side. The bullet caught him at an angle and must have penetrated his stomach. There's no coming back from this.

I hear a loud thump from near the building, followed quickly by another. 'Michael!' I scream.

I press my palms to the wound, trying to staunch the blood as best as I can. I keep my eyes trained on Rogu3 but I see the movement in my peripheral vision as Michael scales back down the school building and runs towards me.

'It's okay. I've got a plan.' I whisper to Rogu3. I don't know whether he hears me or not.

The second Michael's foot lands on the concrete of the grandstand, I yell, 'What do I do? How do I turn him?'

He's by my side in a flash, leaning over Rogu3's body. I pull my hand away from the leaking, gaping hole long enough for Michael to see it. His voice is grim. 'I'm sorry.'

'Tell me what to do to turn him. If he's a vampire, he'll heal. There's no other way.'

'Bo.' Michael's voice is gentle. 'You can't.'

'Of course I fucking can! I drink from him, he drinks from me, then drinks from a human. I just need to make sure I do it right.'

'The chances of him surviving the turn are too slight. And you can't turn someone without their agreement.'

'You did it to me,' I snarl.

'That was different.' He puts his hand on my arm. 'Even if he wanted to be recruited and even if he had a good chance of surviving, it's against the law to turn a child.'

'He's fourteen. He's not a little kid.'

'But he is still a kid. You can't do it. The laws are in place for a reason. You can't just recruit someone because you feel like it. There's a process.'

I stare at him. Maybe there is but Michael doesn't know what I do. I've got the cure. I pick Rogu3 up in my arms.

'What are you doing?'

'If you won't help, then I'll take him to a hospital.'

His face is full of sympathy. 'The wound is too serious. He won't...'

'Get out of my way.'

He sighs deeply but he steps aside. Holding Rogu3's dying body as carefully as I can, I run. Again.

UNABLE TO USE the bike and hold Rogu3 at the same time, I smash the window of the first parked car I come to. I've never hotwired a vehicle before but I understand the mechanics of it. I'm about to put Rogu3 down so my hands are free when there's a jangle of metal and a set of keys lands next to me. I look up and realise it's the teacher.

'Take it. Get him help.'

Our eyes meet in understanding then she quickly turns away to deal with the rest of the still-cowering pupils. I open the passenger door and lay Rogu3 inside, feeling an odd sense of déjà vu. The last time I did this, it was for O'Shea. He made it out to the other side – but then he has stubborn daemon blood running through his veins. I rev the engine and drive off, calling the office as I do.

'You've reached New Order, how may I help you?' Matt's voice is chirpy.

'I need Connor,' I growl.

'Bo? Are you okay? There's a video of you at the Agathos court...'

'Find Connor and tell him to wait outside my flat.' I hang up, swerve round the corner and double check in the mirror that Rogu3 is still with me. He's still breathing. I put my foot down.

I don't bother to park the car, I just stop it in the street outside the office and retrieve Rogu3's limp body. Three protestors are still there, clearly shocked at what they see. No doubt they'll call the police, the press and even the army in to deal with me. I won't have much time.

We make it up the stairs to my flat. Connor is already there, his eyes wide.

'Stay there for now,' I command. I kick open the door and lay Rogu3 down on the sofa. I don't know if I'm doing this correctly but I don't have a choice. I brush away his air and, without even thinking, sink my fangs into his neck.

His blood tastes tainted. I can only think it's something to do with the weakening of his body. I suck for about as long as I think Michael did when he started to turn me. Then I bite my own wrist and offer it up to Rogu3's mouth.

'Drink,' I tell him. He doesn't respond. I press my wrist closer. 'Drink, damn you!'

For a heart-faltering moment, I think he won't do it. But, somehow, primeval instinct takes over and his mouth moves. There's no pain although the sensation is oddly uncomfortable. I count in my head and, when I reach twenty and can see Rogu3's eyes starting to roll back in his head as the unconscious coma of the turn affects him, I yell for Connor. He bursts in.

Connor's eyes fall on Rogu3 and the wound on my wrist. 'Bo, what have you done?' he whispers. 'You're not allowed...'

'Give him your blood.' I'm calm now but I know there's not much time left. 'Now, Connor.'

I don't know if this will work. Typically, after receiving a vampire's blood, a human falls unconscious for up to three days. That's not going to help me; I need to speed up the change, which means I need Rogu3 to sip from Connor before it's too late and he can no longer manage it.

Connor's indecision is clear. He knows the ramifications of what I'm doing. 'It's alright. This is my decision and I have a plan. You just need to trust me.'

He swallows. 'Okay.' He offers me his wrist. 'Here. You'll need to break the skin.'

My disgust at drinking blood has vanished. I waste no time in opening up Connor's vein and gently guiding it to Rogu3's mouth – but he's already out cold. I curse and slap his cheeks. He doesn't respond. I do it again and he jolts, eyelids flickering.

'Come on, Rogu3. Just a tiny bit. That's all it'll take.' I hope. 'You can do it, Alistair.'

Connor looks at me. 'He's drinking.'

I breathe a sigh of relief. As soon as I'm sure he's swallowed some blood, I tell Connor to leave. 'You don't want to be here for this.'

'But...'

'I mean it, Connor. Get out. In fact, go down to the office and get everyone out.'

'It's only Matt. The others have gone home already.'

'Good,' I say grimly. 'The two of you wait outside. If the police arrive, try to stall them.'

'The police?' He's alarmed.

'It's okay,' I soothe. 'You've not done anything wrong. I have.' I glance down at Rogu3 and smooth my hand over his damp hair. 'Go,' I repeat.

Connor leaves, closing the door behind him. I listen carefully until I hear his footsteps heading back down then I run to the fridge. I take out the chocolate, throw it aside and grab X's vial. Unstoppering it, I sniff. It still seems alright but I don't know if this will work. It might be too soon – Rogu3's not turned properly yet. I might be forcing a process that should take up to full lunar month into minutes. I can't risk waiting, however. This is Rogu3's only chance.

I look at his stomach wound: it's already healing. The combination of my blood, Connor's blood and the start of the turn is making fast work of knitting the flesh back together. I hold the vial next to his pale lips, praying there will be enough time. Rogu3 whimpers and I hush him gently.

'It won't be long now.' I stare at the clock on the wall, watching the second hand tick round. The seconds stretch into minutes. The police will be overstretched with what has happened at the Agathos court and the school. In fact, so much time passes that I'm starting to think they won't involve themselves because it's a vampire matter. When I finally hear the sirens, however, I know they're not going to let the opportunity slip to show the world just how monstrous bloodguzzlers are. I wait until the cars pull up outside, then I tilt back Rogu3's head.

'It's now or never,' I tell him. I let every last drop of X's blood slide into Rogu3's mouth. It gurgles in the back of the throat but he eventually swallows. When I'm sure he's taken it all, I stand up, brush myself down and head out to face the music.

CHAPTER 20

PLEA BARGAIN

I'm fully aware of the gravity of my situation but I'm still shocked at the number of people outside New Order. There are six panda cars in an arc around the teacher's abandoned vehicle. To the right, I count five photographers and eight journalists. To the left, the protestors' numbers have swelled. I guess they have their buddies on speed dial. Connor and Matt are facing them all. It's hard not to smile at the relief on their faces when I emerge.

'Hello,' I say feebly. There's an explosion of camera flashes.

One of the police officers steps forward. With a sinking feeling, I recognise Nicholls. Great. 'From hero to villain in less than three hours, Ms Blackman,' she tells me. 'That's rather impressive.'

I'm not sure where she's pulled the hero part from but I have no difficulty in understanding why she's called me a villain. I decide to cooperate openly. 'Take me in,' I say. 'Put the damn vampire handcuffs on me and lock me in a cell. I'll answer your questions.'

'Did you kill a fourteen-year-old boy, Bo?' one of the journalists shouts. I'm disturbed by his use of my first name.

'I should qualify that by saying I will answer the police's questions,' I say.

'Well, then,' Nicholls drawls, 'did you kill Alistair Jones?'

I meet her eyes. 'No. He was shot by a daemon. There are about two hundred witnesses who will attest to that fact.'

'Is he dead?'

I don't know. Every fibre of my being is praying that he's not. 'I don't think so,' I mumble. Apparently she wants my interrogation to take place in full view of the world. To add weight, a camera crew arrives and start videoing the action.

'Where is he?' someone calls.

An engine roars and Michael appears, straddling my bike. He turns it off and examines me coolly. I wonder what he's thinking.

A ripple of hushed whispers runs through the crowd at his arrival. Ignoring them, his expression alters and he fixes me with a viciously angry glare. 'Did you do it?' he demands.

Nicholls whips her head round to face him. 'Do what? What did she do?'

'Bo,' he says, not moving an inch, 'you know I can't help you if you did. You were going to take him to a hospital.'

I straighten my shoulders. 'There wasn't time.'

'Send a team inside,' Nicholls mutters.

Several police officers peel off and, giving me a wide berth, head towards the entrance. Nicholls steps forward. I have to give the policewoman her due – she's not intimidated in the slightest by me or Michael. A set of shiny cuffs dangles from her hands. 'Turn round,' she tells me.

'Wait!' There's a quiet voice from behind.

Everyone freezes. I slowly turn and see Rogu3 leaning weakly against the door frame. His face is pale but he's upright and he obviously made it down the stairs under his own steam.

I rush forward to help him. As soon as I get close, I scan him carefully. His eyes look normal and there's nothing to suggest he's a bloodguzzler. His t-shirt is still soaked in blood and, when I look down, he gives me a small nod. 'It's fine,' he says. 'I'll still need stitches, but it's fine.'

In a shaky voice, he says loudly, 'I was shot. Bo helped me.' He smiles. 'I'm lucky it was only a flesh wound. Thank you all for your concern but I really should be getting home. My parents will be splenetic.'

I notice a couple of the journalists exchanging glances. One of them asks, 'What does splenetic mean?'

I stifle my smile, reach over and give Rogu3 a tight hug. He winces and I immediately withdraw but he pats my shoulder in reassurance. 'I'm okay, Bo.' He leans towards me and whispers, 'I know what you did and I'm grateful.'

I stiffen. How much does he know? X killed O'Connell because I told him the truth about the cure. My relief changes quickly to hot, tense worry.

'We'll get you to hospital and then home, Alistair,' Nicholls says briskly, throwing me a look that suggests she's not finished with me yet. She takes him gently by the arm and guides him towards a police car.

'Don't ever call me that again, will you?' Rogu3 mutters as he passes.

I flash him a quick grin. Then my gaze falls on Michael, who is staring at me with an expression as cold as granite. I look away hastily.

One of the protestors shakes his head. 'He was unconscious and dripping with blood. She's done something. Turned him into some kind of...'

'Shut up,' Nicholls tells him. She raises her eyebrows at me. 'I appreciate it has been a long night for you, Ms Blackman. We do have a number of questions, however, about both the boy and the courthouse.'

'Agathos daemons,' I blurt out. 'There may still be some around. They obviously have resources. You need to put a guard on Ro—, I mean Alistair. And Nisha Patel, Devlin O'Shea. Probably Harry D'Argneau too.' I remember he wasn't at the courthouse when the attack happened. 'Wait! Harry! He could be...'

'He's fine. We've spoken to him.'

I sag in relief, pointedly ignoring Michael's dark look. 'The danger's not over. They could still attack again.'

Several people look over their shoulder as if an attack is imminent. For all I know, it could be. Nicholls jerks her head towards the door and I nod. We walk inside, away from curious ears.

'We've tracked the terrorists to a flat in Camden,' she informs me. 'About ten minutes after attack on the school was over, a helicopter took off from that area. There was no recorded flight plan but we tracked it to a small airfield near Brighton. They're currently in the air and apparently on their way to Venezuela. The ones who are still alive.'

'No extradition treaty.'

Her mouth turns down. 'Indeed.'

'Are you sure that's all of them?'

'No. But we have enough CCTV footage and evidence from the flat to piece the story together fairly quickly. We'll know within the next twenty-four hours.'

'They're not terrorists,' I tell her.

'They bombed the Agathos court and invaded a school. They're certainly spreading terror.'

I shake my head. 'No, that's not their motive. It's to do with Tobias Renfrew.'

'I already heard that theory.' She sniffs.

'You don't believe it?'

She gazes at me speculatively. 'These days I don't know what to believe. You're free from any charges, Ms Blackman, although I would like to talk you in more detail at the station.'

'I can come by after dark tomorrow.'

'That will suffice. And there are guards in place for most of the potential targets.'

'Most?'

She quirks an eyebrow. 'Would you like one too?'

'Uh, no, I'm good.'

'I thought you'd say that.'

'We can't let them get away with this,' I say, as much to myself as to her.

'We won't. I guarantee it.' To my surprise, she holds out her hand. I shake it.

'Why are you being so nice all of a sudden?' I ask her suspiciously.

'I wouldn't want to get on the bad side of the Red Angel.'

I blink. 'The what?'

She smirks. 'I'll see you tomorrow, Ms Blackman.' Nicholls pivots and leaves. I watch from the open doorway as she gestures at the other police officers and they all get into their cars and depart.

Matt and Connor bounce up. 'That was hairy!' Connor says. Despite his light tone, he's obviously unsettled by the events upstairs. I want to reassure him but Michael's dark figure looms behind them.

'A word, Bo?'

I nod and turn, leading him upstairs to the flat. The sofa is still soaked in Rogu3's blood. He eyes it silently for a moment and then looks at me. 'What happened?' he asks quietly.

I lick my lips. 'The wound wasn't as bad as we thought.'

His expression is derisive. 'Don't treat me like an idiot. That boy was dying. What did you do?'

I glance down at my feet, realising in panic that the vial is lying on the floor. Attempting to look natural, I sidle towards it and kick it under the sofa. 'I helped him,' I say. 'He's alive. That's what counts, right?'

Michael glowers. 'Tell me.'

I stop dancing round the truth. 'I can't. I'd like to but I really, really can't. Suffice it to say it won't happen again.' That vial was my one and only shot. X made it very clear there would be no more.

Michael leans forward. 'You told me you don't trust me so I answered your questions, Bo. I told you the truth about who I was. Now it seems that you're the one who's not trustworthy.'

I gaze at him helplessly. 'I'm sorry. I just can't tell you.' If I do, I add to myself, X will rip out your heart. I think worriedly about how much Rogu3 and Connor know. X may still take umbrage at my actions.

Michael's face shutters. 'So be it,' he growls. He stalks out. For a moment, I'm tempted to call him back, to do or say anything to make him understand. He wouldn't understand, though. And I have no idea what I'd say.

I sit on the arm of the sofa, away from the damp blood-stains, and rub my forehead. I thought I'd had some bad days in the past but this night puts them in the shade. It's a miracle there weren't more deaths. And in that respect, I guess it's been a success.

I check my watch. To ensure my friends' safety, there's one more thing I have to do. I have time.

❀

I PARK outside X's plush apartment building. The windows are dark and it's impossible to tell whether anyone is inside. I don't even know if X really lives here – it didn't look lived in when I came here before. I run my hands nervously through my hair, get off the bike and walk up to the gleaming red door. The paintwork is so shiny, it looks like it's still wet. I can't see a doorbell or knocker so I raise my fist to knock. The door opens before my knuckles scrape the surface. I peer inside. There's no one there.

Pulling back my shoulders, I step inside and walk up the stairs. When I round the corner to X's living quarters, I wonder whether I've made a mistake. The room was sparse before, but at least it had some furniture. Now I'm confronted with a vast empty space. If it weren't for the large leather chair in the centre, and the pair of feet poking out from underneath, I'd turn round again and leave.

I hear X's deep, unmistakable voice. 'Ms Blackman. I've been expecting you.'

He sounds like a Bond villain. That's disturbing, considering I'd pegged Medici as a wannabe Bond. When the chair swivels round, I'm half-expecting to see a fluffy white cat in X's lap. It is just him, however. He's in daemon form and his tattoos swirl and shift across his skin. He's doing nothing more than sitting in a chair but he still exudes absolute danger. His black eyes don't help.

'Mr X.' I feel like I should curtsey or something.

'It's just X.' His mouth curves into the semblance of a smile. 'Although it's not hard to understand why you feel the need to be polite.'

'How are you?' I ask unnecessarily.

His smile broadens. 'Fabulous.'

I twist my fingers together. 'Thank you for the information about Miller's other victims.'

'Miller?'

'Terence Miller. The serial killer-slash-rapist.'

'Ah.' He seems amused. I can't for the life of me think why.

I cut to the chase. 'You killed O'Connell.'

'I rather think you wanted me to.'

'No,' I say hastily.

He laughs. 'And now you're here to beg for clemency for your little friends.'

'I didn't tell them!' I burst out. 'They don't know about your blood.'

'The boy knows you turned him yet he remains human. The one you drink from knows that also. As for Michael Montserrat, well,' X purrs, 'he suspects.' He holds up three fingers. 'One, two, three, little Bo. I made it very clear what would happen if you let the truth slip. You knew it with O'Connell. You know it now.'

'But I didn't let the truth slip! They don't actually *know* anything. They don't know about the vial. They don't know about you. I've not mentioned Kakos daemons to anyone.' I'm desperate. 'I've not broken the terms of our agreement.'

He stands up. 'Actually, you have. The blood was for you but you gave it to another. Some might say it was a selfless act.' He bares his teeth. 'But it'll all be for naught if I kill the boy now.'

'You're stronger than I am,' I begin.

'I'm stronger than everyone.'

I ignore him. 'You're flexing your muscles. You enjoy playing with me like I'm some kind of toy. So if you want to punish someone, then punish me. They don't suspect a Kakos daemon is involved. Leave them alone.'

His twisting tattoos coalesce, their hard edges blurring. 'You forget I can read your mind,' he says. 'You might sound tough but I can feel your terror.'

'Do you get off on it?' I snarl.

X laughs again. 'I'm not a monster. Besides, I have treated you more than fairly. You're here because you know I have cause to visit them.' The way he purrs over the word 'visit' makes my stomach twist. 'Visit,' he repeats. 'It's not a scary word.' His eyes gleam.

'Please, X,' I whisper.

'Pretty please with a cherry on top?' He licks his lips slowly. 'And whipped cream?'

I stare at him mutely. He walks towards me, reaching out with one long index finger and trailing it down my cheek. I try not to flinch but my skin tingles from his touch.

'I wonder what it would take...' he murmurs, not finishing his sentence. He gives himself a little shake. 'Very well then. As your friends do not know the truth, I shall give them a pass. In return for a small favour.'

I'm too wary to feel relief. 'What?'

X shrugs. 'I don't know yet. I'll have to think it over.'

'You can't do that,' I assert. 'You can't demand some unnamed favour. It could be anything.' How stupid does he think I am?

'Ms Blackman, you're stupid enough to try and negotiate for mercy with a Kakos daemon.' He raises his eyebrows. 'It's not something we're generally known for.'

'Didn't you tell me you were turning over a new leaf? Joining normal society?'

'Normal society? You mean where women are abducted in broad daylight, brutally raped and then killed? Or where daemons try to shoot children because of hacked-off ears? That kind of normal society?' I can't answer him. He folds his arms. 'Those are my terms. A favour. To be fulfilled in the time and manner of my choosing. Take it or leave it.'

He knows I have no choice. Without bothering to speak, I think the words, enunciating them in my mind. Fine. You prick.

He winces. 'There's no need to shout. And I think I preferred Mr X.' He gestures at the door. 'You may leave,' he says. Then, in an appallingly bad Russian accent, 'Goodbye, Mr Bond.'

You got what you came for, Bo, I tell myself. Get out while you still can. I turn and leave, ignoring X's laughter echoing behind me.

CHAPTER 21

TWO

Connor holds out his wrist. I look at it then at his face. 'Would you mind if I tried your neck?' I ask.

There's a flash of obvious delight. 'Really? You think you can manage it?'

'Sure,' I say, mustering as much confidence as I can. Until now, I've had the promise of a cure to hang onto. I may not have been sure I was going to take it but its potential supported everything I did. I knew that there was a way out from vampirism and I could go back to being normal. But I've given that exit strategy away to Rogu3 and I'm not going to feel regret about it. What's done is done. I need to work harder on self-acceptance.

Connor stretches his head to one side to provide me with easier access to his jugular. By now, I know that drinking blood is more a case of mind over matter. When I drank from Rogu3 I didn't hesitate because he would have died if I'd been squeamish. So I let my fangs grow, move over and do what needs to be done. I wipe my mouth when I'm finished.

'Same time tomorrow?' Connor asks.

'Actually,' I demur, 'I'm going to try someone different.'

Even with the hatred towards vampires that's swirling around the country at the moment, there are still plenty of willing vampettes around.

An expression of hurt crosses his face. 'You don't need me any more?'

'Connor, I'll always need you,' I reassure him. 'But you need your strength. I'm told the phone has been ringing off the hook at New Order.'

He grins. 'Have you seen the internet and what they're saying about you?'

I shake my head, puzzled. He gestures at the computer in the corner. 'Look.'

THE RED ANGEL OF MERCY

The country watched aghast last night as shocking events unfolded at the Agathos Court. Terrorists stormed the building because, it's been reported by sources close to the scene, they were attempting to retrieve a severed ear belonging to Tobias Renfrew, the eccentric billionaire who has been missing for over fifty years.

What the daemon terrorists hadn't counted on was Bo Blackman, a vampire who bravely abandoned the Montserrat Family to strike out on her own. Video footage has emerged of Blackman saving one woman before plunging back into the fiery depths to help others.

Her heroic actions weren't confined to the Agathos Court. She hightailed it next to Banbury School, where she confronted the daemons again, dispatching two of the killers.

Not only is Blackman brave enough to abandon the might of a Family, but she is also a true heroine for saving the lives of innocent victims. 'She's an angel,' stated Margaret Morrison, the receptionist at the Agathos Court.

I feel faintly nauseous – and it's not from Connor's blood. There's even a picture to go with the article: I'm silhouetted against the glow of the fire and the red lights of the emergency vehicles. Most of my face is in shadow but there's a grim set to my mouth. I look less like an angel and more like a rampaging idiot.

'I didn't kill those daemons,' I protest. 'Michael did. And I have serious doubts that Meg called me a sodding angel.' I shake my head. 'They've got it all wrong.'

'The phone's been ringing because people want to talk to you,' Connor says. 'We wanted to make vampires look better and you've done that. The video of you coming out of the court-house with that woman is everywhere.'

'But,' I point out, 'they're making too much of the fact that I left the Montserrat Family. Like I don't agree with other vampires.' I screw up my face. 'No, I don't think this is good at all.'

'I am pleased you spotted that,' my grandfather says, appearing in the doorway. 'We need to be very careful how we handle this. The last thing we need is for you to become the poster child for vampires striking out on their own because the Families are evil.'

'I don't want to be any kind of bloody poster child,' I grimace.

'You'll need to agree to a few interviews,' my grandfather continues, as if he hasn't heard me. 'I'm thinking breakfast tele-vision. Maybe one of the better broadsheets as well.'

'I'm not doing that!' I protest.

'You have to, my dear. Good press can turn on a penny. We need to make this as positive as we possibly can, especially when it comes to the Families.' I grit my teeth. This is ridicu-lous. Sensing my thoughts, my grandfather looks at me sternly. 'New Order is all about better PR. This is the perfect opportunity. Besides, if nothing else, the statement from that despicable man Miller has been completely buried. It may emerge at a later date so we need to be on guard but, if we handle this correctly, we might just turn the tide of public opinion.'

I pull out the sheet of crumpled paper which O'Shea gave to me and wave it around. 'These daemons are still on the loose! Michael might have killed a few of them but we still don't know who's behind this or if they're going to strike again.'

'The police are convinced that the perpetrators have fled the country. Negotiations are under way with the Venezuelan government but I don't hold out much hope.'

I shake my head. 'They have too many resources at their disposal. I find it hard to believe the ringleaders have simply gone.'

'They attacked the heart of the Agathos justice system. And they failed. They won't want to be anywhere near here for a very long time. Terrorists are not taken lightly.'

'But I don't think they are terrorists. Why would terrorists be so interested in some fake ear? And who the hell does the ear belong to, if not Tobias Renfrew?'

'Not every mystery can be solved, Bo.'

I ball my fists in frustration. 'I promised Nicholls I'd meet her to make a statement and answer her questions. I've got a few sodding questions of my own. Maybe she can answer them.'

'You're going to be chasing your tail.'

I sniff. 'At least I'll be chasing something.'

I MARCH into the police station. I don't care where in the world they are, I'm not ready to let the people who almost killed Rogu3 get away with it. I've barely given my name to the desk sergeant when Foxworthy appears. If anything, he looks worse than the last time I saw him. Given his case with Miller should have been wrapped up, I'm surprised at his pallor.

'Hey,' I say. 'I'm here to see Nicholls. Are you looking for the daemons too?'

'No. They've gone to Venezuela; there's nothing we can do. It's up to the government to sort it out.'

I stare at him. 'After what they did? Foxworthy, we can't just let crooks get on a plane! We need to go after them!'

'It's not my call. Not everything is conducted at our level, Blackman. Sometimes you need to let the experts take charge.'

'It's been less than twenty-four hours. I'm not dropping this. Where's Nicholls anyway?'

'She said you can come in another time. There's no rush for the statement now we know for sure that they've absconded.'

'That's sodding ridiculous! I came all this way to talk to her.' My eyes narrow. 'I thought we were getting along better now. Instead you have me running around the city pointlessly.'

He looks at me. There's something dark behind his eyes that makes me pause. 'The dog's going to be okay,' he says. 'The vet called earlier.'

'Kimchi?' Finally there's some good news. 'That's fantastic!'

'Once he's well enough, he'll be transferred to Battersea Dogs' Home.'

I frown. I may have something to say about that. I realise the darkness is still there in Foxworthy's eyes. 'It's not Kimchi that's bothering you, is it?'

Foxworthy raises his eyes to the ceiling and presses his lips together. 'Nicholls has agreed to question you later because I thought you'd want to come with me.'

'I don't understand,' I'm starting to get a bad feeling in the pit of my stomach. 'Come with you where?' He sighs. 'Foxworthy, what is it?'

'We've found another body,' he says.

I scan his face. 'What do you mean?'

'A woman aged twenty-one. She's been identified as Fiona Lane, a magic arts student at St. Martin's. She's been raped and killed. Her body is at a disused quarry on the edge of the city.'

Blood drains from my face. 'No. It can't be…'

Foxworthy's eyes are haunted. 'Two wooden stakes were driven through the palms of her hands.'

WE STAND several feet away from the spread-eagled corpse. Eventually I tear my eyes away, turning so I don't have to look at her any more. 'The bodies were in Miller's garden. Plus, Miller fit Corinne's description. This has to be a copycat.'

'That would make sense,' Foxworthy agrees in a defeated tone, 'except we didn't release the part about the stakes.'

I search around desperately for an answer. 'I'm sure there are plenty of people who know about that detail. Lots of people were involved in the initial investigation.'

'I hope you're not suggesting a law enforcement officer is responsible for this.'

My shoulders slump. 'Was Miller the wrong man? Did he have a friend who borrowed his garden? Was he innocent after all?' It sounds beyond implausible. At this stage, however, confronted with the horror of what was once Fiona Lane, I'm prepared to believe anything.

'I don't think that can be true.' The inspector looks at me patiently.

I realise he's waiting for me to connect the dots. I glance around, trying to clear my mind and focus my thoughts. 'Corinne said that when she first regained consciousness her attacker was wearing a balaclava. Later he wasn't. Maybe that's because there were two of them and one – obviously not Miller

– was concerned about not revealing his identity. Plus, we're now in a quarry in the middle of sodding nowhere. All the other victims, even the early ones, were abducted or attacked in busy public places.'

Foxworthy nods. 'We've established that Fiona Lane was visiting her boyfriend. He lives in a house not far from here. She was supposed to arrive this morning on the early bus. It's a fifteen-minute walk from the bus stop to his house, I'll show you the route later. It's pretty much deserted; there are some houses scattered around but very few people passing. When she didn't show, he assumed she got caught up with friends or slept in. It's only because the foreman made a routine visit to check the safety barriers around the quarry that she was discovered at all.'

'It's a complete departure from his previous killings.' I take another look at the body. 'She's not as bruised and battered as Corinne was either.'

'No,' Foxworthy agrees.

'It never made sense that Miller could do what he did when he was only a few metres away from so many passersby. But if he had an accomplice...'

'...it would make it a hell of a lot easier.'

I press the base of my hands into my eyes until it hurts. 'There are two of them. Miller had a fucking companion.'

'Yeah. And he's obviously not ready to stop killing.'

'It's not over,' I whisper. I cast my eyes around the high, craggy walls of the quarry. It feels like I'm stuck in some hell pit, surrounded by suffocating darkness. High above, the moving light of a plane crosses the sky. My eyes track it until it disappears. 'We need to go back to Corinne.'

Foxworthy squeezes my arm. 'We'll catch him, Bo.'

I look at him balefully. 'Promise?'

He doesn't answer. We start to walk away, the hard dirt

crunching under our feet. Up above, at the lip of the quarry, I see the silhouette of a man struggling with two others.

'I want to see her!' he yells. 'I want see Fiona!'

'Her boyfriend?' I ask quietly. Foxworthy nods. 'Why don't you let him down?'

'Because then the last thing he'll remember is his girlfriend smeared in blood and pinned to the ground. He won't remember the times they laughed or made love or what she looked like when the sun caught her hair. He'll just remember her sightless eyes and her broken body.'

Fiona's boyfriend starts sobbing and the sound echoes around the quarry. I might be able to close my eyes but I can't close my ears. His grief and anguish pierce my chest.

'We jumped to conclusions,' I mutter. 'If we'd thought about it more, we might have realised there were two of them. Fiona Lane could still be alive.'

Foxworthy is more pragmatic. 'There wasn't any evidence to suggest that. And it's incredibly rare for killers to work in pairs.'

I nod slowly. 'How would they meet? We already know Miller was a loner.'

'We're going back through his life. There has to be some kind of clue.'

I mull it over. It's not as if you'd get chatting to someone and casually reveal that you're on your way to do a spot of rape and murder. Even using the internet to find a serial-killer buddy seems unlikely.

'They had to know each other very well, and probably from a very young age. It's the only thing that makes sense.' My foot slips on a section of scree and I pause to regain my balance. 'Did anything come from looking at the first victim?'

'There was little to go on. Her family cleared out all her

belongings last year. We tracked down some friends but,' he shrugs, 'they had little to say.'

'Can you give me her details?'

Foxworthy doesn't seem too happy. 'We checked her out. You may not have a very high opinion of the police but we know what we're doing. Your buddy Arzo came along too. He agreed with us.'

'I think the police do a great job. I just want to get a feel for her myself.'

'The family may not want to talk to a bloodguzzler,' he warns.

'Nothing new there.'

'I'll email you with what we have when I get back to the station. Maybe the Red Angel can shed some new light on the situation.'

'Piss off.'

CHAPTER 22

THE TREE

It's nice to be trusted. This time Foxworthy lets me walk unfettered into Corinne Matheson's room. The guard is no longer in attendance outside, no doubt because it seemed pointless after we apparently got our man. That's not the case any more.

'Shouldn't there be someone on the door?'

Foxworthy frowns. 'There should be.' He pulls out his phone, jabs in a number and mutters angrily before hanging up and looking at me. 'They'll be here soon.'

Corinne is lying flat on her back with her eyes closed. Her eyes are puffy; now that her bruises are healing, she looks even worse than before. Her face is a horrifying mishmash of colours, from dark purple to blue to tinges of fading yellow. Her bandaged hands lie motionless on her stomach. The dressings look fresh but blood is starting to seep through one of them. I wince. That can't be good. Still, there's a gentle snore indicating that at least Corinne is getting some rest. A nurse hovering near her bed wags a warning finger in our direction. I nod although I'm wishing I could shake her awake.

I pull up a chair and settle down. It's the middle of the

night; Corinne could be out for hours. The nurse changes the bag on Corinne's IV line and departs.

'This could take all night,' I hiss at Foxworthy. 'We might not have time to spare.'

He looks outside the door for a second. 'The nurse has gone. We can try waking her.'

Corinne's face is peaceful. I gnaw on my bottom lip. 'It wouldn't be fair. She needs as much sleep as she can get. We can come back in the morning.'

'In daylight?'

'Before. It won't get light until just before eight.' I look him up and down. 'You're dead on your feet. You should go home and rest.'

I can tell from the way his spine stiffens that he doesn't think much of my suggestion but he'll be no good to anyone if he's too tired to function.

'What will you do?'

'I'll wait here for an hour or two in case she wakes up then I'll head out either to Miller's house of hell, or to see what I can dig up about the other victims. It's night time.' I give a self-deprecating grin. 'I do my best work when the sun is down.'

Corinne moans softly in her sleep and both of us whip round. Her hands jerk and one leg kicks. I place a hand on her forehead to soothe her. She relaxes slightly and snores again.

'We can't wake her,' I reiterate, glancing at Foxworthy's exhausted face.

He nods reluctantly and checks his watch. 'I'll be back before seven.'

'Take longer if you need it. Without proper rest, you'll be useless.'

'I'm not taking advice from a damned bloodguzzler!'

I wink. He rolls his eyes, straightens his posture and strides out of the room as if to prove that he's not as weary as I think. I smile after him. We have more in common than we realised.

I stand up and stretch, looking around the room. Other than a bunch of flowers on the table near Corinne's head, it's exactly the same as the last time as I was here. I search around for a card, wondering who sent them. There's nothing there. The flowers can't be more than a couple of days old but they're already looking worse for wear. A large daisy droops dejectedly; I reach out and try to prop it back up but only succeed in knocking off several petals. I give up and lean back in my chair, watching Corinne's chest steadily rise and fall.

After a while, my phone buzzes. I frown at the screen: it's the details of Joy Palazzi, the first identified victim. Foxworthy. He must have taken a detour via the station before going home. Much as I appreciate the information, the man just doesn't know when to take a break. I juggle the phone from hand to hand while I decide whether to stay with Corinne or venture out. Then there's a knock on the door and I almost drop the damned thing.

It's another nurse. He looks at me nervously. 'You're the one who was on the news.'

I shove the phone away. 'Yes.' Come on, Bo, I urge myself. Be nice to the human. I stand up and stick out my hand. The nurse can decide whether to lean over and shake it; if I go near him, he'll take fright and run a mile.

Instead of shaking my hand, he places something in it. I look down in surprise. It's a blood bag. 'I thought you might be hungry,' he whispers.

Words fail me and I gape at him like an idiot.

'She doesn't have anything to do with those daemons you're after, does she?'

I shake my head, still holding the blood. 'No. And you don't have to give me this. I'm not going to attack anyone and drink their blood. Even a new vampire like me has self-control.'

The nurse looks alarmed. 'Oh! No, I didn't think you would. I just thought, you know, that maybe you'd need the energy...' His voice trails off and he shuffles his feet. Maybe my newfound status as a heroine has some benefits after all.

I thrust the bag back at him. 'You guys probably need this more than I do,' I say, trying to be kind.

'We had a lot of donors after the Agathos attack. There's plenty going spare.'

'Please. I insist.'

He swallows and takes it back. 'Okay.' I try to ignore his worried look as he wonders whether he's offended me.

'But thank you,' I tell him. 'It was a really lovely thought.'

He smiles. He's really a sweet guy. If I was human... I push the thought away.

'Will you take this instead?' he asks, anxiously. As well as the blood, he's holding a badge that says 'I love London General'.

'Are you sure?' I ask doubtfully. 'If people think you have vampires roaming the corridors wearing the hospital's seal of approval, it may not do you any favours.'

He grins. 'But you're not just *any* vampire. You're the Red Angel.'

I smile weakly and take it, pinning it to my t-shirt. It hangs lopsidedly. I guess I can remove it as soon as I leave.

'She probably won't wake for a while, you know,' the nurse says. 'We have her on strong painkillers.'

I look at Corinne. As if in response to his words, she moans again. I nod. 'I might come back later.'

'My shift doesn't finish for another six hours. If I'm still here when you return, I can get you some more blood then.'

I feel a rush of warmth for him. 'Thank you.'

'You're welcome.' He blushes slightly and leaves.

I pat Corinne's arm. 'I'll be back,' I promise her as another face looks into the room. I give her new guard a businesslike nod and head out after the nurse.

~

MATT MEETS me in the quiet cul-de-sac where Joy Palazzi grew up. It's sickeningly close to both the park where she was attacked and the street where she was run over. I reflect on the irony of her first name. Regardless of what her formative years were like, no one would suggest her life was joyful, not when it was cut short so brutally.

I stare up and down the street. It's a typical, middle-class suburban area. The gardens are well-kept, the cars are big and shiny and Neighbourhood Watch signs abound.

'What are we doing here?' Matt asks loudly.

I hush him. It is already after midnight and the residents are clearly all in bed and asleep. Red Angel or not, I doubt they'd take too kindly to being woken up by a vampire, even if I have a good reason to be here.

'I just want to look around.' I point to the nearest house. 'That's where Joy lived.'

He looks it over. 'Nice.'

At first glance, he's right. The detached house is a good size with a pretty red-brick exterior and large bay windows. It's south facing so the sun must stream in during the day. There's an apple tree in the garden and a path leading towards the back. All in all, a good place to grow up in.

On closer inspection, things aren't quite so rosy. There's a rusting lawnmower hidden by the trunk of the tree. The grass has grown up around it. There are clumps of weeds all over the lawn. The front door, which was once probably very grand, now has peeling paint. All the curtains are drawn – and they look as if they've seen better days. I think of Mrs Lamb. Terence Miller and his accomplice are responsible for the destruction of so many lives.

I walk to the neighbouring house. This garden is better kept. I can see ornaments in the window sill and I guess that an older couple live here. Miller was in his late twenties; I'm convinced his murdering buddy will be about the same age. I walk from house to house, working out what I can about the occupants. I have no way of knowing whether these people were around when Joy was attacked but the housing market has been iffy, to say the least, over recent years so maybe they were. I decide that the family across the road has small children and several pets and mentally cross them out. Another one seems to belong to an elderly lady.

Matt, bored with my wandering, sits on a garden swing and starts to hum. I ignore him and keep searching. I know I'm not going to find a house with a sign in it saying 'Hi! I'm your friendly local serial killer!', but in my bones I'm certain that Miller's accomplice came from this area. Maybe he saw Joy going to school every day. Maybe he went to school with her.

'Matt!' I hiss. He's staring out over the rooftops and doesn't hear me. I try again. 'Matt!'

He blinks then gives me a lazy smile and ambles over. 'Yeah?'

'Did you find a list of addresses for Miller?'

'Yes.'

I wait impatiently. Somewhat flummoxed, he gazes at me vacantly.

'Well? Did he live anywhere near here?'

Matt taps his mouth, thinking. 'No. But there were a few gaps when he was in temporary accommodation.'

Damn. I'm still convinced that Miller and the prick who is

still at large have known each other for years and that one of them at least knew Joy in person. Foxworthy said that Miller had been bounced around different foster homes. Granted, none of them were near here but...

'Do you think we could get one of those?' Matt asks suddenly.

'A swing?' Maybe bringing along my fellow vampire recruit was a mistake. Matt often has insights to share but right now he seems more preoccupied with children's playthings than anything else.

'No, silly. A tree house.'

I sigh, exasperated. 'Matt, we work in the centre of London. There aren't any suitable trees.'

'I live at the Montserrat mansion,' he reminds. 'There are lots of good trees in that garden. You know that. You've climbed some of them.'

I roll my eyes. 'Come on. This is a waste of time.' I start back to the motorbike. Maybe Miller's house will yield more secrets.

'I particularly like the big one in the corner,' Matt continues. 'Do you know, if you climb to the top of it you can see right into the girls' bedrooms?'

I stop. 'What did you say?'

Matt's eyes dart from side to side. 'I ... er ... nothing! I didn't mean to do it! Well, I did but I didn't really see anything. Bo, I'm sorry.' He drops his head in shame.

'Where's the tree house, Matt? The one you were talking about before.'

Without looking up, he points a finger. I follow it, eventually spotting the rickety planks. They're so well concealed by foliage that I'd never have noticed them.

'Come on,' I breathe. I make a beeline for it.

I'm forced to scale several garden fences. In the last one, a dog starts barking. I'm torn between willing it to shut up and thinking of poor Kimchi. Matt, following at my heels, opens his mouth. With a sudden premonition, I clamp my hand over it. 'No barking back at the dog,' I tell him sternly. He pouts.

Leaping over the last fence, I see a strip of land between two rows of back gardens that face each other. A small stream runs down the middle and trees, some only just starting to shed their leaves with the onset of autumn, line the way. I check my bearings then pick my way down, twigs snapping under my feet. Matt jumps into the water and splashes along next to me.

'There's a rope swing,' he says, awestruck.

I see that he's right. It's frayed and old; it'd be a miracle if it could bear anyone's weight these days, even a child's. I hold Matt back, frowning at him.

'Can't I just have a little go?'

'No, you'll end up falling. It's been here too long.'

I'm surprised it's not been cut down. Then again, considering the undergrowth and lack of recent trails, this area has probably been off limits to local children for years. Probably since Joy's abduction. Besides, who needs rope swings and tree houses when you've got Playstations and XBoxes?

I continue to the tree in question. It's a large imposing oak with branches that extend far across the night sky. The tree house is several feet up. I stare at it doubtfully, not sure it'll hold my weight, then I walk round the trunk, judging its girth. At one side, although the soil is heavily compacted, the ground feels unusually uneven. I press it with my foot. Something's not right.

Bending down, I scrape away the loose soil. Someone has been digging here. Not recently, but then I'm not looking for recent.

I glance up at Matt and his muscle-bound body. 'You're too heavy to climb up. See if you can dig out this earth. There might be something there.'

Matt looks disappointed but nods. I skirt back to the tree-house opening. If there was a ladder here it's long gone, so I jump upwards, pulling myself onto the nearest branch. It snaps under my weight and I'm forced to leap back to the trunk, my arms and legs encircling it as if I'm giving it a big hug. I shimmy upwards like an island dweller on the hunt for coconuts – except that this is no pretty palm tree. The bark is damp and rotting in places and it's hard for my short arms and legs to grip round it. With a sloppy technique, I push up as quickly as possible then squeeze into a gap between the tree house and the actual tree. I stand up, wary of the creaking, unsteady planks under my feet. One big storm and this entire structure will tumble down.

The moon leaks in from the gaps in the roof, illuminating the small area. I step forward gingerly to peer out of the window-shaped hole at the front. The tree house protests loudly. Gritting my teeth, I edge over: from here to Joy Palazzi's house, there's a clear line of sight. At least there would be, if there wasn't an overhanging branch in front of me. I wonder if she ever came here.

Twisting back, I double-check I'm not missing anything. There's a large spider's web in the corner and a few empty soda cans. I can't see anything else other than graffiti etched on the flimsy walls: a lopsided love heart; a testament to the long since forgotten boy band, Bros, and an odd symbol. I trace my fingers over it. It's like two Ws flipped onto their sides and linked at the bottom. It might be from a couple of teenage witches. I take a snapshot on my phone and head back down.

Matt is on his knees, covered in dirt and staring sadly at the hole he's created.

'What is it?'

His bottom lip judders. 'Animals. It's like a pet cemetery.

The kids who played here must have buried their pets.' He sniffs.

I look at the collection of tiny skeletons that he's unearthed. I bend down and pick one up. The skull is detached and the bones are notched all the way along as if something has gnawed at them. Or tortured them, pre-mortem. Deciding I need to get Foxworthy onto this so he can send some forensic specialists, I back away.

'We should go, Matt.'

'Shall I take these?' He points at the yellowing bones.

'No. Don't disturb them any further.'

Silently, we walk back the way we came. It's not far but it's a relief when we re-enter the first back garden – it feels like a return to civilisation.

'Bo?'

'Yes, Matt?'

'I don't think I want a tree house after all.'

I fervently agree.

It's almost four o'clock by the time I get back to the hospital, leaving Matt to make his own way back to New Order. He has strict instructions to find the names of all the residents of Joy's neighbourhood for the last five years. The revelation that there is a second killer on the loose may have surprised me but we're now hot on his heels. We're closing in on him and I won't let Medici get to this one first. He's all mine.

The hospital is quiet. I pass a few tired-looking doctors and dimly lit rooms where patients are struggling to get through the night. Other than that, the place is deserted. There's no sign of the friendly nurse from earlier. He probably has night rounds to complete.

I pad towards Corinne's room, lost in thought about a pair of boys who met on a suburban estate and escalated from killing small animals to murdering both human and triber women.

At first, I think nothing of it when I hear the footsteps behind me. It's not until I start paying attention that I realise something is wrong. They are fast paced and catching up on me – but they also sound measured, cautious. Without turning round, I sniff the air. Unfortunately, the strong antiseptic scent of the hospital masks everything else. Just turn around, Bo, I tell myself. It's only a hospital worker. It's stupid o'clock and they're probably tired, that's why the footsteps are so heavy.

Instead of heading to Corinne's room, I twist right. I don't alter my pace and I make sure my posture stays relaxed. The footsteps don't come after me; I hear them continuing down the original route. I let out a breath and backtrack to turn the tables and follow my follower.

Gut instinct counts for a lot. I get back to the main corridor in time to see a figure disappear into Corinne's room. There are no scrubs or white coat in evidence; either Corinne has some very unusual visiting hours or this is something else entirely. I take out my phone and text SOS to Foxworthy, then I speed up. I fling myself into Corinne's room just in time to receive a smack in the face.

'Two for the price of one,' a distorted voice exclaims. 'How fortuitous.'

Cold steel circles my wrists. The draining sensation is both familiar and horrifying. Instantly, my movements are sluggish and heavy. I try to lift up my arm and hit back but everything's in slow motion. The voice laughs.

I blink several times, trying to clear my vision. The first thing I see is Corinne, wide awake. Her breath is coming in rapid gulps. 'You,' she gasps, 'you're dead.'

Belatedly, I realise we never spoke to Corinne about the possibility of a second man. Whoever he is, he's wearing a balaclava and he's even sporting dark glasses to obscure his eyes. I guess he learnt from Terence Miller's mistakes.

I lunge forward but he strikes me down easily and I go flying across the hospital floor, ending up in a sprawled heap in the corner. That's when I spot the slumped body of the guard. There's a trickle of blood from his mouth but he's still breathing. Thank goodness for small mercies.

I put my hand out to force myself to my feet. I'm barely halfway up when there's a whoosh of air and all I see is blur of red swinging towards my face. Fire extinguisher, I think dully, identifying the weapon before I pass out.

CHAPTER 23

I LOVE LONDON GENERAL

Consciousness trickles back. I'm still sapped of strength so the handcuffs must still be in place. There's a screaming pain in my arms and my shoulders feel as if they're being ripped out of their sockets, alerting me to my unnatural position. I'm strung up and hanging vertically, my toes only just scraping the ground like a carcass in an abattoir. I can hear harsh, ragged breaths from several feet away and a dank smell pricks my nostrils.

I open one eye just a crack. The last thing I need is to alert my assailant to the fact that I'm awake. Wherever I am, it's damned dark. Piercing through the gloom, I see an uneven stone wall. The slabs are edged with moss.

In the far corner, there's a bucket. I fix my eyes on it: it's shiny and new and I can see a sticker poking out from the far corner. Very, very gently, I pivot a centimetre to my left to examine it. The font is unmistakable: IKEA. I frown. Whoever put me here was prepared; it might be an old disused space, but he went out and bought supplies. Except the bucket isn't for me. I can't move. When I hear a hiccupped sob, I realise who's with me.

As silently as I can, I inch round again to face another windowless wall. Corinne is hunched in the next corner, hugging her knees, still wearing her hospital gown. I ignore her for now and keep twisting until I reach my physical limit. Then I do the same in the other direction. There's a door to the right that looks depressingly solid; other than that, the room is empty.

I wait for a few minutes, straining to hear beyond Corinne's muted sobs. There's a scuffle behind me, suggesting we share our cell with a creature of the four-footed variety, but I can't hear anything else.

I try to think. We were attacked in a hospital in the city. The corridors were quiet and it was the middle of the night but it would still have been difficult to spirit both of us away, even if we were comatose. He'd have to wheel us out one after the other, increasing the risk of being spotted. The balaclava would hide his face from prying security cameras but if he'd passed anyone, they'd have known something was wrong. It might have been the dead of night but there were still plenty of night-shift porters, nurses and doctors around. It bothers me that this prick manages to get away with such public crimes.

I flex my toes and ignore the burn in my arms and shoulders so I can assess the damage to the rest of my body. My face hurts – but then a sodding metal fire extinguisher slammed into it so that's no surprise. The energy-sucking handcuffs make it difficult to test my strength but it's not the first time I've worn them. I use my previous experience to search past their magic.

My skin feels prickly so it must be daytime. The gnawing ache of hunger in my stomach suggests it is late. I reckon I've been out for about ten hours. Dusk is already approaching again. That's good; my thirst for blood isn't. I wish for a moment that I'd taken up the nurse's offer of a blood bag. It wouldn't have done much – to truly satiate a vampire's hunger, we need to drink directly from the vein – but it would have given me a bit more time. I'm only a fledgling and, like a newborn baby, I require regular feeds to stay alert and capable.

Fortunately, however, I'm not alone.

'Corinne,' I whisper. My voice is barely audible. 'Corinne!'

She starts. 'You're awake.'

'Keep your voice down,' I urge. 'He might come back.'

'I thought I was safe. You told me I was safe.'

I squeeze my eyes shut for a moment. 'I'm sorry,' I say finally. 'Can you tell me what you remember from the hospital?'

There's a loud sniff but she takes a deep breath and gathers herself together. 'He came in wearing that mask thing. I knew instantly...' The horror of her situation overcomes her briefly. I wait. There's a scraping sound and I know it's her fingernails digging painfully into the cement floor. She forces herself to focus. She's a strong woman.

'What about the guard?'

'I'd been having a nightmare, I guess I'd been screaming. He'd come in to check on me. When the man ... the bastard ... the one who's going to...'

'Let's call him Troy,' I interrupt. It's a silly name but the more I can encourage Corinne to think of him as figure of ridicule rather than the person with all the power, the more chance we'll have to get out of this alive. Besides, the city of Troy was sacked, burnt and destroyed – and I'm going to destroy him.

'Um ... Troy?' She clearly thinks I'm mad.

I shrug then wish I hadn't as shooting pains surge through my body. 'Humour me.'

'Well,' she continues, sounding even more unsure, 'when Troy came in, the guard barely had time to react. One second he was standing, the next he was lying on the floor.'

I frown. 'Did Troy hit him?'

'He must have. It was so fast that I didn't see it.'

I shake my head. 'You didn't even cry out.'

'I didn't have time,' Corinne answers, suddenly defensive.

'No, that's not what I mean. He must have...' There's a muffled sound from somewhere outside. 'Quiet now,' I hiss. 'Act like I'm still unconscious.'

'Huh?' Corinne asks. Then she subsides as there's a clanging noise and the door lock slides open.

I roll back my eyes and drop my head, concentrating on my breathing to make it shallow and even. If he realises I'm awake, there's no telling what he'll do. Hopefully he's not here to kill either of us; considering we're both still alive, I reckon he has grander plans than an anonymous end in an underground tomb.

I hear the door open with a protesting creak. Wherever we are, it's not somewhere that's used often. Troy is careful, standing at the threshold and checking we're both where he wants us to be before he ventures inside. When he's satisfied, he strides over to me, snatching a hank of my hair and yanking it upwards to peer at my face. I keep my features slack. He prods my cheek with a gloved finger and I steel myself to avoid reacting.

'Are you awake yet, little bloodguzzler?' he coos. His voice is distorted like it was in the hospital. When I don't react, he kicks my shin hard. I swing limply backwards, my toes dragging.

'Leave her alone!' Corinne yells from behind me. She no longer sounds so frightened.

'What do you care, bitch? You're just a whore.' Despite his warped voice, there's venom in his tone. He throws something at her. 'Eat this. Don't worry. Your time will come soon enough.'

'Let us out!'

'Hm, let me think about that.'

'You bastard!' she shrieks.

'You're right,' he answers. 'I am a bastard. But then my mother was a whore just like you. Eat the fucking food.'

He turns back to me, lifting my head again. I feel cold steel sink into my temple as he drags a blade down my cheek towards my chin, slicing open my face. Warm blood pours out. 'That's for Terry,' he says gently. 'But don't worry. There'll be more to come.'

He releases me and stalks out, the door closing behind him and the lock settling in place. I stay where I am, head drooping. A puddle of blood is forming on the floor next to my feet as the wound on my cheek drips. I grit my teeth and focus on breathing. One one thousand. Two one thousand. Three one thousand. It's not until I've reached a hundred that I finally move again, pulling my head upright.

'Are you okay?' Corinne trembles.

I nod then remember she can't see anything. 'I'm fine,' I tell her. 'Was he still wearing the balaclava?'

'I couldn't see. It was too dark.' Her panic is rising again.

'It's alright, Corinne. I need you to stay calm and think about this – is there anything familiar about him? Anything at all?'

'I ... I ... don't know. What do you mean?'

'His voice,' I mutter. 'He's not just disguising his face. He's disguising his voice too. That means he thinks you might recognise him from the way he talks.'

For a long moment, Corinne is silent. When she finally speaks, her voice is small. 'Do you think he's one of my clients? If he is, he's not a regular. His body shape isn't familiar.'

I mull it over. Considering his vehemence when he addressed Corinne, I don't think he availed himself of her services. I could be considered responsible for the death of his buddy, Terence – the way he sliced my cheek makes it clear he thinks that – but there's a lack of anger towards me. His cutting was cold, calculated. He seems to be reserving all his spite for Corinne. It's as if her profession is so repulsive to him he can barely bring himself to speak to her. Maybe that's because of what he said about his mother. If she was a prostitute, it's possible he was put into care temporarily as a result. He might have met Terence Miller that way.

'Not a client, Corinne. Someone else.'

She sighs, obviously thinking it over. 'Nothing's ringing a bell,' she admits eventually. 'Does it matter? He's going to rape and kill us. Does it really matter who he is?'

'He's not going to do that. I won't let him.' I feel strangely confident. An eerie sense of calm has settled over me.

'Why hasn't he done anything yet? I wasn't kept prisoner before.'

I know the reason why, I just don't think I should tell her. The two of them deviated from their pattern by attacking Corinne and I bet he thinks that's why they didn't succeed. Human. Witch. Daemon. Vampire. Fiona Lane was a witch; I'm obviously a vampire. He's looking for a daemon to fill in the gap, then he'll come for me. Once he's finished with me, he'll return to Corinne. That's why he's given her food: he wants to keep her alive until he's ready to snuff her out. It's a sobering thought that he's out for more innocent blood before he returns to us. But Corinne is still the key – I just don't know why.

'Let's not focus on his twisted motives,' I say briskly. 'He's a psychopath. We need to worry about getting out of here.'

'Yeah?' she says sarcastically. 'And how exactly are we going to manage that?'

I inhale the damp air. 'I need your blood, Corinne.'

'You're hungry? That's what you're worried about?' She's incredulous.

I explain patiently. 'It's not about hunger, it's about

strength. Every minute I don't drink, I get weaker. I need to be at full capacity to get us out of this.'

'It'll weaken me.'

'I won't take much, Corinne, I promise.'

'There's no point.'

I harden my voice. 'A moment ago, when he was here, you were brave. You stood up to him. I need *that* Corinne, not the Corinne who's cowering in the corner. If we work together we can get out of this. Buck the hell up.'

She doesn't answer but I hear her get to her feet and shuffle over. She peers at me. 'Is my blood going to help you get out of those restraints?'

'One thing at a time.'

Corinne sighs. 'Fine.' Her face is dirty and tear-streaked, making her dark bruises almost invisible. She pulls away her shirt and stretches towards me so my teeth can reach her neck. 'It's a good thing you're so short,' she mutters.

She comes closer and I extend my fangs. If only Dr Love could see me now, I think sardonically, he'd be really proud. I'm taking his advice and going elsewhere for my sustenance. I sink my teeth into her neck and drink as much as I dare, pulling away before I get too greedy and take too much. I really am getting better at this.

I close my eyes, enjoying the surge of renewed energy. 'You're going to have to pick the lock on the cuffs,' I tell her. 'It's not as hard as you think. You'll just need patience. There are going to be pins inside. You just need to find each pin and push it up so that...'

'I know how to pick a damn lock,' she mutters. I open my eyes and stare at her in surprise. 'I'm a whore, remember? Some men like feeling helpless. Some men like making me feel help- less. I've used cuffs before. It pays to be prepared in case the key gets,' she licks her lips, 'lost.'

I have the feeling she's speaking from experience. 'Oh, good,' I respond awkwardly.

'I can't pick it without a fucking tool though, can I? He checked your pockets when you were out cold and took everything you had.'

I smile. That part's easy. Troy didn't take everything. 'Check my t-shirt,' I tell her.

Corinne frowns but does as she's told. When she sees the hospital badge fixed to my chest, her eyes widen. She nods her head thoughtfully and unpins it, removing the safety pin from the back and twisting the tip. 'The man's an idiot,' she asserts.

'Yes,' I agree, 'he is. And that's why we're going to get out of here.'

She smiles grimly. Her hands are still swathed in bandages although they're no longer pristine white. If there were any other way to do this I'd use it, but we're out of options and Corinne knows it. She sets her jaw in determinedly and uses her teeth to pull at the edges of the bandage on her right hand. Tears well up in her eyes as she releases her fingers and she hisses in pain. I have to give her credit, though; she doesn't stop and she doesn't complain. Once she can wiggle a few fingers she twists off the bandages on her left hand. Despite the black stitches, the terrible wounds are achingly obvious. She swallows down the pain and reaches up to the cuffs. They're connected to a chain which, in turn, is attached to a bolt on the ceiling. If the cuffs weren't magical, I'd have no problem in pulling myself free. But even then, there's a chance I'd bring down half the ceiling with me. Corinne tightens her lips and her brow furrows in concentration. For my sake, I'm glad she's here.

I lean back to give her as much space as possible. The cuffs rattle as she forces the pin inside and starts fiddling. It's an awkward position for her and beads of sweat appear across her upper lip. Her arms are straining and I can tell it's a struggle.

Rather than interrupt her, however, I let her work. It takes some time but finally there's a click and I fall forward, almost knocking her over.

'Is that all the thanks I'm going to get?' Corinne's voice is weak.

I look up at her. Her face is pale and she's starting to wobble. Ignoring the numbness in my own legs, I leap up and catch her as she passes out. I lay her limp body down carefully and quickly massage my arms to get some feeling back into them. Then I turn my attention back to Corinne and re-bind her dressings. There's a lot more blood seeping from them now; her efforts to free me have made it flow freely from the ragged wounds. Given that I just fed off her, she can't afford to lose any more blood. Concerned that the bandages are too grubby, I rip my t-shirt and use the material to bind her hands as tightly as I can then wrap the rest of the bandages round too. The result is hardly neat but it's the best I can manage. I'm going to have to get her to a doctor.

She moans slightly as she comes round and tries to sit up. I hush her, gently pushing her back down. 'You did it, Corinne,' I whisper. 'You got me free. Now I'm going to return the favour.'

Her eyes are starting to look glassy and I curse. Picking the lock took more out of her than I realised. I do what I can to make her comfortable and turn to the door. Despite its age and the fact that it's made out of wood, it's remarkably sturdy. I put my ear to it and listen, on the off-chance that Troy is nearby. I can't hear a thing, so I tug at the doorknob and rattle the lock. I could kick through it but I can't risk the noise. I don't want to give Troy any time to prepare a counter-attack, not with Corinne as vulnerable as she is.

I take a couple of steps back and try to decide the optimum route to take. That's when I hear the scuffling again. I glance to my side and spot a long-tailed, mange-ridden rat run to the corner. Forcing down the shudder that ripples down my spine, I realise it's disappeared. There's a gap in the stonework. I cast my eyes up to the ceiling in gratitude. Thank you, Mr Rat.

Crouching down, I pull away the surrounding moss. Several of the blocks are crumbling where the stone meets the floor. I curve my fingers round the gap and tug and a chunk falls into my hands. I keep scrabbling, digging out the earth around the damp floor and yanking away as much of the stone as I can. As soon as I've widened the hole enough, I push myself through. It's a tight squeeze and my hips get stuck for a moment but I make it. I stand up and dust off my jeans.

The dungeon door is bolted and there's a set of narrow steps leading upwards. There's another door at the far end but it's an odd size, more suited to a child than an adult. Even though I'm small I would have to double over to get through it. I'm puzzled by its purpose. Still, before I go back for Corinne, I need to make sure the coast is clear. I feel the blood coursing through my system as my adrenalin kicks in.

'Come on, Troy,' I whisper to myself. 'Enjoy your last few moments on this planet because you're not going to know what's hit you.'

Staying light on my feet, I move forward, pausing at the foot of the stairs. I look at the small door; Troy is too large to get through such a tiny space. I can't hear anything so I take a step up, then another and another. There's another door at the top but, thankfully, it's unlocked. I hold my breath and twist the doorknob. A chink of dull light appears and there's a gust of fresh air. I suck it in deeply. I can see worn flagstones and another wall, although this time it's made of wood rather than stone. I open the door further and peer out.

It's a small structure – and completely empty. Something doesn't feel right. I chew my lip and think, then I realise what it is. I can hear running water outside but there's nothing else.

London, like all big urban dwellings, never truly sleeps; there is always noise, even if it's a distant hum of sound. Water aside, I can't hear a damned thing. It's completely unnatural. Even if Troy had taken us out of the city, there would still be the sounds of nocturnal creatures. I tiptoe across and open the door to the outside world. Where the hell are we?

I'd know the River Thames anywhere. On the far bank, the glittering spires of London rise up towards the heavens. I feel a surge of relief at the familiar sight – until I glance to the other side and freeze. This doesn't make any sense.

It's an island, just scant feet away from the tiny castle-like building. From source to mouth, the Thames is full of such little land masses and this one, if I'm not mistaken, is one of the more famous. It definitely looks like Oliver's Island but there are no structures there like the one I just exited, not these days. As far as I'm aware, the only building on Oliver's Island was torn down decades ago.

I turn back and stare at it, then touch the wood. It does feel old. The wheels of my brain click round. I stretch out to the other side, my fingers reaching across the water. It's there: it may be barely tangible but there's definitely some kind of membrane. It's as if we're in a bizarre bubble. That's why there's no sound other than the flowing river: we're in a time capsule, not the sort you bury in the ground but the kind that is frozen away from the rest of the world. Just like Connor and those other people who think they can preserve their ailing bodies through magic so they can be resurrected at a later date.

I look up to the sky, fixing on one cloud to be sure. The ripple of the leaves on the small island next to me indicates that there is definitely a wind but I can't hear the rustle and the cloud isn't drifting. Unbelievable. Despite the severity of the situation, I can't help grinning. What a discovery. And how in sodding hell does Troy know about it?

I try to remember what I know about the history of Oliver's Island. It's named after Oliver Cromwell because of the legend that he once took refuge there. There are stories about a secret tunnel, leading from the island to The Bull's Head, a public house close to the shore. It was supposedly used to hide Catholics from their bloodthirsty Protestant counterparts but no one has ever found evidence of it. I think about the tiny door downstairs. Bingo.

I run back inside and down, flinging open the dwarf door. Inside it's dark and smelly but it's definitely a tunnel. There's no sign of Troy, which is irritating.

'I'm still going to find you and make you pay,' I say, not bothering to whisper. Then I slide back the bolt to get Corinne. Priorities. She needs a hospital.

CHAPTER 24

FLOOD

The tunnel seems endless. If I was on my own it wouldn't be an issue but trying to drag Corinne's comatose body along while I'm doubled over is incredibly difficult. I'm tempted to leave her and come back when I can muster up reinforcements but I can't risk our abductor returning while I'm away.

When we finally reach the end and a rickety wooden ladder, my back is screaming in agony. I stare doubtfully upwards. The ladder is at least twenty feet high and ends at a small trapdoor. I don't think I ever had cause to venture through trapdoors in the past; now I seem to do it all the time.

I rearrange Corinne's limbs, ensuring her head is upright so she doesn't choke, then heave myself upwards. When I get to the top, I push the trapdoor but it doesn't budge. I curse aloud. Troy must have covered it when he left in order to hide it. I thump against it and start calling. It may not be a good idea to alert anyone on the other side to our presence but I don't have any other options.

'Hey!' I yell. 'Is anyone there?'

Silence comes back at me. I increase my efforts. 'Hello?' I

punch against the wood. 'We're trapped!' I hammer out a stac-cato beat. Come on, I pray, someone be there. I keep pounding and yelling. My voice echoes back down the tunnel, growing hoarser and hoarser. Desperation seeps out my pores. This can't be where our escape ends. Hope starts to drain away – and that's when I hear a shuffle from above.

I freeze. Is Troy returning? Or is it someone else? I knock hard on the wood, my knuckles bruised and bleeding. 'Help!'

There's a loud clatter, followed by a thick voice muttering, 'Yes?'

It doesn't sound like Troy. 'Down here!' I shout.

'Down where?' The voice is puzzled.

I grit my teeth. 'Here!' I thump louder.

I hear more shuffling and the clink of metal. 'Hey, there's a door!'

'So sodding well open it,' I grind out.

There's some banging and creaking, then what sounds like a bolt being slid back. The trapdoor flips open to reveal a baffled, slack face peering down. The face beams and a hand waves. 'Hi! Are you here for the party, too?'

I pull myself out and look at my saviour. He's a burly guy who's clearly three sheets to the wind. He sways slightly and grins then gives me a closer look and frowns, rubbing his eyes and peering again. 'You're the Red Angel.'

I ignore his comment and point downwards. 'My friend is there. I need some help getting her up.'

'I thought the Families bumped you off,' he slurs.

I stare at him. 'What?'

He shrugs amiably and claps me on the back. 'That's what they're saying.'

'Who's they?'

'Everyone.'

Dread filters through me. 'What day is it?'

'Saturday.' He taps his head. 'Sunday?'

I start to relax when another suspicion occurs to me. 'What date?'

He checks his watch. 'Fifteenth.'

My shoulders sag. A week, I've been gone a whole week. I couldn't have been unconscious all that time – it has to be something to do with the damned time bubble. Anything could have happened in a week. I swallow hard and get over it. I don't have time to worry about that now – I need to get Corinne out. I look at the man; he reeks of booze and is clearly going to be no help in pulling her out.

'Where are we?' I ask.

'Pub.' He leans towards me and I get a whiff of stale whisky. 'I came down here for a sneaky fag. Damn smoking ban.' He pulls out a crumpled pack of cigarettes and waves it in my direction. 'Want one?'

I admit I'm tempted. Instead, I wave him away and look around the small space. It's a cellar filled with kegs and boxes. We must be underneath the pub itself.

'I need a rope,' I mutter. I start looking for one. I push kegs around, ignoring their clatter as they roll and bounce off each other. The man pulls out a phone. 'I have a friend who has one,' he says cheerfully.

I snatch the phone from him and jab in a number. Ambulance and fire brigade, then Foxworthy, I think. My finger hovers over the green send button. No. Troy will come back here if he thinks Corinne and I are still imprisoned. I can't risk it getting out that we've escaped. I gnaw on my lip. I need someone else, someone who's not likely to be followed. With the Renfrew daemons out of the way for now, I know just who it should be.

The man blinks at me. 'You okay?'

I smile tightly. 'Yes.' Then I call O'Shea and tell him what I need.

~

IT TAKES the daemon an achingly long time to arrive. When he finally opens the cellar door and gazes at me with wide eyes, the pallor of his skin worries me. I think he must still be recovering from the events at the Agathos court when suddenly he rushes in my direction, almost bowling me over. His arms wrap tightly round my body and he squeezes hard.

'I thought you were dead,' he whispers.

I blink back tears at the emotion in his voice. 'Nope. You're not that lucky.'

'I should have known you'd make it,' he sniffs. 'Was it Montserrat? Did he do this?'

I pull away and stare at him. My drunk friend in the corner nods to himself. 'Told you it was the Families.'

I keep my attention on O'Shea. 'Why would you think that?'

'It's what everyone's saying. He got pissed off with you leaving his Family and becoming a hero, so he bumped you off.'

'And you believed that?' I'm incredulous.

O'Shea shrugs awkwardly and looks away. 'Hey, I like the guy but...'

I shake my head. 'That's idiotic. If he supposedly killed me, then who took Corinne?'

'The hooker?' I scowl at him. 'She was just collateral damage,' he continues. 'You're the Red Angel. You're the one the media is focusing on.'

'For fuck's sake,' I mutter. But I have far more important things to worry about than my stupid celebrity status. Hopefully my fifteen minutes will be over soon. 'Did you bring a rope?'

He nods, reaching in his bag then tossing a heavy coil of hemp in my direction.

'And Foxworthy?'

'Seemed remarkably relieved that you were in one piece.' O'Shea arches an eyebrow. 'Is there something you should be telling me?' I gaze at him, exasperated. He grins back. 'Yes, your pet policeman is checking the nearby buildings.' I open my mouth to speak but he forestalls me. 'And he's doing it discreetly. Don't worry.'

'Good.'

'I've also arranged for a runner to deliver a message about your welfare to New Order. They've all but shut down business, you know. I'm not sure whether it's down to your disappearance or the media glare. Still, granddaddy will be happy.'

'Thank you.'

His expression sobers. 'An alert has gone out to all female daemons. I can't guarantee they'll take it seriously, though.'

'We need to make it hard for Troy, that's all,' I say absently. 'And give him enough reason to come back here before he starts looking for a daemon victim.'

'Troy? If you know who he is, why don't you just go after him?'

'I don't know who he is,' I say grimly, 'not yet. Troy is the name I've given him.'

O'Shea is confused and I don't bother explaining. I hook the rope round my shoulder and start descending again.

'What about him?' he calls down. 'The drunk guy?'

'Keep him there!' I shout back. 'I need him!'

I clamber down to the bottom of the tunnel and check on Corinne. Her breathing is steady but I'm concerned about her newly opened wounds. The blood flow has stopped but infection is still a worry. I crouch down beside her and lift up her one good eyelid. 'Corinne?'

She moans slightly; at least she's semi-conscious now.

'I'm going to tie a rope round you and pull you up to the surface,' I tell her. 'It's going to be painful but it's necessary.' I have no idea whether my words are sinking in or not, but it makes me feel better saying them aloud. When I'm sure the rope is secure around her waist, I take the other end, climb back up and pass it O'Shea. 'Don't pull it until I say so,' I warn.

'Okay.'

I rejoin Corinne, moving behind her so I can balance her body and stop it from bumping against the tunnel walls. When she's in position, I call up. With a slight grunt, O'Shea starts to heave her upwards. I straddle my legs round Corinne's body, one arm holding onto the ladder and the other supporting her head. It's slow going and I'm dripping with sweat after only a few rungs but, inch by inch, we make it to the top.

O'Shea bends down, reaching under her armpits to hoist her up the last part. Panting, he checks her pulse. 'Strong.'

I nod. 'She's a tough lady.' I give him a hard look. 'She's had to be.'

He spots the puncture wounds on her neck but doesn't mention them. 'How are we going to get her out of here?'

I point at the guy in the corner. He's smoking a cigarette, his eyes unfocused. 'The two of you are going to sing your way out with Corinne in between you.'

'Ah. The old pretend-to-be-legless trick.' O'Shea looks doubtful. 'Are you sure he'll manage it?'

'He's a big bloke, he'll be fine. Just don't let him fall on her. Which hospital are you using?'

'Not a hospital. Foxworthy's found a small clinic near here. It's out of the public eye so it'll be easier to hide her. I'll stay with her myself.'

I relax slightly. 'Thank you. I mean it. As soon as she's safe, you need to get out a story about flooding. Make sure it's broadcast all over the city and this area is mentioned as a potential danger zone. It's the only way we can be sure Troy will come back.'

'It's not rained for a couple of weeks, Bo.'

'Which is why you need to be convincing.'

'What are you going to do?'

I smile grimly. 'I'm going back to wait for him. Even if it takes him days to return, it'll seem like no time at all for me.'

O'Shea knows better than to argue. He scoops Corinne up and beckons to the big man, who grins and lurches towards them.

'Make sure he keeps his mouth shut,' I instruct firmly, as the pair of them manoeuvre Corinne between them. 'And O'Shea?'

He turns his head. ''Yeah?'

'Are you okay? You know, after the stuff at the courthouse?'

He reaches over with his one free hand and tousles my hair. 'I'm fabulous, darling.'

I peck him on the cheek then watch the three of them depart. The song O'Shea chooses to bawl out is particularly bawdy. I cross my fingers tightly; this had better bloody work.

I'M NOT happy about scuffling back through the tunnel to wait in the time bubble next to Oliver's Island. I carefully close all the doors after me and bolt the door to the little dungeon again so it looks undisturbed. I squeeze back through the gap in the wall, replace the disturbed earth and stones and adjust the hanging handcuffs until I'm satisfied they're ready. Then I hunker down ready for Troy's return.

The eerie silence, bereft this time even of rats, is broken sooner than I expected. The footsteps halt outside the door while I move as quickly and quietly as possible, stretching my arms up into the cuffs and making it appear as if they're still locked. I'll only have a fraction of a second to catch him off-guard. My body tenses as I prepare for attack. The bolt grates open, clanging in its catch, and the door swings open.

I don't even look, I simply yank my hands free and leap at the shadowy figure in the doorway, knocking him off his feet. I land on top of him, circling my hands round his throat and holding his torso tightly with my knees.

Then I glance at his face and pull back as if burned. 'What in sodding hell are you doing here?'

Michael grins at me. 'It's good to see you too.'

'You could compromise everything!' I hiss. I'm starting to believe that every time I think I'm about to be attacked it's going to be Michael Montserrat instead, grinning at me so my stomach flip-flops.

'Don't worry. I was very careful.' He shifts his body slightly, making me aware of the tight muscle bunched under my groin and thighs.

I jump up to my feet and glare. 'How do you know? If just one person...'

He gives me a droll look. 'Please, Bo. Do you really think that after all my years as a vampire, I don't know how to stay hidden?'

I don't yield. 'If you've ruined this, there'll be blood on your hands.'

'I haven't.' He stands up and brushes himself off. Then his expression softens. 'I'm glad you're alright.' His expression is earnest. 'I was worried.'

'I'm not a helpless little girl,' I tell him, although I can't keep the smile out of my eyes.

'No, you're not.'

Putting my hands on my hips, I gaze at the sharp contours of his face. 'What are you doing here?'

'Helping you catch this bastard.'

I shake my head. 'It's too dangerous. If he spots you before…'

'Bo.' He tucks an unruly curl behind my ear. 'He won't. Besides, two of us have a better chance of taking him down.'

'You could have sent someone else. It didn't have to be you.'

His eyes gleam. 'But I'm your friend. And this is what friends do for other friends. You're not a lone wolf.'

'I think the only wolfish one around here is you,' I mutter under my breath. Michael grins. Wolfishly. I sigh. 'Go on then. Get in.' I gesture him inside. 'I'll have to bolt you in.' He's too large; he'll never squeeze through the little gap in the wall like I did.

Wary of the time, I quickly lock him in then push back through the enlarged rat hole. Even though I'd covered most of it up, it's easier this time with Michael's help. He understands the process without me needing to explain, scraping away enough dirt and stone and then yanking on my ankles to pull me through.

'You see?' he says, 'teamwork.' Before I can respond snarkily, he looks around the small space. 'A time bubble.' He shakes his head. 'Who'd have thought it?'

'Yeah,' I admit. 'I'd like to know how Troy knew about it.'

'Troy?'

I wave a hand in the air. 'That's not his real name.'

'But we're the Trojan horse. I like it.' He smiles for a second before his expression turns serious. 'Foxworthy told me to tell you that Corinne is safe.'

'How long has it been since she left here?'

'Two days.'

I take a deep breath. 'It's been just over an hour here.'

'Then I guess it won't be long before Troy joins us.'

I bite my lip. 'No.'

'This is a good plan, Bo.'

'Only if he shows up.' I find it hard to take the praise. 'Did Foxworthy say anything else?'

'The preliminary coroner's report is back on the women. They all suffered an incredible amount.'

I sense there's a 'but' coming. 'There's something else, isn't there?'

Michael nods, his mouth set in a tight line. 'Corinne Matheson's attack was more sustained and brutal than the others.'

I absorb this information. 'It's always seemed personal where Corinne was concerned,' I say slowly. 'She just didn't fit the profile of the others. Or the pattern.'

'What are you thinking?'

'This time bubble thing. You'd not heard of it before, right?'

'I know there are companies playing around with this kind of thing. I don't think they've had much success though, despite what they advertise. Nothing they have is powerful enough to create this.' He waves his arm around the room.

'I don't suppose any of the older vampires have heard of something this powerful? Did you ask around?'

He sighs. 'There was one I spoke to who'd heard a rumour about it but she didn't know for sure if it was true.'

'And how old is she?' I prod.

'Two hundred and thirty-three.'

I balk slightly at the age; I don't want to live that long. I focus on the topic in hand. 'A historian,' I say, thinking aloud. 'A historian might know about it.' My stomach churns. 'He distorted his voice. I thought it was because Corinne might recognise him but it wasn't Corinne he was disguising himself from.' I look up at him, wide-eyed. 'It was me. I know who he is.'

Just then there's a noise from outside. I set my jaw and Michael nods. As he moves catlike to the far side of the door, I take up my position back at the cuffs. My pulse is fast and angry. I inhale deeply, holding the breath in my lungs, then I drop my head down and let the open cuffs take most of my weight. The bolt on the other side of the door jiggles before sliding back. It's time to rock and roll.

HE STANDS IN THE THRESHOLD, breathing heavily. I keep my head bowed and limbs limp but I know he's looking for Corinne.

He laughs sharply, his voice still garbled and metallicised. 'You may think you can hide from me, whore, but you know it won't work. There are four walls and this is the only way out.' He takes a step inside. Michael is flat against the wall behind the door. Troy only needs to take one more step and we'll have him.

'I was going to do this properly,' he grunts. 'I was going to give you a fitting end. Unfortunately circumstances are moving beyond my control and we need to end things here instead.' He shrugs. 'It's not what I wanted but it'll have to do. For you and the little bloodguzzler. I'll take care of her first while you watch. Then it'll be your turn.'

I sense rather than see Michael tense, ready to pounce. This is going to happen quickly. He punches the door, slamming it into Troy's balaclava-covered face. Troy howls and I leap away from the handcuffs – just in time to see the syringe in his hand. My eyes widen in alarm. Michael deals a swift uppercut to his stomach but he hasn't seen the syringe yet. I launch myself forward, shoving him out of the way just in the nick of time, then I roll to the side to avoid it myself.

'Where is she?' he snarls. 'Where is the whore?'

I spring lightly to my feet. 'You mean Corinne. Say it,' I taunt. 'Say, "where's Corinne?"'

I see spiteful anger reflected in his dark eyes. 'Fuck you,' he hisses. 'She might get away for now but I'm not an idiot. There's always a back-up plan.' He pulls a glowing orb from his pocket. Ghostly blue swirls are visible within its depths. For a moment, I'm confused then I realise what it is.

'Have fun, boys and girls.' He raises his hand and, before I can stop him, he smashes the orb on the floor. There's a loud popping sound. He's burst the time bubble and water is already pouring into the small room. It's coming from everywhere and there's no chance of stopping it. This isn't a physical leak, it's time returning to the present. The entire area is going to be submerged within minutes.

I tilt my chin up and stare at Troy. I don't care.

'Bo!' Michael yells, scrambling to his feet.

I ignore him, kicking up at the syringe as hard as I can. It falls with a splash: the water is already five inches deep. I rush the man, colliding hard with his stomach and pushing him backwards. His arms flail and he hits me several times but I'm a vampire. I'm always going to be stronger and faster. I grab his wrists and pin them to the ground. His legs thrash but I pay them no attention. 'You're a rapist,' I hiss. 'A rapist and a murderer.'

He blinks at me, struggling to keep his face above the water. 'What of it?'

I grab the balaclava and pull. He twists from side to side but I yank it off. Then I look at him. 'Hello, James,' I say. 'How's the wife?'

'Don't you dare...'

I snatch a hank of his hair and thrust his head underwater, holding it there. I pull it back up and he gasps and splutters. 'You went after Corinne because you didn't like the fact that people mistook your wife for her. Isn't that right?'

He doesn't answer. I plunge his head underwater again. I

feel oddly calm. I yank his head up again. 'Isn't that right?' I hiss in his face.

'Do it,' he says. 'Kill me. Just like you killed Terence.'

'I didn't kill Terence,' I tell him. 'But you've made it personal so I may change my mind about you.'

I slam his head down. The water is creeping up and up. I feel a hand on my shoulder. 'Don't, Bo.' Michael's voice is measured and steady. 'He's not worth it.'

'He fucking deserves it.'

'Yes,' he says, 'he does. But you don't. If you do this, there's no coming back. Believe me.'

I grit my teeth. I can already feel James Matheson's limbs starting to weaken. He's not fighting as much as he was. I curse, then stand up, pulling him to his feet. My hands are trembling. I could have killed Matheson easily right here and now and, despite Michael's words, I'm not sure I would have had bad dreams about it.

'Stairs,' I mutter.

Michael nods, taking Matheson's body and pushing him up. The water reaches my waist as I force my way through behind them. It's bitterly cold but my vampire blood protects me. My vampire blood made me strong enough to take this prick down. I push down my feelings of guilt at what I almost did and my pulse sings. This is good.

The force of water against the door at the top makes it diffi-cult to open so Michael hands Matheson to me. His teeth are chattering and his lips are turning blue.

'You're not going to die,' I tell him. 'You're going to have your day in court. You're going to face Corinne and let her look you in the eyes. Then you're going to face the other Corinne – your wife – so she can see what a monster you really are.'

He doesn't respond. Michael slams his shoulder against the door, forcing it open. I hand over Matheson then turn round to take one last look. There's barely any breathing space left; I estimate there's less than a minute before the entire place vanishes in the murky depths. Good riddance, I decide. I join the other two on the surface.

We cross the room, heading out into the dark night and onto the verdant green of Oliver's Island, and collapse on the shore. The wooden tollbooth creaks and starts to crumble. The planks of wood don't crash into the water, they simply vanish. The noise is tremendous. A flock of nesting birds, disturbed by the sound, fly up into the sky, cawing their disapproval. I blink twice and then it's gone. There's a faint breeze, rippling across the river. And absolutely nothing else.

I pull myself to my feet, glancing back at Matheson who is sprawled on the rocky beach. 'How did you do it?' I ask softly. 'How did you commit all those crimes in public without anyone noticing?'

It's Michael who answers. 'The time bubble – it was portable. He could move it to wherever he wanted. I bet if you go back through old newspaper reports, you'll read about women screaming for their lives, screaming as they're raped.' A muscle moves in his cheek. 'As they're killed. And when people go to investigate, there's nothing there. All he and Trevor had to do was keep shifting through the years and they'd never get caught.'

I nod. 'That's why Fiona Lane was left in a quarry instead of somewhere more public. You already had this place set up for Corinne. You needed the bubble here.' I bend down. 'You only had the one.'

Matheson looks away. I give up, standing up straight and thrusting my hands in my pockets. I look out across the glittering banks of the Thames as the water laps softly at my feet. Michael joins me. 'What are you thinking?'

'That if I were an eccentric billionaire who was about to

charged with murder, I might find a time bubble device rather useful.'

'Tobias Renfrew.' I nod. 'It's an interesting theory,' Michael murmurs. His dark eyes turn to me. 'How are you, Bo? Are you alright?'

I think it over and I smile. 'I'm a vampire.' I meet his eyes. For a moment he seems anxious then he relaxes and smiles back.

There's a crunch from behind us. I spin round, just in time to see Matheson pulling out a wooden stake. He raises it up, ready to fling in my direction. Michael snaps out his hand, catching Matheson round the throat with such force that his face turns purple. Then Michael throws him backwards against the nearest tree. Matheson slumps down, his head at an odd angle.

I stare. Michael has an oddly satisfied look on his face. 'You knew,' I say slowly. 'You knew he had a stake with him. You knew he was going to try something.'

'The final decision was his. He knew he'd never win against two vampires, Bo. He committed suicide.'

'But he wanted to take me down with him first.' Michael doesn't answer. He doesn't need to. 'I thought there was no coming back from this kind of thing.'

He meets my eyes. 'There's not.'

'But it's not your first time, is it?'

'No.' He squeezes my hand. 'He made his decision, Bo.'

I don't pull away. Instead, I look back out over the water. A small boat is chugging in our direction and I can make out Foxworthy's familiar figure, silhouetted against the crescent moon. There's a loud bark and I realise Kimchi is with him, vigorously wagging his tail. Michael releases my hand and I fold my arms and watch them approach. And I don't say another word.

CHAPTER 25
A QUIET LIFE

'You've had a busy week,' Dr Love comments, eyeing me with a practised look of professional solicitude.

I let out a short laugh, although there's little humour in it. 'I guess you could say that.'

'How are you coping with being the centre of attention?'

I shrug awkwardly. 'The protestors outside New Order have given up. Apparently they've decided we're on their side now. Whatever that means. The rest of the Red Angel thing is a pain in my sodding arse.'

'You're getting a lot of calls?'

I sniff. 'Every man and his dog want an interview.'

'And you're declining them all?'

'My grandfather thinks I should do a couple. He says it'll be good for the cause.' I know I'll cave in eventually. It's not worth the hassle to keep arguing with him.

Dr Love nods sagely. 'You don't think your heroic status is justified?'

I snort. 'Hardly. I'm no hero.' I look away, no longer able to meet his eyes. 'I'm no bloody angel either.'

He leans forward. 'What do you mean by that?'

'Look, Doc, I'm doing well. I took blood from someone different this week, just like you asked. And,' I say, crossing my heart with index finger to indicate my sincerity, 'I'm starting to enjoy being a vampire. Being a vampire meant I could save my friends and stop Matheson and Miller from their saga of evil.'

'They were indeed evil,' he agrees.

'The police traced them back. They'd known each other years.' I think about the strange carving on the tree next to where Matt and I uncovered the animal skeletons. It wasn't two Ws at all, it was two interconnected Ms. It wasn't Miller who grew up in that area, it was James Matheson.

'Matheson met Miller in foster care. He was only there for a month or two when his mother was briefly in prison. But a month or two was all it took for them to recognise kindred spirits.' It's hard to keep the disgust out of my voice.

'So you should be pleased neither of them is around to continue their killing spree.'

I take a deep breath, wondering if I can really trust the good doctor. 'That's the trouble,' I say in a small voice.

'That you're pleased?'

'I'm thrilled. I didn't want Medici's goons to kill Miller because deep down I think I wanted to kill him myself.' It feels strange to say it aloud. 'I thought I wanted to hand him over to the police, to do things properly. That's what I told myself.'

'But it's not true?'

I shake my head. 'No. I wanted to see him suffer. And when Michael – I mean, Lord Montserrat – stopped me from killing Matheson, I knew he was right. But when he ended up dead anyway...' My voice trails off.

'You were pleased?' Dr Love prompts.

'I was.' I pick at a hangnail. 'The ex-CEO of Magix is dead. Not at my hands but as a result of what I did. I knew it was going to happen and I did it anyway.'

He frowns. 'I don't follow. He was behind bars. I thought all the signs pointed to a Kakos daemon.'

'I can't go into details,' I mutter. 'But he's dead because of me.' I can feel the weight of his gaze. 'I know the world's not black and white. I'm not that naïve. But...'

'But?'

I look up. 'But I've always known the difference between right and wrong. I've always known which path is the moral one. Don't get me wrong,' I say, 'I'm not perfect and I'm not pretending that I have been. But someone once told me I shouldn't lie to myself and now I think I'm facing up to the truth. My own truth.' I swallow. 'I'm not a good person. I wanted them to die. All of them. There's a group of daemons hiding out in Venezuela and, as soon as I can work out how to find them, I'm going to go there and make them pay for what they tried to do to my friends.'

'Some might call that justice,' Dr Love interjects mildly.

'No, it's not justice. Justice is cool-headed, impartial and logical. What I want to do to them is nothing like that. What I feel about the deaths of O'Connell and Matheson and Miller is nothing like that.' I bite my bottom lip so hard that I draw blood. 'Maybe that makes me evil too. Right and wrong are not so clear any more.'

His eyes are untroubled. 'This might be the first time you've been honest with me.'

'I'm scared.' My hands are trembling so I shove them beneath my thighs. 'There's a line and I'm almost at it. Once I cross it, I'm not sure I can ever come back. It's why I've been avoiding Michael. There's a darkness in me and it feels like it's growing. I'm afraid it's going to come out and I'll never be able to put it back.'

'Bo,' the doctor says softly, 'you're not evil. These feelings are natural. Anyone who's been a victim of crime wants vengeance.'

'But not everyone can get it.'

He watches me for a moment, his face impassive. Then he reaches down, opens a drawer and takes out something. It's a small, round, white pebble. 'Take it,' he urges.

I pluck it out of his palm. It's cool to the touch and very smooth but there's no hint of magic. It's just a pebble. I look at him, confused.

'It's a symbol,' Dr Love explains. 'A placebo, if you like. If you feel like this in the future, if you feel this darkness you speak of is growing and you don't know what's right and what's wrong, hold the stone. Use it to ground you.'

I heft it from hand to hand. 'I don't see how it will work.'

He smiles. 'Trust me. I'm a doctor.' His gaze is so benevolent I'm tempted to ask him for a hug. 'So,' he says lightly, 'other than the Venezuelan daemons, what's next for the Red Angel?'

'I don't know.' I massage my neck. 'There's always Tobias Renfrew. He's wrapped up with those sodding daemons somehow.'

Dr Love throws me a sceptical glance. 'He's been missing for decades. Dozens of people have searched for him. How will you find him?'

I shrug. 'I don't know.' I close my fingers round the pebble and squeeze it tight. 'Maybe I should just let sleeping dogs lie.'

Kimchi, curled up at my feet, opens his eyes and lets out a small bark. I reach down to scratch the soft fur behind his ears.

'You should take a rest,' Dr Love suggests.

I put the pebble into my pocket and feel my old self surge to the fore. 'Actually, it's funny you should say that. As soon as we're done here, I'm heading off for a nice relaxing drink at a little bar I know.'

'Really.' His voice is dry.

I manage to smile. 'Really.'

~

I'M FORCED to go through the same rigmarole as before – knocking on the door and waiting to be allowed entry – but this time the vampire gazes out at me with a less hostile expression. 'If you're the Red Angel,' he says, 'you should be with us. Medici is red.' He grins, baring his fangs which are a disturbing shade of yellow. 'Blood is red.'

'I just want a drink.' I hold up my palms in submission. 'Nothing else.'

He waggles one bushy eyebrow. 'If you want more, let me know.' Although I can't see it from this side of the door, I'm fairly certain that he's cupping his groin suggestively towards me.

I push down nausea and reach inside my pocket, my fingers brushing lightly against Love's pebble. 'Are you going to let me in?' I inquire, as if I don't really care either way.

He grins, opens the door and bows. 'It's not every day we get celebrities gracing us with their presence.'

I keep my lips tightly buttoned, walk up to the now-familiar bar and sit on my usual stool.

'Bloody Mary?' the bartender asks, polishing a glass.

'Yeah,' I say. 'And make it a real one.'

If she's surprised, she doesn't show it. She beckons over one of waiting vampettes. 'Sure.'

'Mary' wanders over with a wide smile. Her pupils are dilated. I don't smile back, I simply reach over and curve my head down. She tastes both alcoholic and spicy and I realise she's been drinking vodka and Tabasco to enhance the flavour of her blood. It should disturb me but it doesn't.

When I've had my fill, Mary leaves me in peace. The bar is

quieter than I expected. I recognise a few faces. One woman, seated with a friend in the far corner, is sending me sidelong glances. There's a pleasing lack of hostility. Considering my illegal incursion into the Medici stronghold just days before, I expected to suffer some setbacks in my bid to cultivate a Medici contact. Instead I feel a zing of excitement that increases when I check out the table in front of her and realise that she smokes.

I pull out the same crumpled pack of cigarettes from my pocket and lay it carefully on the bar top. The door outside bangs to admit a new customer but, before I can see who it is, the bartender passes me my drink. I thank her and tap out a cigarette. Making a show of searching my pockets, I look frustrated at my inability to locate my lighter. I'm careful to keep my eyes down; I don't want to be too obvious. When I feel someone brush against me, however, my stomach flips in delight.

'Do you need a light?'

I look up and immediately recognise with shock that it's Joseph, the good Samaritan. The woman I'd thought was a potential is no longer looking in my direction and I can feel tension coiling in my veins. This could be bad.

'Thanks,' I mutter.

He pulls out a Zippo lighter engraved with the Medici coat of arms and flicks it open, sparking the flame. Not sure whether he's about to thrust it in my face and kick me in the stomach, I lean down carefully to light my cigarette. Even though we're inside and there's no breeze to speak of, he cups his hands round it. Then he bends his head. 'Something's about to go down,' he says in a low voice. 'Whatever you do, don't trust her.'

Ice runs down my spine. I pull back, lit cigarette in one hand and tightly clenched fist in the other. He gives me the perfunctory smile of a stranger and moves away.

I turn back to the bar, puff on the cigarette and wait. Was he referring to the woman behind me? Is she about to come over? I glance at her reflection. She's standing up.

Taking a deep breath, I try to remain casual. I throw a confused look at Joseph to enquire whether this woman is who he meant, but he's sitting with his back to me. I take another a drag as the woman walks up.

'See you, Yuko!' she calls out cheerfully. The bartender smiles and waves. Then, bafflingly, the woman strolls out without so much as a word to me.

I stub out the cigarette, tossing down money on the bar top. 'Cheers,' I say, as sunnily as I can. 'See you again.'

Yuko acknowledges my farewell, scooping up the money while I try to follow the woman.

The doorman gives me a wink on the way out. 'Leaving so soon?'

'Gotta take my dog for a walk,' I tell him. Then I escape into the cold night air and search for a sign of the woman.

She's nowhere to be seen. I curse. If Joseph didn't mean her, then who was he referring to? I look around again, checking the small street in case she's waiting for me. There's no one: she's already gone.

I'M STILL FROWNING when I walk into the New Order office. Peter has apparently already left for home and Arzo is shrugging on his coat to do the same.

'Evening, Bo.'

'Hey.'

The phone rings and Connor answers. He flicks a glance at me. 'Do you want to talk to the *Daily Flag*?' I shake my head. 'They'll pay you twenty thousand for an exclusive.'

I gape. 'Pounds?'

Arzo looks at me pointedly. 'You're a popular person. You're going to have to talk to one of them. We can't afford to let the opportunity to spin our own story slip by.'

'I know,' I groan. 'Just give me a day or two to get my head together first.'

He nods at me. As if on cue, my grandfather appears. 'Bo.'

I peck his cheek, then check anxiously for the cat.

'She's not here,' he says. 'It's not fair to bring her along when you have that mutt around.'

I try not to look too happy. Judging by the stern look I receive in return, I don't do a very good job.

'Something's just happened,' I tell them all quietly. Matt looks excited, bouncing up towards me. The others turn expectantly. 'I was just at Medici's bar and...'

There's a loud banging on the door and a figure bursts through. Kimchi barks wildly and I immediately take an attack stance. Knees, then throat, I decide, before the figure collapses in a heap on the floor. Arzo wheels forward. The figure raises her head, revealing not only her identity but also her scratched and bruised skin.

'Help me,' Dahlia whispers.

Everyone rushes towards her – apart from my grandfather and me. I give him a grim look, which he returns in spades. I squeeze the stone in my pocket and take a very deep breath. So much for some quiet time, then.

ABOUT THE AUTHOR

After teaching English literature in the UK, Japan and Malaysia, Helen Harper left behind the world of education following the worldwide success of her Blood Destiny series of books. She is a professional member of the Alliance of Independent Authors and writes full time, thanking her lucky stars every day that's she lucky enough to do so!

Helen has always been a book lover, devouring science fiction and fantasy tales when she was a child growing up in Scotland.

She currently lives in Edinburgh in the UK with far too many cats – not to mention the dragons, fairies, demons, wizards and vampires that seem to keep appearing from nowhere.

www.ingramcontent.com/pod-product-compliance
Lightning Source LLC
Chambersburg PA
CBHW061525210726
48287CB00006B/1834